3∘

© 2011 **McSweeney's Quarterly Concern and the contributors, San Francisco, California.** INTERNS & VOL-UNTEERS: Becca Cohn, Courtney Drew, Jennifer Florin, Rebecca Giordano, Victoria Havlicek, Jordan Karnes, Magnolia Molcan, Alexandra Slessarev, Angelene Smith, Mike Valente, Libby Wachtler, Mark Waclawiak, John Wilson, Valerie Woolard, Rebecca Power, Megan Roberts. ALSO HELPING: Eli Horowitz, Michelle Quint, Russell Quinn, Jill Haberkern, Andi Mudd, Walter Green. COPY EDITOR: Caitlin Van Dusen. WEBSITE: Chris Monks. SUPPORT: Sunra Thompson. OUTREACH: Juliet Litman. CIRCULATION: Adam Krefman. ART DIRECTOR: Brian Mc-Mullen. PUBLISHERS: Laura Howard and Chris Ying. MANAGING EDITOR: Jordan Bass. EDITOR: Dave Eggers.

FRONT COVER AND SPINE ART: Jessica Hische.
Printed in the USA.

HIYA FOLKS,

My name is unimportant. I'm in the Canadian Forces. I just recently returned from Afghanistan, where I was working with your country's 10th Mountain Division. Aside from the spurs and cavalry hats, they may be some of the nicest people I've ever met, including the racists. We tried to bring them around.

We were playing poker over there and an eighteen-year-old PFC picked up a Dan Brown novel from a package he'd just received from his parents. He looked at the title and said, "What is this? I can't read anyway."

Disturbed, I took him aside and said, "Tomorrow, same place, the picnic table, I'll teach you how." The only book I had was *McSweeney's 35*. He and I walked through every short story; incidentally, he enjoyed the letters the most. He was killed later that night in an IED ambush. We drove into a compound and they locked the gate behind us and detonated initial, secondary, and tertiary devices. I was thrown clear and suffer no health issues. The PFC ended up covering my gun with guts. I let them dry out and fall off and felt that to clean him off wouldn't be right. I miss him. He was from Alabama and loved his little sister who wrote him once a week with pictures of her baby.

When I received Issue 36, just today, I found it cathartic to open a head. Instead of what becomes, what remained is what truly matters: ideas. Not a Tim Horton's coffee mug, but generous, beautiful ideas, stored there.

If I could make a job change, I would scrap inceptor and remain an extractor. I would use my fabled retirement pension, which requires too much time dehumanizing and chasing humans, to buy the drugs and kit required to go into other people's minds and remove that "one simple idea" from us all.

You guys are super neat and thanks for the help. Keep up your good work.

DEEJAY
KINGSTON, CANADA

DEAR MCSWEENEY'S,

Last month, I went to a pastors' prayer summit with a bunch of other New York City clergy. I don't always fit in at clergy gatherings, so I was glad when they broke us up into groups and gave us an icebreaker question. The question—or prompt, I guess—was "Tell us about something that you did in your ministry that others would be surprised that you did." I couldn't really think of anything, and no one was speaking up, so I blurted out, "I wore a dress in front of my congregation." I kind of figured that this was a good time to share an embarrassing moment, and my church had just done some videos that involved guys dressed as ladies. It was a funny story.

No one in the group laughed. One lady said, "That's interesting." I explained that it was for a video, that I'd dressed in a dress, and another person said, "Ohhhhhh…" The ice was officially broken.

Then the guy next to me shared: "Well, I think people would be surprised that I'm still alive, because I've had three heart attacks!" There was an eruption of "Amen"s and "Hallelujah"s. Another pastor grabbed his Bible, opened up to a verse about someone speaking from the grave, and said that the verse was about the three-heart-attack pastor, and that God must have a special plan for him. Then he turned to me and said, "I'm fresh out of verses about guys wearing dresses."

PAUL CURTIS
BROOKLYN, NY

DEAR MCSWEENEY'S,
For the last several months our neighbor has been keeping her cat in a tube. The tube looks like a Slinky covered in black mesh, and its one open end connects to the house's kitty door. The tube allows the cat to leave the house, but no one is fooled. The cat's not really outside. It's in a tube, and the tube is outside.

The tube's diameter is about thirty inches. It can extend to a length of about fifteen feet, and sometimes it shrivels to about four feet. The way the tube shrivels and extends for unknown reasons—and its overall cylindrical shape—would lead any responsible person to describe it as penile. And this just a block away from an elementary-school playground.

I don't know the cat well enough to know how it feels about the whole thing. I've really only had one social moment with the cat, a few weeks ago, when I was coming home from a jog. The tube was almost fully extended, curved to the west a little bit, and the cat was toward the end of it, just sitting there. When we made eye contact I noticed that its face looked like it had been stored beneath a heavy object.

I'm not a cat owner myself. Never have been. My parents had a gray tabby, Ashley, until I was five, but she died before I could properly call myself a cat owner. My dad told me that Ashley walked on a yard that had pesticide on it and then licked the pesticide off her paws. Ashley died of pesticide poisoning, my dad said. But now I'm thinking this was just one of those stories parents tell to cover up the gruesome truth behind a pet's death.

My dad may have killed Ashley. I hadn't thought of this before, but it would explain some things. My mom is a cat lover. My dad despises animals of any sort. His financial advice, for example, is (1) buy gold, and (2) don't ever, ever own a pet. My parents never speak of Ashley. They've never had another pet. Whenever someone asks my mom why she, a cat lover, doesn't own a cat, she says, "Steve won't let me get a cat."

How do I talk to my neighbor about all this? Surely she knows her cat is in a tube. I've never spoken to her. I know that she's attempting to grow raspberries. I know that just after Christmas a plaque appeared next to her door with the Chinese character for "omen from heaven extending to all living things." These aren't what I'd call excellent conversation-starters. I've never actually seen our neighbor, now that I think of it. My wife claims she's seen her, but my wife describes her as "that old lady with the gray hair."

When I came home from work this afternoon, the cat tube was extended and curving almost all the way into the driveway. The cat was nowhere to be seen.

RORY DOUGLAS
SEATTLE, WA

DEAR MCSWEENEY'S,
A few years ago, I read an interview with Helen Hunt. It was only an okay interview, but she shared her grandmother's coconut-macaroon recipe, which I've been meaning to try ever since. I can't remember if the interview was in your publication or in *Redbook*. Can you look into this and let me know? Thanks so much,

JEN STATSKY
NEW YORK, NY

DEAR MCSWEENEY'S,
Pretend for a moment that you're shopping for a new gas range. In fact, let's imagine you're doing a little kitchen remodel, as people do, and you're going to treat yourself to some new appliances. You and your partner have a long list of features you want or don't want in this new gas range, and you spend a lot of time in awful places like Home Depot and Best Buy twiddling knobs and caring about things like warming drawers. And let's say you finally find one that's perfect—I mean *perfect*—in every way. It has the thing that does the thing, it's got five whatevers, it's adequately shiny, and it has enough BTUs to cook a nice French meal for ten people, even though you will mostly use it for making scrambled eggs and "garbagedillas," which are quesadillas made with bits and pieces of leftover food. This range looks fantastic, it's the right size, and it's the

right price. Like I said, it's perfect. Except for one thing.

On the console, there is a button that says CHICKEN NUGGETS.

What if that one button, those two words that bring saturated joy into the fatty hearts and minds of so many American children, was so offensive to your culinary sensibilities that you couldn't find any way to overlook it? What if you knew that every time you approached your new cooktop Cadillac, you would see only that button? Or not only that button, but also the button next to it that says PIZZA. What I'm saying is, what if you knew you would clench your jaw, trembling in bathrobed silence there on the new Marmoleum, taunted by your decision to let this button into your home, until you finally exploded with rage and started shouting "This is what's wrong with America!" before stumbling backward to collapse in sorrow, pounding your fists on your reclaimed-fir butcherblock countertops while your wife shook her head and pointed out again that all of this outrage is coming from the same man who is known for bringing Funyuns to social gatherings?

Could you buy that range? Could you live with it? Because I can't. You suck, Frigidaire.

SLOAN SCHANG
PORTLAND, OR

DEAR FEDEX OFFICE (KINKO'S),
I have been a customer of your establishment for over fifteen years now. The first place I drove to when I got my license was a Kinko's. I was making a comic book and had some copies to make, and your store was close and convenient. I have probably spent over $2,000 at Kinko's around the country.

I wanted to write you to let you know about an incident that happened about four minutes ago. It was not a particularly terrible incident— or, rather, it was fairly terrible, but it wasn't out of the ordinary for a visit to Kinko's, as I still like to call it.

I went this evening to the "Kinko's" at 54th and Lexington, in Manhattan, to make two copies and then find out about shipping those copies to California. I prefer to send things through the post office (not just because it's usually cheaper, but— and this might be hard to believe— because the people at the post office near me are usually nicer than the people at Kinko's), but since it was late at night and I wanted to get this package out right away, I thought I would give Kinko's a try. An employee told me it would probably be about $18 to get my envelope to California by the time I wanted it to get there. I said that sounded fine, and went to fill out the paperwork.

When I finished, that employee was helping someone else, and so I waited. Eventually another employee came over to me, but didn't say anything. After a minute I explained again what I was interested in doing, and he told me it would cost $38. For some reason, he was very terse.

I asked if there was a cheaper option, and he said, "I'm just telling you what the computer is telling me." He sounded mean, at this point. Mean! I then asked when during the day it would be delivered, and we realized that he had put the wrong day in the computer. He corrected this, but still the cost was coming out far higher than $18. After three or four back-and-forths, I gave up.

I have shipped things before, to a similar part of the country, for amounts less than $20—even sent more things, of a higher weight, than the three sheets of paper I was trying to send. But it seemed impossible to convince your employee of this. I looked around to try to figure out what I could do. There was nothing, so I grabbed my drawings and my umbrella and walked back home.

I was oddly affected by how poorly this man treated me. I didn't know what to do, so when I got home I wrote this letter. I also drew a picture of the employee, so you will know whom I am talking about, since I forgot to ask his name. Do not fire him—that is not what I want. Maybe just tell all of your employees to be a little nicer. Here is the picture of him:

Thanks,
JASON POLAN
NEW YORK, NY

DEAR MCSWEENEY'S,
I wrote you yesterday asking about an interview with Helen Hunt that you may or may not have published. While doing laundry this morning, I remembered that she was wearing a tealish sweater on the cover, either yours or *Redbook*'s. Thought that might help. Thanks again,
JEN STATSKY
NEW YORK, NY

DEAR MCSWEENEY'S,
I'm baffled that none of the bohemian Brooklyn bars I frequent feature an audio-book jukebox. Books on tape are

all the rage this season, and the drinking public needs its fix. With your help, and a little start-up capital, I'd like to pioneer the device before some rube steals the concept.

You figure we start out small: one audio-book jukebox containing ten or so complete, unabridged works. I guarantee that, within weeks, the bar will be packed to the walls with kids itching to drop in a fiver and groove to some Rand or "pump up the Tolstoy." And when the masses ignore closing time, rowdily insisting on finishing just one more chapter before they hit the road, we blare *The Great Wartime Speeches of Winston Churchill* to clear the joint out. We can even program the jukebox for special promotions, like "The *American Psycho* Splicer": buy four tracks from any book on tape and get the fifth track free—the fifth track being a random selection from *American Psycho*.

So what do you say? I don't need much money to get this product off the ground; the trial model will be extremely affordable to build, and I have an in at the local library. We just have to return the audio books to her after four weeks. Run the numbers on your end and get back to me with your decision.

Semi-related, I've recently discovered that drinking in excess to certain books on tape helps you unlock their alternate endings.

Best,
DAVID HENNE
DEER PARK, NY

DEAR McSWEENEY'S,
I live in St. Paul, Minnesota. A nice place where God tries to ice-murder all inhabitants every year. If you survive, you have defeated God, so that gives you a nice boost of confidence heading into springtime.

On a recent spring day, I took two of my three kids to see a Minnesota Timberwolves basketball game. I encourage my kids to follow the exploits of the Timberwolves—they can be very instructive. The Timberwolves' players are not generally all that interested in playing basketball, and you get the sense that they are only playing the game to get a little exercise so that when they adjourn to play Xbox for the rest of the night, they won't feel so guilty. I tell my kids not to make the wrong choices in life or they could end up playing for the Timberwolves themselves. I did not take the third child to the game, because she is too young to be exposed to such things.

Prior to the game, we decided to stop for dinner at the Subway restaurant on Fairview and Grand Avenue in St. Paul. You know the one. It's by the movie theater and kitty-corner from Whole Foods. We like Subway. My son gets the meatball sub so he can drip sauce on his shirt and look like a slob all day. My daughter enjoys a turkey sandwich so bereft of additional ingredients that it's a crime to pay what I do for it.

After she ordered her turkey sandwich, I thought turkey sounded pretty good too. So here's what I did: I ordered a turkey sandwich with Havarti cheese. Turkey and Havarti. One of my favorite combinations. Can't go wrong. A surefire winner.

But the order did not fire sure. It was not a winner. "Turkey and *what?*" asked the incredulous sandwich artist.

"Turkey and... Havarti? You don't have Havarti, do you?"

"I don't even know what you're talking about!" she said with kind of a chuckle. "That's not a real thing, is it?"

"Of course it's a real thing," I stammered. "It's Havarti cheese. It's creamy and delicious and goes well with turkey."

"*Havarti?*" she asked, turning to her fellow sandwich artists, who offered only confused expressions and shakes of the head.

She thought this: I had entered a Subway with two young kids, decided to make up a complete nonsense word, and pretended that it was a form of cheese. This, deduced the sandwich artist, was a choice I had made.

McSweeney's, have you ever been in a situation where you're telling the truth but someone doesn't believe you? And the more you insist on the truth, the more it sounds like you're lying? This was me. I had to defend Havarti's existence. But it's as if I was defending a legitimately fictitious cheese. "Do you have any Blamptonshire cheese? How about Flogvers? Or a lovely slice of Greevenheimer?"

It was at this point that I thought about hauling the kids across the intersection to Whole Foods, where I'm sure Havarti could be had, and buying a slice just to bring back. I might have even done it. I'm kind of a jerk like that. But then I worried that maybe I was a snob. I never thought of Havarti as being an elite cheese, a cheese for the cheese cognoscenti—but did I truly understand what made a cheese elite, McSweeney's?

A Subway is a hell of a place to have an existential crisis. I told them fine, pepper jack. Whatevs, you know?

We went to the Timberwolves game and they lost badly to the Phoenix Suns as thousands of Minnesotans watched. It was a grim, self-flagellating exercise.

Okay then, McSweeney's. Bye. I love you.

JOHN MOE
ST. PAUL, MN

DEAR McSWEENEY'S,

It's been a few weeks now and I have not yet received word back from you re: Helen Hunt's grandmother's coconut-macaroon recipe. It's possible I was not entirely clear in my original letter: please do not respond only if the interview was published in your quarterly; I need to hear from you either way. And, if you have access to *Redbook*'s archives through some sort of magazine-publishing database, please also send me a copy. All my best,

JEN STATSKY
NEW YORK, NY

P.S. Please read the interview in its entirety before you send it to make sure it is the one where Helen Hunt gives her grandmother's coconut-macaroon recipe and not some other interview where she does not. She seems like the type who gives a lot of interviews.

DEAR PHOEBE,

You know that moment of resignation when you know you're just about to get hit in the face? Well, you don't. You're fifteen months old. But you will. I wish I could protect you from it. I'm sorry to have to tell you this. Anyway, I've been approaching life lately with this sort of useless, too-late flinch on my face—waiting for the inevitable punch. Since you and your beautiful, red-haired mother left, I've been in a bit of a lonely daze. Tired but sleepless. The house too quiet. At night I tried running up and down the stairs to make some noise, but that didn't work. All I'd wanted was some peace to finish a book that I will never finish, and there it was— and so of course I began going out of my skull. Four and a half Schlitzes at the Mill didn't help, either. So here I am. I arrived the day before yesterday. Brother Francis greeted me after Vespers. He sat me in his office and he explained how things work around here. He handed me a paper with the schedule:

VIGILS: 3:30 A.M.

LAUDS: 6:30 A.M.

MASS: 7:00 A.M.

READING/PRIVATE PRAYER: 8:00 A.M.

TERCE: 9:15 A.M.

WORK: 9:30 A.M.

SEXT: 11:45 A.M.

LUNCH: 12:00 P.M.

NONE: 1:45 P.M.

WORK: 2:00 P.M.

READING/PRIVATE PRAYER: 4:30 P.M.

VESPERS: 5:30 P.M.

READING/PRIVATE PRAYER: 6:00 P.M.

SUPPER: 7:00 P.M.

"Everything's optional," Brother Francis said. "But if you're going to skip a meal, let me know and I'll inform the cook."

"Everything optional?" I asked.

"For you. Not for us."

"I don't have to do anything, go to anything?"

"You sound disappointed."

"I was hoping—" I wasn't sure what I was hoping. "I was hoping you'd whip me into shape."

Brother Francis stared at me. Then he squinted at his watch. He's a kind man, used to lost souls wandering in here day after day, but he's also busy as hell.

"I'm Jewish," I apologized.

"Why should that matter? We welcome all creeds here. Last week we hosted three Hindus on retreat." He threw me a bone. "We do lock the door at ten."

"Awesome."

"But if you should find yourself locked out, you can always hit the bell outside the front door, and the night porter will—"

I didn't last long, not being locked up. I still needed to at least *pretend* to escape. So this morning, after Lauds, I drove to Dubuque to get a cup of coffee. Nothing against the coffee here. It's actually pretty good. And there's a coffee room where you can get it 24-7. Just like at the Comfort Inn. Even so, I had to run from something. Spring has finally come to eastern Iowa and the fields are green, jungle green, the sort of carpetish green that makes you want to roll around out there with someone you don't know. Perhaps this is an inappropriate thing to say. (Shmoo, don't share this with anybody beautiful and red-haired.)

In Dubuque, looking for the Starbucks, I drove down Grandview Avenue where the bright yellow recycling boxes gleamed in the driveways of house after house. I tried to have a spiritual experience over those recycling boxes. It nearly worked. You should have seen them. The people of Dubuque never forget to put out the recycling and they always sort it very well, too—in very yellow boxes.

So, as I said, the lie is that I am here to finish a book I know I will never finish. At some point, I may actually work on it. In the meantime, I am sitting here in the monastery library reading François Mauriac's *Life of Jesus*. Mauriac says something interesting in the first chapter, which is as far as I have gotten since I keep putting the book down to think of you. Mauriac says that the Bible says nothing at all about those years that the carpenter Yeshua, son of Mary and Joseph, lived in the straggy village of Nazareth, of which there is no mention in history and which the Old Testament does not name.

There he lived for thirty years—but not in a silence of adoration and love. Jesus dwelt in the thick of a clan, in the midst of the petty talk, the jealousies, the small dramas of numerous kin…

This doesn't sound so bad compared to being nailed to the Cross. Let's hear it for small dramas. Send a little my way, Jesus! But back then, of course, he wasn't the world-famous Son of God. No, wait, he *was* the Son of God, even then, it's just that nobody knew it. Did he know it? Or did he just feel that there might be something on the horizon besides carpentry? Mauriac also says Jesus was one of three carpenters in Nazareth, and he wasn't even considered the best. So maybe he felt he had to branch out into another line of work just for the sake of doing something different. You know, make his mark another way. So he started making miracles, and that was the start of it. Or the end of it, depending on how you look at it.

But before all that, Mauriac imagines what Jesus and Mary might have talked about for all those years over the dinner table after Joseph died. There she was, sitting with the future King of the World, "whose reign shall have no end," and she knew it. But Mauriac says there must have been times over those long years when she questioned the prophecy. All that time, she kept it to herself. He conjectures that they must have talked mostly about tools. I like that. It's probably right. When in doubt, talk about tools.

One last thing: The monks here at New Melleray are famous for their coffins. In the gift shop they sell jam, hymnals, used books—and coffins. They are beautiful coffins made of walnut.

PETER ORNER
PEOSTA, IA

DEAR McSWEENEY'S,
Turns out my friend read that same interview years ago and ended up bringing Helen Hunt's grandmother's coconut macaroons to the shower! Only, they were actually Andie MacDowell's grandmother's coconut macaroons and it was in *Marie Claire*. Oh, and apparently, the bride is allergic to coconut. Thanks for helping me dodge a bullet!
JEN STATSKY
NEW YORK, NY

P.S. Those macaroons were delicious, though. You should try them.

DEAR McSWEENEY'S,
Imagine a mighty robot hero, made of the strongest metal known, able to transform itself into a sleek and powerful starship at your command. It's Transfobot! By pressing the number

keys 1 through 5, you can change different sections of Transfobot's body into the sleek hull, swept-back wings, and awesome thrusters of a starship. The 6 key makes Transfobot change all at once, and the 7 key blasts off!

The following BASIC program—designed to be typed into and enjoyed on your IBM-compatible computer—has been tested and found to work on the following computers and hardware configurations: IBM PC with color/graphics monitor adapter, with disk BASIC D2.00 or advanced BASIC A2.00, IBM PCjr with cartridge BASIC J1.00, and Tandy 1000 with GW-BASIC 2.02 version 01.01.00. (If you use version 00.05.00, please let me know.)

TRANSFOBOT

```
10 DIM r$(24,1),A(5),B(5)Z(5)
20 CLS:WIDTH 40:KEY OFF:SCREEN 0,1
30 LOCATE 12,16,0:COLOR 7:PRINT "Stand by…"
40 FOR H=0 TO 1:FOR I=1 TO 24
50 R$(I,H)="":C=0
60 READ T,KO:R$(I,H)+CHR$(T)+CHR$(KO)
70 C=C+T:IF C<17 THEN 60
80 NEXT I,H
90 FOR I=1 TO 5:READ A(I),B(I):Z(I)=0:NEXT I
100 CLS:FOR K=1 TO 5:GOSUB 1000:NEXT K
110  K$=INKEY$:K=VAL(K$):IF  K<1  OR  K>7
THEN 110
120 IF K<6 THEN GOSUB 1000:GOTO 110
130 IF K=7 THEN LOCATE 24,1,0:FOR I=1 TO
24:PRINT:NEXT
140 FOR K=1 TO 5:IF K>1 THEN Z(K)=1-Z(1)
150 GOSUB 1000:NEXT K:GOTO 110
1000 FOR I=A(K) TO B(K):LOCATE I,12,0:C=0:P=1
1010 T=ASC(MID$(R$(I,Z(K)),P,1))
1020 CL=ASC(MID$(R$(I,Z(K)),P+1,1))
1030 COLOR CL:PRINT STRING$(T,219);
1040 C=C+T:IF C<17 THEN P=P+2:GOTO 1010
1050 NEXT I:Z(K)=1-Z(K):COLOR 7:RETURN
2000 DATA 6,0,5,7,6,0,5,0,7,7,5,0,4,0,1,6,2,7,1,4
2010 DATA 1,7,1,4,2,7,1,6,4,0,5,0,7,7,5,0,6,0,5,7
2020 DATA 6,0,2,0,5,1,3,7,5,1,2,0,1,0,6,1,3,7,6,1
2030 DATA 1,0,17,1,10,1,1,5,6,1,17,1,3,1,1,0,9,1
2040 DATA 1,0,3,1,3,1,1,0,9,1,1,0,3,1,3,1,1,0,9,5
2050 DATA 1,0,3,1,3,4,1,0,9,1,1,0,3,4,2,4,2,0,9,1
2060 DATA 2,0,2,4,1,4,3,0,9,1,3,0,1,4,1,4,3,0,9,1
2070 DATA 3,0,1,4,4,0,4,1,1,0,4,1,4,0,4,0,4,1,1,0
2080 DATA 4,1,4,0,4,0,4,1,1,0,4,1,4,0,4,0,4,1,1,0
2090 DATA 4,1,4,0,4,0,4,1,1,0,4,1,4,0,2,0,6,7,1,0
2100 DATA 6,7,2,0,1,0,7,7,1,0,7,7,1,0
2110 DATA 8,0,1,7,8,0,7,0,3,7,7,0,6,0,1,7,1,6,1,7
2120 DATA 1,6,1,7,6,0,6,0,5,7,6,0,4,0,9,7,4,0,3,0
2130 DATA 11,7,3,0,2,0,13,7,2,0,1,0,6,7,1,1,1,7,1
2140 DATA 1,6,7,1,0,7,7,1,1,1,7,1,1,7,7,7,7,1,1,1
2150 DATA 7,1,1,/,/,6,7,2,1,1,7,2,1,6,7,5,7,3,1,1
2160 DATA 7,3,1,5,7,17,7,17,7,3,7,2,0,7,7,2,0,3,7
2170 DATA 2,7,3,0,7,7,3,0,2,7,1,7,4,0,7,7,4,0,1,7
2180 DATA 4,0,9,7,4,0,4,0,9,7,4,0,4,0,9,,7,4,0,4,0
2190 DATA 9,7,4,0,3,0,11,7,3,0,2,0,6,7,1,0,6,7,2,0
2200 DATA 2,0,2,7,1,0,2,7,3,0,2,7,1,0,2,7,2,0
2210 DATA 1,5,6,10,11,13,14,17,18,24
```

Have fun,

JOEY LATIMER
LA QUINTA, CA

DEAR MCSWEENEY'S,

I'm presently sitting in the back of a van hurtling westward on I-40 en route to Asheville, North Carolina, where I'll be playing tonight with my band The Mountain Goats. A minute ago I looked up from my copy of Keith Richards's autobiography in time to catch a glimpse of Greensboro's Four Seasons Town Centre.

Now, you're probably thinking, What's the big deal? A mall's a mall. Not on your life, pal. That is one very special mall. Y'see, from 1987 to 1990, I worked at the Four Seasons Town Centre branch of the Record Bar chain, selling New Kids on the Block buttons, BODY BY BUDWEISER posters, and the latest hair-metal, country, and rap cassettes to the upstanding citizens and sleazy dirtbags of the Gate City.

My Record Bar career began inauspiciously. I arrived bright and early on my first day only to be told that a maintenance worker had been crushed to death in the Town Centre's ornate glass elevator just hours before. I suppose I could've taken the news as a bad omen and hightailed it out of there right then, but I didn't, for two reasons: (1) I needed that $3.75 an hour, and (2) I knew if I hung in there long enough, I'd meet more than my fair share of weird and wonderful people.

People like…

- Sam, the black-toothed, *TV Guide*–collecting Andre the Giant look-alike who'd corner me just as we were closing in hopes that I could sleuth out the title of a song he'd just heard on the radio. A typical encounter involved Sam drenching my face with saliva while grunting, "She's a killer queen… da da da da da da." Without fail, every lyric Sam sang contained the title of the song he was searching for.

- The frantic man who, just seconds after we opened, sprinted up to my coworker and me, pleading, "Can I use your bathroom? I'm from Danville!"

- The middle-aged Sunday-school teacher who thought that, because I worked in a record store, I could turn her pro–Operation Desert Storm poem/love letter to General Schwarzkopf into a 45 in time to capitalize on the conflict. Though I couldn't help her, I did give her a free Miami Sound Machine cassingle.

- My enigmatic coworker Rusty. I loved Rusty. He sported a Mohawk and an earring, yet often wore cowboy boots and a floor-length duster coat. Rusty was a North Carolina rodeo-going shit-kicker who spun the latest 12" dance singles at local clubs and had an encyclopedic knowledge of *SCTV* episodes. He lived to vault over the front counter and tackle teenage shoplifters. A customer once asked Rusty if the store had "that song about the cat." When Rusty asked her for the melody, the woman began singing (to the tune of "Rock the Casbah"), "Siamese don't like it / Not the cat's fault." Rusty took an especially long lunch at Spinnakers Pub after that.

- The mild-mannered housewife who set up an R-rated Patrick Swayze fan-club booth outside the store one Sunday. We reluctantly okay'd this, hoping it would entice a customer to purchase our lone copy of the just-released *Dirty Dancing* VHS cassette, which we were selling for the very reasonable price of $79.99.

- Courteney Cox, Linda Hamilton, Jon Lovitz, Anthrax guitarist Scott Ian, and Oprah's longtime beau, Stedman Graham. Hey, they may be celebrities to you, but I will forever think of them as my customers. Though my interaction with Ms. Cox was brief, I felt something special as I handed her that *Purple Rain* cassette. I know she felt it, too.

- Mr. Pritchard, a chain-smoking, sixty-something grump I'd help find records to play during his wedding-deejay gigs. Never has one

human been less suited to interact with other humans on their most joyous of days. Mr. P's finest moment came when my boss, Judy, directed him to our Peters Creek Parkway location for a single we didn't have in stock. Pritchard scowled, flicked his cigarette ash into a record bin, grabbed his crotch, and moaned, "I'll show you a Peters Creek!" Did I mention his teenage daughter was on hand to witness this?

In retrospect, I think those Record Bar days were crucial in helping me understand the myriad colorful characters I've met traveling the world in rock bands these past twenty years. Just like you and me, they had their own experiences—good and bad—that resulted in the people they became. I dunno. I guess this is the stuff I enjoy pondering.

Pondering the experiences that resulted in the shirtless, sunburned hitchhiker we just passed holding that ANYWHERE THERE'S BEER/WEED/NOT MY EX-WIFE CARLA sign, on the other hand, is probably best left for another time. Anyway, I should get back to the Keith book. I'm almost at the part where he snorts a small section of the Shroud of Turin. Shadoobie,

JON WURSTER
GREENSBORO, NC

DEAR MCSWEENEY'S,

I recently went on my first trip to Japan. The big things blew my mind, of course—how Tokyo makes New York feel like a quaint little parochial hamlet, for example. But it's the quotidian details that have really lingered with me.

The first night I was there, I was walking down a crazy-busy street—like a highway with mosh-pit sidewalks—and a little Japanese lady was handing something out on the corner. As any intrepid traveler should, I took what she proffered. I expected a flyer I couldn't read, but instead I got a tidy package of facial tissues with a photograph of a bunny's face on it. Were they made from rabbit fur?

Whatever they were, it was January and I had a runny nose and am not the sort of together person who travels with tissues, so I was stoked. Got to some serious nose-blowing. More and more in the days that followed. I came to find that ladies handing out tissues were commonplace in the busier parts of Tokyo—I guess it's standard advertising practice.

But here's the heart of the matter. As many free tissue packets as there were, there were never any trashcans to throw my boogered-up tissues into. Never. Ever. Anywhere. My pockets started to swell with garbage.

On my last day in Japan, I was in Kyoto, getting yen out of a bank so I could buy some hand towels for my girlfriend, and I saw something that blew my mind: a publicly accessible wastebasket. I stopped what I was doing and dug all the shit out of all my jacket and pants pockets and segregated the piles into (a) currency denominations I still didn't have a grasp of, (b) a tangle of work-related receipts I will never file with the IRS, and (c) a mountain of snotty, wadded-up tissues. All of (c) went into the can.

Now, I know this seems totally unmind-blowing, but here in Manhattan nearly every intersection is punctuated with four trashcans. And Japan has so many things that we don't, like vending machines with beer in them and a clean subway system and ubiquitously great fried chicken. But trashcans? As rare as fat, sunburned white people.

So here's the thing, my unresolved cultural query: where are the Japanese putting all their spent Kleenex? Is there a system over there that I don't know about, whereby I could have politely and correctly negotiated the transfer of my blown nose-paper to private, unseen receptacles? Or is Tokyo a metropolis of 40 million people with pockets stuffed full of snot?

Wondering/sniffling,

PETER MEEHAN
NEW YORK, NY

WHERE HE FELL

by ARIEL DORFMAN

HAT'S THAT?"

"What?"

"That. What's that?"

Orlando couldn't decide whether to open his eyes and admit that Karina had woken him up, or to keep them shut and hope that she would go back to sleep herself and that—but no, her whisper had been followed by a hand shaking his blanketed body. She wasn't going to let him off the hook—now those lovely fingers of hers, strong from exploring so much wire and wood, so many carvings, all those stones and tapestries, all that vigorous sewing, now her hand was digging deep into his shoulder, she required his full attention, full attention and nothing less.

"What time is it?"

She shushed him, lowered her response even more. "Listen, just listen," throaty and melodramatic, oh God, she was really on edge, the jet lag, anticipation of the day that awaited her outside, awaited them both on those Paris streets and corners, and sure enough she had refused to knock herself out with a pill—*They're bad for you, Lando, habit-forming, you know, I'll just let nature take its course, you go ahead and stick some strange chemical in your body*, not that any pill in the world could protect him against a wife who insisted on rousing him at, what—he didn't want to ask again about the time, merely blurred his eyes open and caught the glow of the clock. Four in the morning, heaven help me, tomorrow was going to be one of those dawn-to-dusk days, from six in the morning till nine or ten at night, at least fifteen hours, that's what Karina's project would take, but this was not about tomorrow, Karina was asking him once more to listen.

Nothing there, nothing at all, save the silence like an accusation, and—no, she was right, that voice, rising in anger, the words indistinguishable but the meaning, the menace, the blind rage in the night, that was clear. Somebody was growling, almost howling, a man, it was a masculine voice, even a macho voice, and yet that man was crying to himself as well, suppressing a sob—so fervent that it seemed to penetrate them like an arrow, it came from next door, that murderous throb of confusing syllables. And then it ceased, as suddenly as it had begun.

Orlando switched on the light. In the harsh glare, he saw Karina's face, whitened by fear, and then, incongruently, behind her, the thirty faceless rag dolls arranged on the floor in an untidy row, awaiting tomorrow. Awaiting her hands.

"It's coming from the next room, Karina."

"I know, I know. He's been raving like that for a while."

"What do you mean?"

"I've been lying here in the dark, just listening. But he's getting more aggressive. And there's a woman as well. Listen."

But there was nothing to hear. Certainly no woman—and the man must have calmed down, or stopped maybe to catch his breath, or maybe he was doing something else now, didn't need to use his voice to—and now Orlando's ears did capture a plaintive No, no, no, high-pitched and entreating, and then again the man, repeating the same identical ranting tones, as if the woman had not understood the first time and needed to hear it all over again, whatever it was, "*Je vais te*—" That much was comprehensible, I'm going to—what was it that the man was going to do?

"What's he saying?"

"I don't know."

"But you speak French."

Orlando tried a lame joke. "If Molière were to be resurrected only to interpret these words, he wouldn't understand either. Sartre himself would fail, my love. It's just too muffled." But she was not smiling, Karina knew enough about belligerence to imagine what might be happening in that nearby room, and all the more reason not to alarm her even more, tomorrow was too important... had Karina slept at all? How long had she been there, absorbing the fury that once again was snarling what was unmistakably a threat, could it be that the man had really meant it, that he—? Orlando thought he knew what the last word was, Karina had guessed, Orlando was sure that Karina did not need a translator to recognize a voice that fed on its own rage, fed on the muscular joy of being able to let loose every decibel in the universe, if voices could kill...

"Go and listen."

"Where?"

"He's threatening her, Orlando. Go and listen. Out there, man, in the corridor."

"Out there?"

"Yes, outside his door. Go and listen."

It was pointless to suggest that they call the night porter, file a complaint. Karina would brush aside any plan that was not the one she had settled on; what mattered, she'd insist, was not to stop the voice from speaking but to stop what the owner of that voice was going to do. First, though, they had to be certain of what was really happening—because it might all be perfectly innocent, just a quarrel between lovers, but what if she was right, and there was a killer in the room next door and Orlando protested to the hotel management and the maniac found out who had fingered him and decided that Orlando needed to be taught a lesson, targets us, lies in wait and thrusts open the door as we pass by and comes out with a knife or a gun or has hands like a butcher's or—now it was Orlando who was imagining things, scenarios, he couldn't help it, an incessant film flooding through his head, the images kept cascading as he nudged himself out of bed and into the hall, feeling Karina's breath behind him, her heart beating like his, tiptoeing, both of them, down the corridor in their pajamas, what if the man heard them? He was not saying anything now, not one word, and no response either from the woman, what if the man had already—three steps and they were there.

Karina pointed to the door. She wanted him to get closer, put his ear to the wood. Orlando shook his head, no, he wasn't going to risk it, not while there was no sound from the room—but now came the sudden scrape of a chair, and the voice again, almost the exact replica of what they had heard several times already, "*Je vais te—*" and now Orlando could understand the next word, the very one that—and then something new, "*Tu m'as trahi,*" you've betrayed me, I'm going to—Orlando couldn't deny it anymore, couldn't deny what Karina's eyes were demanding, what they knew without his confirming that the word was *tuer*—kill, I'm going to kill you, you've betrayed me—and the woman responding No, no, no, as if they were stuck, the man and the woman inside that room, but also Orlando and Karina hovering outside, all four of them trapped in a loop, a sound track that some crazy disc jockey was replaying over and over and over again, as if—and now Orlando sighed with relief, he gestured to Karina to follow him, just as from inside the room they could hear the man say "*Je t'aime,*" no need to translate that, *Je t'aime, je t'aime...* and Karina nodded dubiously and came along, shuffled back to safety, closing the door as inaudibly as they had opened it a minute ago.

"It's nothing, Karina, no need to worry."

"What did he say?"

"Karina, you don't have to—"

"Tell me, Orlando!"

"That he loves her, that she betrayed him, that he's going to kill her. But—"

"But what?"

"They're not real. Just voices on a machine."

"What? How do you know?"

And Orlando explained that this old hotel had fallen on hard times, that when he had checked in two days ago the man at the desk had told him that some of the rooms, centrally located at a reasonable price in the heart of Paris, were being permanently leased by a media company—editing facilities, that sort of thing, and yesterday Orlando had happened to glance inside one of the rooms, yes, yes, he knew that Karina didn't approve of his incorrigible voyeurism, but in this case it had been providential, because he'd managed to see that in that room, not the one next door but two doors down, two men were hunched in front of a screen, *tap tap tap* on a keyboard, an ad they were working on flaring with cartoon characters and sounds and images before them. That's what this was, Karina, really, really, no need to worry.

True, the receptionist had assured Orlando that no work was done during the night, but we all know how obsessive artists can get, in this case probably a scene for some melodrama wasn't picture perfect and someone had come back neurotically after midnight to match the right *Je vais te tuer* to the shot. That's why he and Karina had kept hearing the same insomniac phrases, the same passionate besotted words, the same No, no, no from the woman—it was all a fiction.

And again they listened, the same tones still coming through the wall, this new rage of the man matching that tired twin macho rage of some moments ago, the woman for a second or third or fourth time denying the charge, placating her lover, trying to save herself, over and over again, the same scene. "Like peas in a pod," Orlando said, smiling at the image, so innocent and childlike in the dead of night.

"How can you be sure? Did you see anybody *there*, in room number nine?"

"What else could it be? If the guy were real, he would have done something by now, killed her at least, don't you think?"

"Not funny."

"Karina, it's just some editor on a deadline."

"The bastard," Karina said. "Keeping me awake all night."

"*Pobrecita*," Orlando said in Spanish. "Try to get some sleep."

"I'm sorry that I woke you up. It's just that I was—"

"I understand. Tomorrow's a big day."

"Don't you think we should bang on the door? Or on the wall? Just so he knows, so he shuts up, not let him get away with it?"

But Orlando didn't want an altercation, not now, not ever, sensed it was best to complain discreetly tomorrow—though it was already today, soon the sun would be casting its light on them as only the sun in Paris can, with that fierce gentleness that had created the Impressionists and devoured Picasso and inspired Miles Davis, had, in fact, legend had it, fallen on Camus as he directed the first reading of *Huis Clos* in this very room, *la chambre ronde*, on a midwinter night longer than this one, but then as now dawn had come, Paris was yawning itself awake, down in the rue de Seine they could hear a delivery truck braking, the crates of fruit and vegetables being slammed onto the pavement, a call from one man to his mate to be careful, calm voices, matter-of-fact voices, voices satiated with croissants and *café crème, du grand*, and *fromage frais* and *du beurre aussi et de la confiture, s'il vous plaît*, nothing like the voices of ferocity and supplication from next door that had already concluded their endless litany, seemed to have decided to call it a night, as if to relieve Orlando of the need to knock adamantly on the wall, pre-empt an intervention that he really wanted to avoid. Tomorrow was already here, maybe they should just get ready for their long day ahead, or maybe...

But Karina wasn't in the mood.

She went into the bathroom, and, after a moment, the shower erupted and water poured onto her skin. He would have liked to have been that water, he had been that water so often, remembered, tried to remember what it was like, that skin, each finger, each slip of a curve, each opening, and yet each time different, each time the first time. But not today.

He looked at the thirty rag dolls scattered against the wall of the room, one for each year. He was glad that the director of the museum yesterday, a slender, wispy, pretty woman, had spoken passable English; he had not been forced to translate for Karina, to help her explain why there would be exactly thirty sites.

"My brother," Karina had said. "Thirty years ago tomorrow. June 19."

"Yes," the woman had answered. "I know. I'm sorry."

"My mother still expects him to come home. One day for the door to open and my brother to step into the room and there he'll be, after all this time."

"How old is your mother?"

"Eighty-eight," said Karina. "She's eighty-eight. She says she won't die until he returns."

This had been yesterday at the Musée Jean Moulin, the museum honoring the liberation of Paris and General Leclerc. Orlando and Karina, following the woman's instructions beforehand, had ventured into the Gare Montparnasse and climbed the unassuming flight of stairs next to track number three, two stories up, to discover the great esplanade there, a gigantic wild garden two blocks long and one block wide, built on top of the train station, surrounded by high rises there in the very middle of Paris, hidden from thousands of passengers and passersby and tourists on the streets outside, a gem above the bustle of the city. Karina and Orlando had stopped in unison and gaped at the spectacle, children being strolled along alleys of exuberant verdancy by bespectacled grandparents, that magnificent field planted on the roof of the station like a promise of resurrection in the most implausible of places, and then, shaking their heads in disbelief, they had entered the museum. There they had received the obligatory guided tour from Madame la Directrice, along with a copy of a book she had written about the days in August of 1944 when the resistance had risen up against Hitler's occupying army, forcing the Allies—a reluctant Montgomery, a cautious Eisenhower, an obstinate General Marshall— to move on Paris in order to avoid a massacre.

"Your book," Orlando had said to the museum director, "it wasn't available in the bookstores."

"Is that so?"

Orlando had made sure he would reach Paris a day before Karina precisely so he could find a book that would guide his wife on her expedition, help him guide her. Even though she hadn't asked him to do anything, had arranged the meeting at the museum, had everything under control, might even resent that Orlando was inserting himself so forcefully into events—*All I'm asking is that you accompany me, that's all, make sure the camera is working, no battery troubles, that and just be by my side, mi amor, that's all.* But Orlando had wanted to surprise her, to gather as much information as he could, he was determined to prove—as if proof was necessary, as if Karina cared for proof—how much he loved her, to bring her a trophy, a book that contained every memorial plaque in Paris, every crook and angle and spot where someone had fallen during the uprising of 1944. Someone must have documented all those heroes who had died for their country; someone must have photographed the markers that Orlando had noticed on other visits.

Nothing. Not one book. Not one pamphlet. "There are more books on that period than there are plaques themselves," the buxom saleswoman at Gibert Jeune had sniffed. "But none like the one you describe." This was at the fourth bookstore Orlando had consulted. She had gone on and on about the plethora of volumes on that period, the saleswoman, and the absolute lack—*Monsieur, I would know,* croyez-moi, *I'd know*—of any documentation on the specific sites of death of those patriots. Not that her unyielding and irrevocable assurances had stopped Orlando from continuing his quest, visiting five, six more *librairies*, until finally in a small shop on the rue Jacob a wizened old man had told him there was a book called *Ici est tombé,* from Editions Tirésias, with photos of twenty-seven such sites, along with interviews with the families and friends of the men who had fallen in the fight against fascism. It would take a month to get the book, did he want to place an order?

No, Orlando needed it by the next morning, he needed to give it to Karina as soon as she arrived from Charles de Gaulle, it had to be on the bed when she plopped down, before she went out with him to the musée—he at least had the satisfaction of going back to the supercilious woman with her thick ankles at Gibert Jeune and informing her that there was indeed a book, *Ici est tombé,* it was called. And the saleswoman was forced to look it up on her *ordinateur* and had to agree that it did exist, yes, Monsieur, but such a small publishing house, it would take at least a month to order, did he want to wait that long or maybe he should get it directly from the publishing house if he was, as it was clear, in such a hurry?

So all that Karina had found on her pillow when she arrived was a desultory piece of paper on which Orlando had written the words *Ici est tombé.* A rain check, an IOU. "I looked for it all day yesterday," Orlando had said. "Sorry I couldn't get it in time—I thought maybe today we could go up to Editions Tirésias. It's near the Porte de Clignancourt."

"Sweet of you, *mi amor*," Karina had said, giving him a peck on the cheek, ruffling the thin mop of hair on his head. "But we have the meeting at the musée. The director there has drawn us a map of the thirty sites. I asked that they be close enough to each other to take in during the course of one day. And there's still the Six Burghers of Rodin that I want to take another look at, and a good dinner, you know Paris better than I do... You choose, I pay, okay? And then we should try to get some rest."

Except that she hadn't rested at all, damn those media people next door, they really had some nerve editing at these ungodly hours, and why in hell did they require the sound to be so obstreperous, were they deaf or something? Karina's shower stretched on and on, but its pitter-patter did not soothe Orlando, almost seemed to be mocking him in some undefined way.

He dressed rapidly and, without disturbing Karina, left the room.

Not a peep, no love betrayed, no promises of death and retribution. Only stillness and peace behind the neighboring door. The bastard! He, that man, whoever, the invisible editor—he was probably off to his own merry arrondissement, was snoring away right now or making love to his wife or his mistress or masturbating or whatever fuckers like him did in order to relax after a hard night's work, the son of a bitch, *fils de putain*.

Though not an insult escaped Orlando's lips when he complained to the receptionist.

"Room nine?" the receptionist said. "You're sure?"

"Yes, of course—right next to ours, next to *la chambre dix, la chambre ronde*."

"There are no media people using room number nine."

Orlando stared at him. "Who's in there, then?"

The clerk smiled enigmatically, as if to imply that Orlando knew quite well who was lodging in there.

"That's confidential information. You wouldn't want me to reveal your name to some other guest, would you? I mean, if he came along and said you had been threatening your wife."

"But he was. If you're right and that room's not being used by some filmmaker to—listen. That man was extremely violent. And he didn't just threaten that woman once, he did it over and over again."

The receptionist smiled again, made a gesture to Orlando to inch closer. "So you saw him go in, recognized him? Is that what you want me to confirm? That it's really him?"

Orlando's face must have registered the sincerity of his mystification, because after a pause the receptionist sighed and said: "You don't know, then? You don't know who's in that room?"

"No, of course not, I've already told you, I've already said so, I—"

"If you promise to tell no one… It's Antoine Ricard."

"Antoine Ricard? The actor?"

"Antoine Ricard, yes."

A scroll of names dropped through Orlando's mind: Truffaut, Chabrol, Rohmer… Ricard had even worked with Spielberg and Jonathan Demme. He was one of the most flamboyant French actors of the last forty years. In the room next door? Yammering menaces at a woman, barking them out over and over, groaning uncontrollably?

"He rents that room from time to time," the receptionist said. "He has his own house, of course, in the 16ème, I think. But like so many artists, he loves our hotel. The women want to make believe they are Juliette Gréco, and the men, take your pick: Sartre, Jean-Paul Belmondo, they all stayed here. So Ricard—wait a minute. Yesterday a script was delivered to him—he must have been rehearsing. I didn't know there was a woman up there, but that's not my business, right? Or yours?"

"At four in the morning? He's rehearsing at four in the morning?"

"Method acting," said the receptionist, obviously somewhat of an intellectual. "Maybe the film calls for something terrible to happen just before dawn and Ricard wants to position himself. He's known for his extreme attention to details, his belief in atmosphere above all, a *je ne sais quoi*... but you're right, he should not be disturbing the peace like that. I'll have a word with him—"

"No, no, no, there's really no need to—"

"You're right. Such an artist! And I'm sure it was just a one-time thing. We've never had any protests before."

Karina took the revelation about the identity of their next-door neighbor with surprising good humor, suggested that if Ricard started to shout again tonight Orlando could knock on the door and ask for his autograph.

"Me? Why me?"

"Because you speak French, *naturellement, mon amour*."

The impish lilt in her voice was an indication that, contrary to what might have been expected, the incident in room nine had lightened her mood rather than souring it. Maybe she would have had a sleepless night anyway. Maybe the French actor and his partner in crime had done Karina a favor by distracting her from the thirtieth anniversary of her brother's abduction, the thirty sites awaiting her commemoration and the thirty rag dolls and Orlando's camera. Strange how something that seems to be terrible—a man about to kill a woman, a woman begging for her life—turns out to be comic, a mere illusion, two actors hamming it up, strange that this could end up being a blessing for someone like Karina whose life had been, like Orlando's, touched by a violence that was far from fictitious.

Just as the violence that had terminated the life, back on August 24, 1944, of Jacques Francesco—right there, the plaque said so, affixed to the wall at the entrance of the hotel:

ICI EST TOMBÉ

MORT POUR LA FRANCE

It was somehow fitting that Karina could begin her project without even leaving the premises. When they had made their way downstairs, she looked at the plaque and then across the street, at the cheese and sausage sellers who, like every Friday, were installed on the curb with large crusts of bread—not yet ready to sell, not at six in the morning, but preparing for a long day, though not as long as Karina's would be, or Orlando's. This was just their first stop but she was going to take her time, slowly, as ever, never rushed, Karina, examining the spot where Jacques Francesco—or was *Jacques* the surname and *Francesco* the given name? The notes from Madame la Directrice did not say—the spot where that young man had been killed. Though maybe not that young, no indication of his age, only that he had died for France. And then Karina had turned to the receptionist who had followed them outside and was now watching her with his gray, incurious eyes.

"Would Sartre have heard the shots?"

"Sartre?"

"Would he have heard the shots. From the room where we slept last night. That was Sartre's room—was he here that night? Did he wake up on August 24 and hear the shots that killed Jacques Francesco?"

"I don't know, Madame. I don't know if he was here at all that day. I have been told that he and Beauvoir lived here for five years, from 1943 to 1948, but I don't think anybody is aware of his whereabouts on that day or any given day." The man's English was surprisingly unblemished, with hardly a trace of French. Where was he from, where had he learned to speak like that?

"And Beauvoir? Maybe he had gone to her room, down the corridor? Maybe he'd have heard the shots from there?"

"Or maybe," Orlando interceded, feeling the need to divert the discussion, conscious that this was the second bizarre conversation that the receptionist had been forced to endure that morning, you don't want to get into trouble with the hotel staff, that was a golden rule of Orlando's, "neither of them was even nearby that day. There was heavy fighting. They may have fled."

Karina pursed her lips. "Well, somebody didn't. Somebody besides Jacques Francesco was here, saw it all, heard the shots, reported this death. Or there wouldn't be a plaque here today. If nobody had reported the death."

Spurred somehow by her own words, as if they'd refocused her on the mission she had set for herself, Karina now began to work. She measured the space on the rue de Seine, the possible perspectives. Had the witness been close, had she watched from a window, from behind a shuttered door, from that corner where customers eager for some bread or breakfast were now lining up in front of Chez Paul—there'd definitely been nothing like that café boulangérie there in 1944, right? Or had there been another man, a companion, someone right next to the young soldier, shifted just an inch to the side at the very instant the bullet whizzed by and killed Jacques, a bullet that could have been meant for the comrade-in-arms, could have found Sartre as he went to retrieve his daily baguette, Beauvoir as she slipped out of the hotel that very afternoon?

Karina did not wait any longer. She dipped into the large American Flyer wheeled carry-on and, with one of the rag dolls in her hand, she crossed the rue de Buci to the Café du Marché, nimbly sidestepping one of the women waiting tediously for the place to open. Karina motioned to Orlando, indicating the exact point from which he was to take the photo, and then, only then, once he was in position, she pressed two buttons into the face of the rag doll and then, in red lipstick, painted beneath them a wide-open mouth about to cry out, a cry that was somehow also subdued, and stepped outside the range of the camera's lens. "Did you get that?" she asked Orlando, and he said yes, that he had.

He had taken two snaps, in fact, as per her instructions, she'd be able to contemplate the scene later on. The doll placed where she presumed somebody, anybody, a man, a woman, maybe a child, maybe a bystander, someone had seen the soldier fall, had been unable to stop the death but willing to tell the story, just like her, just like Karina. She was also going to tell what had happened, twenty-nine more times before the day was done she was going to re-create the story of those who had stood and watched a body collapse in a heap and then transmitted that incident, event, occurrence to their countrymen, so that many years later a plaque could be chiseled with words, a ceremony had been held, hands had fastened the memory in marble onto the wall of the hotel, right next to the door. So that she could do her work decades later, could mark and honor the thirty years since her brother had been kidnapped, snatched from a street in Santiago, vanished without a trace, not one more word from him or about him, not even a rumor, not one whisper about where he might be, who had taken him, what they had done, Mauricio had disappeared from the face of the earth as if he had never existed.

Nobody had reported his death.

Karina had not been there, in Chile, that day. Because of Orlando. Because she had followed Orlando into exile and was by his side, had been by his side for three years by then as they wandered and then finally anchored themselves in New York; Karina was the one who had answered the phone that day, Orlando knew it was something terrible by the way she repeated *Mamá, Mamá, Mamá,* each time more desperately, Karina's mother was crying on the other end of the line in a Santiago thousands of miles away where Karina could not console her, could not accompany her as Mamá looked for Mauricio in the days and weeks and months and years ahead, Orlando knew it had to be about Mauricio that day when neither of them, not Orlando, not Karina, had been in Chile. Thirty years ago. June 19, 1979.

That day she had started the ritual they were returning to now, that was culminating now, here in Paris. That day, as soon as she'd hung up, she'd gone to her clay—talking all the while, giving Orlando the details of what her mamá had sobbed over the phone, that Mauricio had not come home that evening, had not called as he always did at mid-morning, had not met his girlfriend for lunch, had not reached the university at all to take his final exam—how could he, why would he, miss the final exam?—Karina told Orlando all this, Mamá Clara was hoping there might be good news, maybe a minor accident, maybe an ulcer attack and he was in a hospital; or some other explanation, he'd gone off with friends, but his friends were all involved in some way or other in the struggle, and his friends knew nothing about where Mauricio might be, his friends had all gone into hiding so the government couldn't find them if Mauricio, if Mauricio—and at that point Karina had already kneaded the clay into something fluid and cruel and strangely tender, not a face, more like a send-off kiss, fingers on lips blowing a kiss, but not quite lips and not quite fingers and not exactly a kiss. A signature piece from Karina, of the sort that had already earned her a kind of fame at the early age of twenty-nine, an exhibition in that Manhattan gallery in SoHo, just off Mercer, those carvings of hers that seemed to stop time and simultaneously accelerate it, those lips that were not lips saying goodbye before they could say hello, saying hello as they said goodbye, her series of farewells and sighs, a first secret homage to her brother but not yet the dolls that many years later she would start to work on, that she had now brought to Paris. "*Valediction*, that's what I'll call it," Karina had said to Orlando in New York back then once the small statuette of lips was finished, even if it would never be finished, the whole point was that she had caught the lonely bird of that mouth in mid-flight, whether about to land or open or close or spread its wings would never be clear, that would be determined only by the spectator, he who watched, she who had not watched the scene.

For thirty years, on every June 19, Karina had added one more leave-taking to the cycle and succession of memorials, each year different, each year more ferocious and more loving, each year saying hello and saying goodbye to the brother who never surfaced again, except in the sorrow of his mother and in the eyes and hands of his sister. But they had always been modest attempts, savagely heartbreaking and slender, always something she fashioned from whatever material was at hand—nothing prepared, nothing projected ahead of time, just every June 19 a self-effacing, unassuming recollection, almost a transitory token, a minimal recurring refusal to forget, but never something like this, never thirty rag dolls transported to Paris, of all places, never a meeting at a museum, never anything in the streets among people who could watch her work. For thirty years it had been a humble and private ceremony, a dialogue between herself and her brother, herself and her demons, herself and the unstated suspicion that if she had stayed in Chile she could have saved Mauricio, somehow stopped him from going out that day, if she had not accompanied Orlando in his banishment she could at the very least have been there in Santiago, found someone who had seen something, heard something, knew something, anything. Not that she had ever reproached Orlando, not that the chain of artistic carvings year after year constituted a recrimination. No. Each new work, year after year, was only a diffident interruption of her routine, an annual reminder of the need to bridge the distance from the native land she rarely visited, that never even seemed to crop up in their conversation as of late, so that Orlando had been astonished by her decision to go public, expose herself like this, plan in advance, yes, truly astonishing—as if hit by a stone, that's the origin of *astonished*, he could still hear himself discussing the word with her when she had come back from English lessons during that first year in New York. Back then he would make her go over another verb and another noun before they made love, grasp and unclasp her hands roughened by having toiled away all day with her stones, astonished, yes, that she had chosen him out of all the possible men on this planet and of this species, a bewilderment that had never ceased.

"Orlando. Orlando!"

He had drifted off, as he did from time to time, he had forgotten where he was, why he was there, had blurred out completely the rue de Seine and the Café du Marché and Jacques Francesco dying so long ago and Karina's impatient wave of the hand. They had all those other sites to visit, he was supposed to lug the bag around the cobbled streets of Paris, he was supposed to accompany her, waiting affably while she decided where she wanted him to stand, the place where somebody might have seen the body fall, Orlando was to be her memory today.

Their next stop was at 17 Quai des Grands Augustins—two plaques, one on top of the other, René Dova, MORT POUR LA FRANCE, nineteen years old, and Georges Loiseleur, twenty-eight when he died for the liberation of Paris. But what does this mean, Orlando, PRISONNIER ÉVADÉ—had Georges escaped from prison? And Orlando: yes, that's what it meant, Georges had managed to find a way out of some concentration camp and joined the resistance and then on August 19, both he and René—but Karina was already wondering about something else, wasn't Picasso's studio nearby, in the rue des Grands Augustins just around the corner, do you think he heard the shots, do you think maybe he was visiting his friend Michel Leiris near here, in that house over there? Not that Karina was expecting a reply from Orlando, she was asking it of herself, asking it of the dead Picasso as she had asked it of the dead Sartre and the dead Simone de Beauvoir, *Beauvoir* means to see beautifully, right, Orlando, to see from beauty itself? And now she had scurried across the street and started to twist the rag dolls together, two of them, one for René and one for Georges, making them clutch each other's arms or hands or filaments or whatever it was they had sticking out from their torsos, Karina ignoring a woman with a black dachshund on a pink leash who was staring at her as if she were desecrating the Seine itself with her outlandish antics and frantic fingers, the dog deciding to pee on the corrugated metal of one of the bookstalls just as Karina saw that the traffic had stopped at Saint Michel and urged Orlando to cross and take the pictures, two each for each of the fallen. And then they'd walked back toward the Pont Neuf, next on their itinerary, mapped out so carefully and with such fastidious consideration by Madame la Directrice, she had indeed made sure that all thirty sites were within walking distance of each other, all in the 5ème and 6ème arrondissements, except for a few in the 1er, where so many *résistants* had been killed near the Hôtel de Ville and the rue de Rivoli.

And there, at the Pont Neuf, in effect, was René Revel, age thirty-nine, also killed on August 19—"According to the museum director's book," Orlando said to Karina, "there was a barricade here on that day," maybe that was why so many had died so close to—but Karina was not listening. She was frowning at the words below René Revel's name: A ETÉ TUÉ PAR LES ALLEMANDS, the man had been killed by the Germans. It was the word *Allemands* that was beckoning to Karina, Orlando knew her well enough to realize that she was asking herself why the engraver or the family had decided to commemorate this martyr by emphasizing the nationality of the murderers, calling them Germans rather than Nazis, why not Nazis? Karina had to be thinking of her own mother who would never speak a word of the German she had been born into eighty-eight years ago, Karina must be thinking of her grandfather who had stayed behind in Berlin and been murdered himself, Karina was thinking of the day when her then-adolescent mother had heard right here in Paris, also over the phone, the news of her own father's death, and Karina confirmed that this was what was coursing through her mind, that Orlando was right, by taking the rag doll that was supposed to witness the death of René Revel, tell the story of how he had fallen on the Quai de Conti, shot by a sniper who spoke the same language as Karina's mother and grandparents, and making it into a scarecrow of a phone—one of those ancient black ones with handles like the wings of a hawk, the sort that would have been in René's house when his sister answered and heard the news, when his mother answered and was told yes, I saw him fall, *ici est tombé*, I can tell you exactly where it happened, how it happened, what his eyes last saw, come with me when this war is over and we will stand together, you and she and I, and remember René. A phone in Paris that conveyed and received the news, a phone in Santiago that Karina's mother had clutched, the phone in New York in Karina's hands, captured by Orlando's snapshots, all those phones deep inside Orlando's guesses about what his wife was thinking.

And that's how it had gone the rest of the morning. Robert and Lucien at the Préfecture de Police, in front of the market full of birds and mice and rabbits, and then across the Seine, barely glancing up at Notre Dame and then the Place Saint Michel and Karina in the middle of the crowd clapping at a breakdancing trio, that early in the morning, oblivious to the multitude and the sounds around them, forcing Orlando to position himself awkwardly with the American Flyer in front of a man in a wheelchair who wouldn't be able to see the performance, a discourtesy that didn't matter to her, the invalid was occupying the selfsame location Karina was sure one of her witnesses had stood in, and so she molded a figurine that was also in a wheelchair, as if that would have been possible back then, as if anyone that crippled could have been present when the bullets were flying and one of them hit, maybe more than one, smashed into the lungs of Raymond Boisson, 29 ANS, TOMBÉ GLORIEUSEMENT POUR LA FRANCE, and down the Boul Mich and another Raymond and another Robert on the rue Monsieur le Prince, so many Roberts, and Jean Bachelet—like our president, Michelle, Michelle Bachelet, do you think they're related? But Karina wasn't paying attention, something else was worrying her and Orlando was about to ask, was about to make the mistake he always made, interrupting the seesaw of her mind precisely when she needed a few more instants to go up toward the next thought or descend until she had touched the ground and could whittle the idea into an articulation, Orlando rescued from that blunder by...

It was Antoine Ricard. Ricard himself sitting there, on a bench just inside the gates of the Jardin de Luxembourg not twenty paces away from where Jean Bachelet had been shot in the attack on the gardens, the attack on the nearby Sénat where several others had been mowed down, Bachelet dead at thirty-three years of age, remembered by his *camarades du combat du 5ème*, so close to where Antoine Ricard sat hunched over some pigeons. He was feeding them offhandedly, almost with apathy, those enormous hands of his breaking open half a baguette with an almost delicate ennui; he seemed more concerned with the woman next to him, petite, blondish but perhaps with a touch of brown, hair perhaps recently dyed and fading off, firm, well-rounded breasts, so much younger than Ricard and talking to him with the intensity only a lover can drag from some fluid deep inside the body, angry over something or disappointed or—or maybe it was all fiction, maybe it was one more dialogue they were elaborating for the film, *je vais te tuer*, Ricard's character fated to kill her sometime after this scene. Was this a tableau of reconciliation or was it the prelude to an attempted murder, would they repeat tonight the same words over and over and force Orlando to confront the great actor and his concubine or partner or whoever she was, bang on the door and demand silence? Oh how he hated the idea of interrupting Ricard, that famous face of his and those large hands like hams when he swung open the door and saw Orlando in his pajamas in the corridor!

And then the woman in the Jardin du Luxembourg glanced up and realized Orlando had been spying on her and there was a flash of panic in her green liquid eyes, inside the tears a lightning flash arising and quenched just as quickly, or maybe he was imagining it all, Help me, help me, was that what she was saying, hard to know because then the alarm dissolved and she said something to Ricard and he cast the last crumbs to the pigeons as they fluttered around, and without sending even a *dernier regard* in Orlando's direction, gently took the woman's arm and started to walk away into the gardens, toward the fountain where little boys were trying to sail capsized boats and their weary mothers were scolding them.

"Ricard," Orlando managed to stammer, "look, Karina, it's Ricard, the actor, you know, who—"

"Orlando, I have a problem here."

"A problem?"

"A plaque is missing. Something's wrong. I can't find Jean Arnould. He should be here, he's on the map, he was killed on August 25, it says here, but there's no plaque, nothing."

Orlando forced his eyes to abandon the receding back of Antoine Ricard and concentrate on his wife.

They spent the next half hour looking for the missing Jean. It was only when Karina herself (Orlando would not have dared propose it) suggested that they give up, that she'd find a way to replace Jean Arnould, it was past midday and they should have something to eat, there, I bet that café over there has great *soupe à l'oignon*, it was incredible how Karina was able to detach herself from what had just been obsessing her, she'd always been like that, for over three decades, one moment sweating over a piece of mahogany that would not quite bend to her imagination, swearing at it, licking its surface, scratching the wood almost orgasmically, and a few seconds later smiling contentedly and asking Orlando if he had remembered to fetch the clothes from the dry cleaners on his way back from the office. Had she heard him mention Ricard? Had she even noticed the man?

Orlando watched her slurp up every last drip and crust of the onion soup, every last sliver, and steal the ruins of his baguette and dip it into Orlando's *soupe de poissons*, scooping up the last remnants of the brew, and then she turned to the map and ticked off the next settings and victims, Alfred Biard and Marc Bloch, and she wanted to pass by the rue Bonaparte and also a house where Joseph Roth had lived while in exile, escaped from Vienna, her mother loved Roth's work even if she read it only in Spanish, but before that let's share a crème brûlée, Lando, what do you say?

How did she manage it, the switch? How did she go from the bliss of her throat welcoming the sweetness of that dessert—Oh, it's burnt just right, Lando, and fluffy inside, here, take another bite, you'll do me a favor, I'm going to be as fat as a barrel if I don't watch out—how did she go from that bouncy joy of living, go from there to the rue Saint André des Arts fifteen minutes later, the plaque that nobody read as they lined up for their crêpes and their *gauffres*, oblivious to this woman, his wife, who was burrowing inside the pain of someone she had never met, kneading it out into a cry, ridding herself and the witness of the pain but being true to it at the same time, how did she do it? Crouched over the next doll, the eyes either faded or burned into the rag, the mouth about to shutter itself open and say something, what it would pass on to the fallen man's relatives, each doll seeming to be watching not only that death but all the previous ones, an intimation of wisdom accumulating. Orlando didn't know how she did it any more than he understood how she moved from the crème brûlée to the memory of Mauricio, only that she was exhilarated by the journey, fed on it as Orlando, trapped in the last mood, could not. By mid-afternoon he was exhausted and could barely keep up with her, began to snap the photos with a nonchalance similar to the attitude with which Antoine Ricard had been supplying crumbs to the pigeons, almost indifferent. And then the sun was setting, and finally, finally, the rue de Buci, the rue de Seine, the blessed hotel, Orlando thirsting for the shower that had eluded him that dawn, that he had been unable to take because of the ruckus next door, but no, wait, Orlando—Karina turning to him, already swinging wildly again, counting the names on her fingers—we only have twenty-nine.

And then she read the alarm and collapse in his eyes and gave him a playful punch on the arm and brushed a kiss on his lips, *mi amor*, no, don't worry, we're not going out again, we'll just do Jacques Francesco a second time, who says there weren't two witnesses, a woman first from the Café du Marché and a man who was caught in the crossfire, there, farther down the rue de Seine, where the new cheese shop is, Orlando—and she extracted the last rag out of the carry-on and drew dark glasses on the face, deciding that the man had been blind, had only *heard* the shot or shots that split open the life of Jacques Francesco at the door of the hotel, 60 rue de Seine, did Orlando know that some 160 blind people had been executed by the Germans, deported, tortured, why not include one blind person among her collection? Whoever it was he had been damn more attentive than so many who went around with their eyes intact and their hearts closed, *snap, snap*, and that was it, they were done for the day…

When he emerged from the shower, Karina was dialing her mother in Santiago—*We'll go out to dinner as soon as I talk to her, it'll be late otherwise, and no matter what you do, don't tell her what we've been up to, de acuerdo?*—and he listened, drying himself off and then naked for a while, hearing Karina invent a different day. In fact, she was telling Mamá Clara about yesterday, June 18, as if it were June 19, the garden above the Gare Montparnasse and the museum of the liberation of Paris, but not a word about the map or Madame la Directrice, then deftly jumping ahead to recount the *soupe à l'oignon* and the crème brûlée and Orlando had a delicious *soupe des poissons*, Mamá, I stole the last of it, you should have seen his face, *la cara que puso*, and then we went to the Musée Rodin.

So that was why Karina had insisted on going to see the Rodins yesterday. She had wanted to tell her mother about the statues, tell her what she was doing in Paris without lying, report what was, in effect, going to be her next project. "Yes, Mamá, I went to see *The Burghers of Calais*, remember you showed them to me when you brought me to Paris, when I must have been nine years old? I never forgot them, I think they started me on my artistic path, I've never been able to get them out of my mind—those six men who are about to die, who know they're destined to have their heads cut off by Edward III in order to save their city, who volunteered to be sacrificed so the English king wouldn't kill everybody else, and you see them about to confront the moment when the sentence will be passed, when they have to face the fate they chose." There was a pause while Karina's mother asked her something. And then: "No, Mamá, my project won't be about the Burghers themselves, though it's inspired by them, you could say. The series is going to be called *Waiting for Philippa*. She was the queen, the wife of Edward, the one who interceded, she got down on her knees and begged him to spare their lives, she placed herself between those six men and the executioner's sword and her husband relented and offered the hostages to her to do whatever she pleased with, and she freed them."

There was another pause as Karina and her mother and Orlando thought about this and then Karina was off again, perhaps afraid of that silence: "That's my plan, Mamá, I want to assemble a sequence of figures like question marks that ask where she is today, where are the Philippas of today when we most need them. I'm not sure what it will be, how it will turn out, but that's what I'm going to spend the next year or so doing, a compilation, I guess you could call it, maybe videos with some mobiles, maybe some rag dolls, I'm not sure of anything, except that you'll be the first to receive an invitation when I open, yes, I think it might be at the Venice Biennale, yes, Orlando has been *maravilloso*, he's accompanied me like he always does, he's been very helpful, he's right here, would you like to say hello to him?"

And she passed him the phone and Karina had not mentioned Mauricio nor had Clara, although the whole conversation had really been about the brother who thirty years ago had not come home, the son Clara was still waiting for in that lonely house in Santiago. Which meant that Orlando couldn't whisper a word of what the day had brought, Karina's homage to the fallen, he had to make believe he knew everything about *Waiting for Philippa*, the men about to die, even if this was the first time he had heard a word about Karina's next project.

And then he forgot about Philippa, because there was dinner at that old bistro on the Île Saint-Louis and then the slow walk back to their hotel and then the even slower love they made in that room where Sartre and Beauvoir had perhaps also touched each other's bodies but most certainly had been more interested in intermingling their minds, where Jean-Paul and Simone had spoken endlessly about their lovers, brought the stories to their soul mates as trophies to be quartered and analyzed at length, and Orlando did manage to think, So this is what Philippa did with Edward the night after the king spared the life of those condemned prisoners, this is how she opened herself to him because he had opened his heart to her compassion, this is what happens when you are married to the right woman, when you are chosen among all the men of this planet and this species.

He was deep in a dream of Philippa that night, and of Mauricio perhaps, and Jacques Francesco, when Karina woke him again past midnight.

"They're at it again, Orlando. Listen."

The same voice of rage and the same female response, the hoarse bell of Ricard's mad fury and the quiet bell of the woman's prayer, clashing with each other, overlapping, cracking against each other in the night. Now the woman angry, and the man saying he loved her, You betrayed me, no, you're the one who betrayed *me*, she was putting up a fight, she was not going to let him get the upper hand...

"You have to go. You have to stop them."

Orlando imagined his knock and then the face he had seen on so many movie screens and then on television, that face scowling at him and Orlando's deplorable, stuttering French and one of the most eminent articulators of the Gallic tongue responding with sarcasm and brutality, those famous fists of Ricard's, those lips that had pronounced the verses of Rimbaud and the alexandrines of Racine sneering at him, at Orlando's miserable attempt to explain that—what if the actor answered, What right do you have to complain, Monsieur, we didn't interrupt you when you were crying out with joy and pleasure a few hours ago, we didn't ask your lady to stifle her calls of *mi amor mi amorcito mi lindo*, we respected your privacy but you don't respect ours? Karina, Karina, wouldn't it be enough just to bang on the walls, call the night porter, Karina?

"Listen to her, Orlando! Listen to *him*. What if that woman's in danger?"

"What if they're just rehearsing? They're actors, Karina!"

"No. What's happening in there is for real."

"All right, say it's for real—even then, a real quarrel, a real love affair, they'll tell us it's a scene, they won't admit to strangers that they're—"

"But he'll know, Ricard will know that we're here, she'll know she's not alone!"

"And if it's just today, just that today of all days you're—"

"I'm what?"

Orlando was saved from having to answer, to spell it out. Because the argument next door was brusquely, unexpectedly, cut off. Absurd to think that Ricard and the woman, in the midst of their heated altercation, could have heard Karina's whispers, Orlando's hushed rebuttals. But maybe Ricard had sensed their presence, somehow had guessed that he was performing for an audience, maybe the woman had understood that she was not, in effect, alone in the night, maybe they would stop for good now.

"Maybe they'll stop for good now."

Murmuring this into Karina's lovely ear, Orlando could feel his own breath against her cheek and neck, the scent coming back at him warm and with a faint hint of garlic from last night's dinner.

She shook her head, stood up, started toward the door. So resolutely, so forcefully, that she almost tripped over one of the rag dolls that was perched near their bed—how had it gotten there, left the rest of the figurines obediently lined up against the wall of the room? She looked down at it for a moment, perplexed—and then continued on her way.

"What are you doing?"

"Are you coming with me?"

"You don't speak French."

"Are you coming with me or do I have to confront him by myself?"

They would never know of course who was right, Orlando or Karina, if it was all an act or for real, if they had saved the woman from death by knocking on that door or merely interrupted a scene soon to be devoured in the local multiplex. They would never know, not ever, but finally, ultimately, definitely, it didn't matter, did it?

Orlando led the way.

THE SPECIAL
POPULATIONS UNIT

ARAB SOLDIERS IN ISRAEL'S ARMY

an essay by CHANAN TIGAY

O N MARCH 6, 2008, a small infantry unit from the Israel
Defense Forces' Givati Brigade left camp with the rising
sun to comb the Gaza border for arms smugglers, terrorists,
and assorted other unwanted visitors. Israel shares 1,017 kilometers of
borderland with its neighbors, and patrols much of it every day. On the
average morning, these patrols turn up very little. But when this group
of soldiers pulled into the still-cool sand outside their base's gate, the
first of two Jeeps in their convoy caromed over a remote-control bomb
and burst into flames. The vehicle jumped, hit the ground, and rolled
to a stop. Inside, the front seat was slick with blood. A young soldier
lay slumped against the dashboard, dead.

Had he been a typical Israeli soldier, what happened next would
have followed a predictable routine. *Haaretz*, *Yediot Ahronot*, and
Ma'ariv, Israel's three major dailies, would have run front-page
stories detailing the attack and the ensuing military funeral, their
reporting flanked by outsize color photographs of the dead man as
he was in life, a hand still resting on his shoulder where his wife or

girlfriend had been cropped out. Human-interest pieces would have followed—*Yediot* recounting how, during the *shiva* mourning period, the soldier's grieving mother had brought out his soccer trophies, *Ma'ariv* relaying an eerie story about something prescient he'd said the last time he'd visited. Meanwhile, in Jerusalem, the prime minister would convene an emergency meeting of his cabinet to hash out a military response.

When this soldier died, though, things went differently.

Suliman abu Juda, one of several thousand ethnic Arabs who serve, almost unnoticed, in Israel's military, was buried in a civilian ceremony in the unregistered Negev village he called home—a settlement not officially recognized by Israel. In the days following his death, only one newspaper printed his name. The foreign ministry's website, which lists soldiers killed in action, posted a nameless bio of abu Juda, a twenty-eight-year-old father of seven. Next to the profile was an empty box where a photograph would normally go.

The muted response came at his parents' request. It was an effort on their part to avoid retribution from other Arabs in Israel, and from Palestinians who might have opposed their young son's decision to cast his lot with the Israeli army. Abu Juda had two wives; one hailed from the West Bank city of Hebron, an incubator of Palestinian violence. His parents worried that their in-laws' standing, to say nothing of their physical safety, would be jeopardized if their son's name got out. And so abu Juda's death was allowed to pass almost unnoticed.

His faceless online obituary is an apt illustration of the Israeli Arab soldier's predicament. These men—and they are almost entirely men—are despised by much of the Arab world as traitors, and feared in Israel as a potential fifth column. The average Israeli Arab simply *lives* in the Jewish state; Israel's Arab soldiers are its collaborators. Some, like abu Juda, fall in love and marry women from the West Bank and Gaza, and then, quite literally, must raise their rifles against family members.

They are at once Muslims and citizens of the Jewish state; the first line of defense and a "demographic threat."

In the summer of 2010, I traveled throughout Israel—from the unrecognized Bedouin villages of the Negev desert to the charmless military bases along the Lebanese border to the elegant villas of the Galilee Druze—and spoke to dozens of Israeli Arabs who had served in the military. These are not men who enlist in hopes of securing desk jobs or scoring posts in towns with good surf. Many serve in combat units; this being the Middle East, these units see action, and sometimes their soldiers die. Since its founding in 1948, Israel has fought seven wars and two intifadas. More than five hundred Israeli Arab soldiers have been killed in those conflicts. In a country as small as Israel, that's a huge number.

And yet if these men are willing to risk their lives for their country, the thinking goes, Israel must be doing something right. Despite the misgivings Israeli Arab soldiers encounter on every side, many observers point to their service as a critical indicator of Israel's unique position in the region: a stable, multiethnic island thriving in a sea of dictatorships and turmoil. This proposition, I will learn, is tested at every turn.

Shortly after I arrived, I called Faisal abu Nadi, a former officer in the *G'dud Siyur Midbari*—the Israeli army's Desert Scouts Brigade, more commonly referred to as the Bedouin Unit. Abu Nadi is now the chairman of the Forum for Released Bedouin Officers and Soldiers, a small group that looks after Bedouin men in their post-military lives. He once had office space of a sort—a little concrete-and-steel clubhouse he tells me was built a decade ago as a meeting spot for Bedouin soldiers and their families—but three months before I call him, bulldozers on the payroll of a local building council came and razed the structure, which was built, illegally, on state land. About half of the Negev's Bedouin live in illegally built shantytowns that are "unrecognized" by Israel—which tends to mean that they lack electricity and running water, and also that they are subject to demolition.

With no office to receive me in, abu Nadi invites me to his home. When I arrive he leads me past his *shig*, a sitting room where Bedouin men entertain other Bedouin men, and through a courtyard where he keeps a small menagerie of little beasts, all of whom must be extremely warm in the afternoon blaze. I count seven or eight sheep, a white stallion, a dozen pigeons in a coop.

"What do you do with the sheep?" I ask.

"The sheep?" he says. "We eat them."

"What about the pigeons?"

"We take out all the organs, all the innards," he says. "Then we stuff them and eat them."

"And the horse?" I ask.

"That's just for the kids to have fun."

Abu Nadi is a very handsome guy—clean-shaven, graying, buzz-cut hair. Short, probably around 5'6". He wears jeans and a polo shirt and doesn't smile much. He has two wives, he tells me, and plans to take a third. Thus far, his first wife has given him six children; his second, two. She's feeding one of them in the kitchen as we head into abu Nadi's living room and recline on shiny red floor cushions. Above the doorway there's a framed map of the world, over which hangs a rifle—a wedding gift, abu Nadi says, from a friend. Two Hebrew plaques recognizing his military service sit beside each other on a shelf above the window. One of them spells his name wrong: TO FAISAL ABU WADI, it says. *Wadi* is the Arabic word—also used in Hebrew—for a dried-out desert gully.

There's another rifle on this shelf, too, and a saber hanging off-kilter in its sheath along the opposite wall. "It's not real," abu Nadi says, when he catches me staring at it. "It's just for decoration." Then he says the same thing about one of the rifles, and then the other.

Many Bedouin live in pretty rough dwellings—corrugated-metal huts with dirt or concrete floors, fire pits outside for cooking, oil lamps for light—but abu Nadi's house is a house. It's got only one story, and it's not fancy, but it's comfortable.

"The state is liable at any moment to bring a bulldozer and destroy this," abu Nadi says. "You see this?" He gestures theatrically around the room. "It's illegal."

Abu Nadi chain-smokes Time-brand cigarettes, and he lights one before speaking again. "If the state destroyed the clubhouse for Bedouin officers and soldiers—not a pool hall, or a club for the elderly, or for young people—a clubhouse for Bedouin officers and soldiers where bereaved families meet, where youth preparing to enlist meet, where released soldiers and officers spend time... If the state comes and specifically, *specifically*, destroys the clubhouse, what do they say? It's an illegal building. A building that has been there for ten years. It's not new, not renovated. It was there ten years. But it was an illegal building. There are thousands of illegal buildings. Thousands! Why, specifically, this clubhouse? What's happening here?"

This, as abu Nadi knows, is a simple question with no simple answer. The Negev desert comprises more than half of Israel's land mass; at the state's founding, some seventy thousand Bedouin lived there, making up the vast majority of the area's population. Traditionally nomadic, Israel's Bedouin had by then settled largely into semi-nomadism (moving seasonally), or had ceased wandering altogether. Like the Palestinians, most of them either fled or were expelled during Israel's first days. Between eleven thousand and eighteen thousand stayed behind, and they became citizens of the new Jewish state. Since then, their position has been perpetually in doubt.

Eager to develop the Bedouins' historic pasturelands for Jewish settlement and military bases, the Israeli government—through the army—initially relocated its remaining Bedouin to a small corner of the Negev they called the *siyyag*, which means fence. There, the

Bedouin lived under military rule until the late 1960s. Beginning in 1969, Israel established seven Bedouin cities inside the *siyyag*, looking to ameliorate the situation by concentrating the majority of its Bedouin population in these government-planned townships. This has not happened. Today, half of the Negev's 180,000 Bedouin— the population has increased tenfold since independence—live in the townships, and half have spread out into (or never left) the unrecognized villages, most of which are also located in the *siyyag*.

"I think the cardinal sin was not taking their connection to the land seriously," Clinton Bailey, one of Israel's foremost experts on the Bedouin, tells me. "From their point of view, whatever they had, they had legally, in the context of Bedouin law—which in their world was the only law that mattered."

At various points, Israel has offered the Bedouin both money and land in exchange for abandoning their illegal villages, but many communities have viewed the offers as insufficient, and turned them down. Some are wary of leaving behind their traditional work to settle in cities lacking the infrastructure necessary to provide them with new jobs. Others are simply reluctant to start paying taxes. Another obstacle originates with the Bedouin who left Israel in the 1940s, a good number of whom still claim ownership of lands that now fall within the borders of the government-planned townships. Deferring to age-old custom, many Bedouin have refused to move onto land to which another tribe holds claim—which means that large swaths of the Israeli-built townships are considered by their intended residents to be uninhabitable. The townships have other problems as well: unemployment is extremely high, crime is rampant, and educational opportunities are abysmal. Experts also say that even if all of the Negev Bedouin suddenly decided to move into the state's preferred, circumscribed quarters, there simply wouldn't be enough room for them.

And yet despite this, the day I meet abu Nadi, Israel completely razes the Bedouin village of El Arakib, leaving its three-hundred-odd residents homeless. Later that same month, forces from the Israel Land Administration (ILA), a government entity that manages 93 percent of the country's public land, destroy three houses in another Negev village, this one home to the abu Sulb tribe—a venerable family that sends more of its young men to volunteer for service in Israel's military than almost any other Bedouin tribe. Two of the three destroyed houses belong to Arab soldiers in the IDF.

Later, I ask a government source familiar with internal deliberations on the Bedouin situation what bothers Israel so much about these illegal settlements. "A state has been built, and for the state to be built it has to have planning: to plan a village, to plan a road, to plan electricity and water and sewage," he tells me. "And the state absolutely cannot provide services to anyone who just goes and settles wherever he wants, even if he's been there for ten or twenty years."

The inability to pump water and light into every far-flung community doesn't quite explain why entire villages are being destroyed, and my source seems aware of this. "Let's say you have authority to knock down five hundred houses," he says. "So, make some sort of priority. Make sure not to destroy the houses of soldiers. That's it. Simple." He pauses. "But I'm not in the Israel Land Administration. I'm not in the Bedouin Authority."

Israel is far from the only country that has faltered in its efforts to settle its Bedouin. In the 1950s, Syria tried to limit its own Bedouin's movements without much success; Saudi Arabia had similar difficulties, though subsidies from the state have helped smooth those over. Egypt, whose relationship with its Bedouin population has long been testy, has over the years destroyed its fair share of Bedouin homes. It bears mentioning, too, that if Israel were not the democratic state it assuredly is—if, for example, it were almost any of the twenty-one

Arab nations that surround it, where men and women have recently begun to lay down their lives in order to claim their right to speak out—Bedouin veterans like Faisal abu Nadi wouldn't be able to so freely criticize their government. And abu Nadi recognizes all this. He says he wouldn't want to live anywhere else. But anywhere else includes the seven townships Israel built to house Negev Bedouin like him.

I hear different versions of abu Nadi's concerns from many of the Arabs I meet. After a dozen such conversations, it becomes clear to me that the subject I'm pursuing—the question of how Israeli Arab soldiers see themselves, and what their service means for them and for the country—is, like so many questions that hang over this region, really a question about land. In their book *Invisible Citizens: Israeli Government Policy Toward the Negev Bedouin*, Shlomo Swirski and Yael Hasson observe that "the Negev Bedouin constitute the largest social group in Israel of whom it may be said that they still do not stand on solid ground." Bedouin veterans want many things: financial support, jobs, electricity. But at the heart of their demands—and their disappointments—is the desire for a stable place to live, and the sense of belonging that comes with it. "If you solve the land problem, you solve everything," says Elhaam Kamalaat, a Bedouin social worker and longtime army wife. "The rest is just social issues."

For many of the men I talk to, military service was meant to be a solution of sorts. "It's an entry ticket for citizenship," says Col. Ramiz Ahmed, who as head of the IDF's Special Populations Unit is charged with recruiting minorities and assisting them with issues relating to their military service. The army has long represented the most concrete way for Israeli citizens to demonstrate their dedication to the Zionist project; it offers both a stamp of approval and a networking crucible. Until very recently, joining the armed forces was considered an essential step in life among Israel's Jews—up there with birth and death—and opting out, even for legitimate reasons, carried a lifelong stigma. Although most Bedouin do not enlist (they are not required to), those who do hope their service will open doors. It is as such that the army often proves to be a bitter disappointment.

"Those Bedouin who served are angrier at the state than those who didn't serve at all," says Kher Albaz, director of social services in Segev-Shalom, one of the government-planned Bedouin cities. "Every normal person—not just the Bedouin—who enlists to serve a state has expectations. Even the most nationalistic and Zionistic Jew who stays in the army beyond the time that's required has expectations—personal expectations, financial expectations, quality of life, land. Otherwise he's crazy, he needs therapy. That's the name of the game here. And in the case of the Bedouin, it didn't work."

It can be difficult, at times, to tell how true this is—whether things really are not working at all, and will never work, or whether the situation is less clear-cut. A month after I meet him, abu Nadi's story still isn't sitting right. Even given what seems to be a growing penchant for smashing Bedouin buildings, the decision to destroy a clubhouse for soldiers who had served the state honorably strikes me as so senseless as to defy logic.

"It wasn't a clubhouse—it was a *shig*," a high-ranking Israeli military official tells me one Saturday morning. He's just returned home from services at a nearby synagogue and we're at his dining-room table, sipping tap water. At the mention of the clubhouse, he smiles.

"Whose *shig*?" I ask him. "Abu Nadi's?"

"Yes. His family's."

"And he just claimed it was a clubhouse? To get sympathy?"

He shrugs. "I know Faisal and I like him," he says. "But it was a *shig*."

*   *   *

Israel is a tiny country: about the size of New Jersey, with a smaller population. Of its 7.5 million citizens, about 1.5 million are Arabs; of those, several thousand are in active service in the Israel Defense Forces. Currently, about a thousand Bedouin serve, most in the standing army—and half of them, like abu Nadi did in his time, serve as trackers, putting their native mastery of the area's deserts to work.

In accordance with Israel's enlistment law, decisions about who is drafted are left to the defense minister. The Bedouin are not required to enlist, and never have been, and so must volunteer if they wish to serve. Some tribes have done so all the way back to the pre-state period, when the El Heibs joined the Palmach, the underground Jewish army's elite strike force, to form a unit known as Pal-Heib. Since then, their tracking skills have become the stuff of legend—it would be unusual for an Israeli combat force to cross into enemy territory without a Bedouin tracker at its head. If they weren't Arabs, one intelligence source tells me, the Bedouin trackers would be considered the most elite unit in the military.

(On the other hand: at one point I ask an Arab soldier if a Bedouin will ever command the Bedouin Unit. "Never," he tells me. "The unit would fall apart.")

At any given time, some two hundred Israeli-Palestinians also serve in the army—young men whose forebears did not leave Israel at the state's founding. Depending on whom you're talking to, and what their politics happen to be, these individuals may be called Israeli Arabs, Arab Israelis, Palestinian Israelis, Israeli Palestinians, or simply Palestinians. A handful of Circassians—Muslims who migrated to Palestine from the northern Caucasus in the late nineteenth century— serve as well. Unlike the Bedouin, they are required to do three years of military service.

The Druze, Arabs whose faith began as an offshoot of Shia Islam, are by far the most numerous among the IDF's Arab conscripts. Ever since a 1956 "blood covenant" between Israel and Druze religious leaders, Druze men, like Israeli Jews, are subject to compulsory military service. This requirement excludes those Druze who live in the Golan Heights and never took Israeli citizenship after Israel captured the area from Syria in 1967; the Golan will be the centerpiece of any peace agreement with Syria, which for years has demanded its return as a precondition to negotiations. If the territory reverts to its former owner, Druze who served in the Jewish army would not last very long.

Initially, Israel's Druze served only in a special platoon for minorities and in *Herev*, the so-called Druze Unit. In recent years, however, the entire military hierarchy has been opened to them, and Druze have begun to serve even in the most elite units. The highest-ranking non-Jewish officer in the history of the Israel Defense Forces is Maj. Gen. Yusef Mishlab, a Druze, who served as coordinator of government activities in the Palestinian territories and headed the Home Front Command when the U.S. invaded Iraq in 2003. As Israel prepared bomb shelters and distributed gas masks in advance of a possible Iraqi attack (Saddam had launched Scud missiles at Israeli cities during the first Gulf War), the man overseeing the effort was Arab. The Druze may represent the most hopeful sign of genuine army-enabled Israeli Arab integration.

All these distinctions, though, make little difference to the type of person who would lay a mine in an IDF soldier's path, or blow up a bus in Netanya, or fire a missile into Israel in the name of God.

At over six feet tall, Alaa al-Din A'Naim towered over the other members of his unit. He was so strong that his commanders in the Desert Scouts Brigade assigned the nineteen-year-old trainee the shoulder-bowing task of carrying a MAG, a thirty-pound machine gun other armies mount on Jeeps. On November 14, 1995, during a routine training exercise near the Gaza Strip, a member of A'Naim's team stumbled over an undetonated grenade, left behind by an M203 grenade launcher. Of nine soldiers taking part in the exercise, only A'Naim died—although he held on for eight days before his broken body gave out.

"I came home from work that day at five or six," says Salim A'Naim, Alaa's father. I am visiting him at his home, in a small, unrecognized Bedouin village overlooking the ancient city of Nazareth. The Muslim holy month of Ramadan has recently begun, and A'Naim hasn't eaten all day. As his wife and daughters lay down dishes for the evening's meal, we take seats on the porch outside.

A'Naim, who bears a striking resemblance to the actor Anthony Quinn, speaks slowly and emphatically about Alaa, whom he refers to repeatedly as "the soldier." His other sons are soldiers, too—Yusef, who joins us on the veranda, was nearly killed in Gaza during the now-famous raid in which Hamas gunmen kidnapped Israeli tank-gunner Gilad Shalit. A sweet, skinny guy with his head shaved bald, Yusef was guarding Shalit's tank when it was attacked; since then, he's carried a quarter-pound of shrapnel inside his torso. He flips open his mobile phone now, and shows me a picture of himself from before the raid. In it, a thick, muscular version of the shadow sitting in front of me proudly flexes his biceps. "I used to work out," he says.

Shortly after grenade fragments perforated Yusef's brother's body, Alaa was airlifted to a Beersheba hospital for emergency surgery. His parents made the two-hundred-kilometer drive there in a taxi. "Every twenty or thirty kilometers they'd call us from the hospital," A'Naim says. "'Where are you? Where are you?' Every twenty or thirty kilometers, 'Where are you?'" When they arrived at last, medics were wheeling Alaa out of the operating room. "We ended up right next to him in the hall—him on the bed and us walking, together," A'Naim says. Alaa's big body, which his father had once thought indestructible, hardly fit on the gurney. "I kissed him, kissed his feet," A'Naim says. "He was unconscious for eight days after that."

He says "eight days" very slowly, as though the phrase were a ghost he's urging forth from his lungs. Then he pauses, looks to the speckled tiles of his porch, and shakes his head. "On the eighth day the doctor called us into the room. I still remember what he said to us. He said, 'I am the chief doctor. Even with American soldiers in their war in Vietnam, of three million, four million soldiers, maybe two or three had injuries like the one Alaa has.' That was the day he died, and it was like an earthquake. An earthquake. A cab came and took us home. It was a black day here in the North."

A'Naim pauses again just as the muezzin's call to prayer rings out from a nearby mosque. It's a perfect segue into the next part of the story. The sad part.

Immediately after Alaa died, his body was brought home and deposited in the mosque from which his father and I have just heard the *adhan* chanted. The A'Naim family gathered together and made their way there, to see the local imam recite the traditional burial rites before they took the shroud-covered corpse to its final resting place in the Muslim cemetery atop a nearby hill.

"We were outside the mosque—people from the army, the police, civilians, everything, waiting to be called in," A'Naim says. Ten minutes passed, then twenty, then thirty. The mourners, huddling outside in the chilly November rain, grew anxious. A murmur passed through the crowd: *What happened, what happened, what happened?*

A number of relatives headed into the mosque to check on the delay. When they emerged, grim faced, several minutes later, the men headed straight to A'Naim.

"The imam refused to pray over Alaa," he tells me. "The Islamic Movement opposed praying for the soldier because he served in the army."

The Islamic Movement is a hard-line anti-Zionist group with

connections to the Muslim Brotherhood. Its northern branch, which operates mosques near the A'Naims, is significantly more extreme than its southern counterpart. I ask A'Naim what went through his mind when he heard of their involvement, and he smacks the air by his ear. "First of all, a person like that, I don't want his prayer," he says, referring to the imam. "What hurts me—excuse the phrase—is that his entire clan isn't worth my son's shoe. That hurts me. It hurts. But I had no strength at the time. If I'd gathered my strength, I don't know what would have been. It would have been another tragedy. It was a tragedy when he refused to pray, and he might not have stayed alive."

Instead, the mourners located a Bedouin imam who agreed to officiate. They then made the short trip to the cemetery—only to find that they would, again, be refused entry because the dead man had been an IDF soldier. But this time members of Alaa's unit who had traveled in to bury him would have none of it—they opened the cemetery by force, pushed aside its proprietors, hoisted the body onto their shoulders, and buried Alaa in a grave overlooking Nazareth's Old City.

As the ceremony ended, Alaa's commander stuck a plaque for fallen soldiers into the raised earth above the grave. When A'Naim returned the following morning to pay his respects, the marker had been dug up and smashed.

A few days after our first meeting, A'Naim invites me out to the Nazareth cemetery. We park, leave the car, and wind our way silently through dozens of tightly spaced gravestones, up one hill and down another, until we reach the fence at the far end of the grounds. A'Naim stops and gestures to the dirt before us, where a series of half-buried concrete cinder blocks trace the approximate shape of a shrouded corpse in the dry earth. Most of the graves in this section are bordered by flowers; all have headstones. Alaa's grave is unmarked but for the encroaching piles of browning pine needles, thick like hair on a barber's floor. Sighing, A'Naim gets to work.

He brushes off the cinder blocks around the grave, silently collecting handfuls of pine needles and dirt and filthy stones. He finds a hose and waters two tiny shrubs that have sprouted where the military plaque once stood. Then he stands, shuts off the hose, and, palms upturned to God, says a silent prayer.

On the way home he tells me that the imam who refused to pray for his son hasn't been seen in the area since the day after the funeral, fifteen years ago. "He disappeared," he says. "Left town. There are members of our clan who want to kill him. They're still looking."

A'Naim does not expect the Israeli government, or the army, to help him overcome the prejudices of his neighbors. His demand is different. Shortly after Alaa died, the army installed electric cables and water pipes in A'Naim's village, bringing the bereaved family plumbing, light, and a new sense of normalcy. Now he wants to move his son to a resting place closer to home. His village, like abu Nadi's, is "unrecognized"; there is no cemetery.

"Our dead are scattered in three different villages," A'Naim tells me. "And we're constantly asking: first of all, recognize us. After that, it's very easy to establish a cemetery, right?"

It would be easier still to put up another marker on his son's grave, or to move the body to a burial site closer to the rest of his tribe's dead. That A'Naim has chosen not to is itself a highly political act.

"That's not a grave," A'Naim told me as we passed through Nazareth, on our way back from the cemetery. "It's an embarrassment— for the state and for the army." Not an embarrassment for forward-thinking Muslims like the A'Naims, who recognize the benefits of living in a modern democracy; not an embarrassment for the Islamic Movement's leaders, who preach Israel's destruction even as they enjoy those benefits. An embarrassment for the army and for the state, which can't or won't recognize the village where Alaa A'Naim once lived.

When I return home, I call Dan Shafrir, A'Naim's lawyer, to get a sense of why a man who has paid an awful price for his children's service to the nation has had such a difficult time gaining recognition for his village. Shafrir tells me that in the 1950s, the state evacuated A'Naim's tribe from the area around Givat Ha'Moreh, in northern Israel, to make way for Jewish housing near the city of Afula. While the move to their current village was made with the full knowledge of Israel's Interior Ministry, he says, there was never any official documentation. Today, Shafrir has thousands of pages of documents relating to A'Naim's land claims, including letters from government offices acknowledging the need to help.

"If you read carefully, the letters say that Israel has the moral obligation to help Mr. A'Naim," he says. "The problem is to turn the moral obligation into a real obligation." Shafrir believes that A'Naim has a good chance to do just that; the process is stalled, he says, because A'Naim, whether out of a more pessimistic view of the legal system or a belief that the system should come to him—or perhaps, Shafrir says, due to nothing more than bad advice from previous lawyers—has yet to file his case.

Technically, Israel has been in a state of emergency since its founding in 1948. On May 14 of that year, about two hours after David Ben-Gurion, Israel's first prime minister, declared the establishment of the state, Egypt (and, a short while later, Iraq, Jordan, Lebanon, and Syria) invaded the newborn country and instigated a conflict that Israelis call the War of Independence and many Arabs refer to as the *Nakba*, the Catastrophe. Today, the Knesset votes each year to extend the emergency footing. This, coupled with a general sense among many people here that Israel, surrounded on all sides by Arab nations, is in a constant state of existential peril (a suspicion that has only been exacerbated since the ouster of Egyptian president Hosni Mubarak and the ensuing unrest elsewhere in the Arab world), makes the presence of a large minority of Arabs threatening. This perceived threat has itself grown more acute with the Islamic Movement's rise. Traditionally lackluster in its religiosity, much of Israel's Bedouin population has, over the last several decades, fallen under the sway of homegrown Islamists. At the same time, the old-style "sheikh culture," in which village headmen sat atop the Bedouin tribal hierarchy, has begun to decline, and the Islamic Movement has moved to fill the leadership vacuum. A significant increase in Bedouin crime—which increasingly spills out of Arab areas—has not helped the Negev Bedouin's case among the greater Israeli population either.

(About 80,000 Bedouin also live in the verdant Galilee region; most of that number not only live in legal settlements, but are said to be about thirty years more socioeconomically advanced than the tribesmen of the Negev, who still endure drought and other desert deprivations. An additional 30,000 Bedouin live in central Israel.)

Shmuel Rifman, mayor of the Ramat Negev Regional Council, an umbrella organization of collective farms, kibbutzim, and community villages in the Negev, tells me that as the Bedouin have dispersed through the *siyyag*, they have not only hemmed in the neighboring city of Beersheba, precluding expansion of the Negev's capital, but also wreaked havoc. "They steal sheep, transformers, army equipment, copper," he says. "There's nothing they don't steal. Anything that will move, they steal. A night doesn't pass when it doesn't happen. It's part of the Bedouin culture." A state that wants to maintain sovereignty, Rifman argues, cannot allow its citizens to go wherever they please. "In today's system," he says, "the Bedouin wake up in the morning and they're sitting here, then later they'll put another tent on a hill over there, and gradually they'll occupy the area."

Rifman insists that the solution is not to recognize more Bedouin villages, but to encourage a mass migration of Jews to the Negev to ensure that, despite the Bedouin's astronomical birthrate, Jews will continue to outnumber them for years. It's certainly one way to approach the problem. But Moshe Arens, who served stints as defense and foreign minister in a series of right-wing governments, says the solution lies elsewhere.

"Instead of looking at the Bedouin as Israeli citizens who should be approached and coached into being loyal to the State of Israel and serving in the IDF, there are people who look upon them as some kind of enemy population," Arens tells me over coffee and Danish. "It's a very bad situation." Widely credited as having opened the military up to more widespread Arab service during his tenure as defense minister, Arens says the army may just be the answer. "The IDF is the big equalizer. It's been the melting pot for the Jewish population as well. It's been the melting pot for the Druze population. It could be the melting pot for the Bedouin."

For now, the vast majority of Israeli Arabs do not enlist, unwilling to serve a state they see as inherently inequitable. It's hard not to think of what Kher Albaz has told me already—that the military melting pot, and its promise of greater integration and opportunity for the Bedouin, has yet to actually work. Part of the problem, too, is that many of those Bedouin who *do* enlist are the least educated among their tribesmen—unable to find decent-paying work elsewhere, they settle on the army. But because they lack basic skills, they don't advance through the ranks.

When I talk to enlisted Bedouin, though, educated and not, they say that ultimately, despite the doubleness they feel; despite the dueling loyalties, the contradictions and the pain; despite the fact that, to outsiders, the Israeli armed forces seems the most unlikely of organizations in which to find a group of motivated Arabs—despite all this, they say, the army is the only place in all of the Jewish state where, for three or four or five years, Arabs truly feel Israeli.

"It's the only place you find real equality," says Adam Jorno, an Israeli Palestinian who served as a combat soldier in the 1990s. "I think that we, the Arabs of Israel, need to take a position. You're either here or there. You have to be an integral part of the country, and that includes military service. There are those who say, 'Oh, I don't want to kill my brothers!' So don't be a combat soldier. Don't go shoot Arabs. Go do another kind of service. You don't have to be a fighter, but contribute to the country. Or take yourself and live with Hezbollah in Lebanon and fight against Israel."

Jorno's name wasn't always Jorno. Once, his name was Khleikhel. But several years ago, when he was commanding a checkpoint along the border between Israel and Gaza, overseeing the entry of several thousand Palestinian laborers into Israel each day, a woman approached him and asked for a favor. He didn't know her, but he quickly realized that she was a member of his very large extended family. She was building a house, she told him, and wanted to expedite construction. Could he arrange the permits that would allow two Palestinian workers to sleep over in Israel?

"It's a small country, and our family is big," says Jorno. He's a successful lawyer now in Rosh Pina, not too far from Safed, representing Arab soldiers in the military courts. "They must have heard that there was an officer named Khleikhel at the crossing and said, 'Let's go get him to use his pull for us.' It was a red flag for me. If I help someone like that, who knows what might happen? I don't want to let someone sleep here, and then there's an attack and I'm to blame."

So he changed his name to Jorno. After that, he says, his relatives couldn't make the connection. "That's it," he says. "I disappeared."

Jorno's concerns about being linked to terrorists are not unique. Reports surface from time to time about non-Arab soldiers receiving unofficial instructions to withhold vital intelligence from Bedouin trackers, for fear that they are colluding with terrorists or smugglers operating in the border regions. These fears, painful as they may be to men like Jorno, cannot simply be dismissed as ignorance or racism.

In July, I travel to northern Israel to meet Hassan El Heib. El Heib is the mayor of Zarzir, a Bedouin municipality located ten kilometers from Nazareth, and a lieutenant colonel (reserve) in the IDF. A gruff man with a distinct military bearing, he hails from the first Bedouin tribe to ally with the Jewish *yishuv* in pre-state days. He uses the majority of the time we're together to hammer home the Bedouin's long-standing military service, and to stress the common fate linking Israel's Jews and Arabs. "We aren't smugglers and drug dealers," he says. "If Israel's economy is good, it's good for all of us. A terrorist that comes here and carries out an attack, kills all of us. We have to guard the house."

What El Heib doesn't initially mention is that his own brother is one of the exceptions to this claim. While serving in Lebanon in 1996, Lt. Col. Omar El Heib was gravely wounded by a roadside bomb planted by Hezbollah guerillas. Omar lost an eye in the attack, and was left partially paralyzed as well, with shrapnel lodged in his head. Despite his injuries, he continued to serve. Several years later, though, Omar was accused of passing military secrets to Hezbollah in exchange for money and narcotics. In 2002, a Tel Aviv court found him guilty, agreeing with the prosecutor's contention that he had handed over maps, troop-deployment details, and the locations of high-ranking commanders. He was sentenced to fifteen years in prison.

When I raise the issue, Hassan El Heib doesn't deny that his brother did what he was accused of doing—but he does his best to distance himself, and the larger Bedouin community, from claims that Omar's motives were terroristic or nationalistic. "After he was injured, his mental capacity was like an eight-year-old's," he says. "How many Jews with a *clear* mind have spied against the State of Israel? If my brother did these things, it wasn't ideological. He was caught up with a group of criminals, that's all."

After he was caught, Omar El Heib was stripped of his military rank and dishonorably discharged. If Hassan El Heib's claim about his brother's mental deficiencies is true, it is unclear what he was still doing in the army at the time of his arrest.

In 1969, the same year the first of the Bedouin cities was constructed, the state established legal machinery allowing Bedouin to submit claims relating to their relocations to a land settlement officer at the Ministry of Justice. By the early 1970s, some three thousand such claims had been filed, impacting nearly one hundred thousand *dunams* (25,000 acres). And so, in 1975, the government moved to formulate an official response to the Bedouin "land problem" in southern Israel, adopting the recommendation of the Albeck Committee, which a year earlier had determined that the entire Negev—including the *siyyag*—constituted state land on which Bedouin were "unable to acquire any rights, not even by virtue of protracted possession and cultivation." Cognizant that humanitarian considerations would likely preclude high-court backing for mass eviction of the Bedouin from the *siyyag*—the very territory to which they had been forcibly moved by the Israeli military nearly three decades earlier—the committee proposed compensating Bedouin who relinquished their lands and moved to approved Bedouin settlements. The Albeck Committee recommendations have remained the basis for numerous government proposals, panels, and committees that have since sought to solve the land problem, all of which have championed policies that can be boiled down to three attributes: they deny Bedouin ownership of Negev lands; they support compensating the Bedouin for appropriated land; and they have not worked. According to *Invisible Citizens* authors Swirski and Hasson, forty years after those first three thousand land claims were filed, most are *still pending*.

Druze soldiers in the Israel Defense Forces, 1949. Courtesy of IDF Archives.

Defense Minister Moshe Dayan eulogizing Lotfi Nasser El Deen, killed on what was to have been his last day in the army, in 1969. Courtesy of Amal Nasser El Deen.

A Bedouin tracker inspects a mark in the sand, 1953. Courtesy of IDF Archives/BaMachnaeh.

Circassian soldiers training in the Jezreel Valley, 1949. Courtesy of IDF Archives.

Soldiers in the Minorities Unit at a parade marking Israel's first Independence Day, 1949. Courtesy of IDF Archives.

A banner in the village of Daliyat al-Karmel, offering a reward for information leading to the discovery of a missing Druze soldier. All photos from this page on, except for those on page 88, by Chanan Tigay.

Faisal abu Nadi walking through the rubble of what he says was a clubhouse for Bedouin soldiers.

TOP & BOTTOM: *The village of El Arakib, shortly after it was first demolished.*

The remains of a demolished home in El Arakib.

El Arakib's residents rebuilding, hours after their village was razed.

Breaking the Ramadan fast with the A'Naim family, in their unrecognized village near Nazareth.

Faisal abu Nadi's village, as seen from the roof of his home.

The unrecognized Bedouin village of Wadi Naam.

Arab trackers at Biranit, a military base perched on the border with Lebanon. Several were fasting for Ramadan.

The Memorial for Fallen Druze Soldiers, with a tank donated by Prime Minister Yitzhak Rabin.

Salim A'Naim says a prayer at his son's grave in Nazareth.

TOP & BOTTOM: *The Memorial for Fallen Bedouin Soldiers in northern Israel.*

Rafik Halabi at his desk in Daliyat al-Karmel.

Majdi Mazareib, chief tracker in Israel's Northern Command.

Amal Nasser El Deen in his office at the Memorial for Fallen Druze Soldiers.

Hassan El Heib, mayor of Zarzir.

A Druze village in northern Israel, as seen from the Memorial for Fallen Druze Soldiers.

Yusef A'Naim, before his injury. Courtesy of Yusef A'Naim.

Former defense and foreign minister Moshe Arens (in sunglasses).
Behind him is Hassan El Heib. Courtesy of Hassan El Heib.

In 2007, the government inaugurated the latest committee—an eight-member group headed by former high-court judge Eliezer Goldberg. The Goldberg Committee was charged with laying out a formula for compensating the Bedouin for expropriated land and locating substitute plots for those who were to be evacuated; after a year of study, the committee released its report. While agreeing with earlier decisions denying Bedouin land ownership, it nevertheless found that the Bedouin maintain "a certain degree of rights" to lands on which they have lived for years. The committee called on the government to recognize forty-six illegal Bedouin villages.

It seemed like a promising sign. In the lead-up to the report's release, many Bedouin were cautiously optimistic that, at long last, their situation would be settled. And the Committee's findings suggested that steps might indeed be taken in that direction. But no sooner had the Goldberg Committee issued its recommendations than Prime Minister Ehud Olmert rejected them, appointing a *second* committee to examine the Goldberg Committee's work and see where it might be altered.

Israel's national postal service doesn't deliver to Umm El-Hiran, the unrecognized Bedouin village where Raed abul Ghiyan's clan has been squatting for fifty years, so the father of two picks up his mail at a post-office box several kilometers away, in the government-sanctioned city of Hura. One afternoon in 2004, while sorting through a small stack of envelopes in his car, abul Ghiyan, who is thirty-four now but looks older, spotted one that stood out—green print, perforated edges, and the familiar return address of his military unit's liaison office. It was his *tzav giyyus*, the annual order to report for reserve duty. Into their forties, most Israeli men are required to spend between two weeks and a month of each year in the reserves; abul Ghiyan had been a soldier in the Desert Scouts Brigade, and the *tzav giyyus* meant he would be heading back shortly for his yearly military stint.

Back at home, his wife stopped him before he could tell her what had come in the mail. "Take a look at what's stuck to the door," she said. He's recounting this to me while we recline on thick, embroidered pillows in the courtyard between his house and one belonging to his parents. A gaggle of young children runs noisily past, and abul Ghiyan, who keeps his thinning black hair brushed forward and thickly gelled, calls his kids over to say hello.

"So I go to the door," he tells me when they've run off again, "and pasted there is a *tzav harisa*—a destruction order." By order of the Israeli government, abul Ghiyan's house would be destroyed in thirty days if he didn't first tear it down himself.

"I started laughing," he says. "I held the reserves order and the destruction order up next to each other and laughed. I was in shock a little. How can this be? That in one day I got both of these?"

The irony of his situation is made even more acute by the fact that, in 1954, his family was relocated to the spot it was about to be uprooted from by Israel's military government. "They destroyed our houses near Shoval and forced us to move here," he says. "Then they gave my grandfather a gun and said, 'Guard the border against Jordanian incursions.' They wanted us here as a line of protection from the West Bank."

In 2004, he says, the government decided to uproot the family again, this time to make way for a new Jewish village. "Instead of Umm El-Hiran, they want to call it just Hiran," abul Ghiyan says. "A person volunteers to serve in the army, and this is the gift he gets?"

In the days after receiving the destruction order, abul Ghiyan says that he appealed to officers in the army, to members of the Knesset, to government ministers. "Until the story got into the media, none of them had answers," he says. "But when the story got on television, newspapers, radio, then their behavior started to change." After several weeks of protests and appeals, the Israel Land Administration issued a stay on the demolition. Seven years later, the stay holds—and the fate of the village continues to hang in the balance.

Meanwhile, abul Ghiyan waits, raising his children in a home that may not be there in three, six, eight months. And while he waits, he does his annual reserve duty.

From as early as six or seven years old, Bedouin boys learn that the earth is everything. Sent into the field to graze their family's livestock, young Bedouin find themselves faced with safeguarding their families' entire livelihoods. This, it turns out, provides them the perfect training for life as army trackers.

"As kids, we didn't know what a computer was," Lt. Col. Majdi Mazareib, chief tracker of Israel's Northern Command, tells me in an office so spare it's clear he rarely visits. With his bald head, dark skin, and intense bearing, he could have been mistaken for a pharaoh in another eon.

"We walked barefoot sometimes; most of the time, maybe," he says. "You survive in the field. You don't have any limits. You don't have a Polish mother who calls you in at one o'clock and says, 'Come eat.'"

As far back as he can remember, Mazareib hunted. He built traps to catch birds for his family. He learned how to raise bees. "The minute you go out into the field, you hear the noises, you touch the plants, you touch the rocks. It's not a formal course, not like your parents send you to a class. It comes naturally," he says. "At the same time we had a herd of sheep, and for part of each year we'd go down into the valley with them. We'd be in the fields of the Jezreel Valley for months. We slept in a tent. When you go out with a herd, you're a leader. Imagine a Bedouin boy, eight years old, his family's business placed in his hands. It's a lot of responsibility. You have to make sure the herd eats properly, drinks properly, that you don't lose any. Now, what's the connection between being a shepherd and a tracker?"

Mazareib's cousin and assistant, Dayan Mazareib, comes in and pours us sweet tea. They have an easy rapport, and it's easy to picture the two of them out in the field together, trying to occupy themselves through long months of boiling days. Mazareib turns back to me.

"It begins with the fact that while you're watching the herd, your friends come and you start playing with them," he says. "While you're playing, you're not paying attention, and the herd keeps going, and you lose them. Then you have to search for them—and that's when you start developing the senses: to run, to search, to know. That's a kind of tracking. And that can be suitable for the army."

Jewish soldiers describe Bedouin trackers as wizards of a sort. Oftentimes, a tracker can't point to exactly what it is that has raised his antennae; it's just a sense. In other instances, very specific signs lead to a particular discovery. Soldiers regale me with stories of trackers who, having spotted a series of footprints etched in the border sand, go on to (accurately) tell their officers how many people have infiltrated; how old they were; how much they weighed; whether they were men or women; and, in some cases, that one had a limp, or was pregnant. Some infiltrators wear specially fitted shoes that slip on backward, so it appears they are leaving Israel rather than entering; trackers can spot this ruse with ease, much as they can tell when an infiltrator has fastened sheepskin to the soles of his feet in an effort to leave no discernible prints at all.

Mazareib tells a story about would-be terrorists caught crossing into Israel from Egypt. Under interrogation, the men admitted that they had been most worried about covering their footprints, citing the IDF's trackers as their greatest concern. "If they see four Jeeps, it doesn't frighten them," Mazareib says. "But if they see one tracker, following their tracks on foot, that drives them crazy. You can neutralize every piece of technology eventually. There's no replacement for a tracker."

Trackers also die in higher proportions than other soldiers. When they are working with a combat unit, they travel at the front, ahead of the other men. "The fact that I'm at the head of the force, if I go with the naval commandos or *Sayeret Matkal*"—an elite recon unit— "that means I'm no less good than they are," Mazareib says. "There's sometimes a price, when an explosive is detonated, or there's sniper fire and trackers are killed. But there's also an advantage. If I trust someone else to go ahead of me, he can lead me into mines, and I can be killed then, too. So I prefer to go at the front."

In his ethnography of the Sinai Bedouin, Joseph J. Hobbs suggests that "one reason for the retreat of pastoral nomadism is that non-nomads do not understand how Bedouin live and view life. This ignorance is a source of fear and repression. Rather than try to change the nomads, sedentary powers-that-be might, with more understanding about the desert people, benefit from the detailed knowledge and extraordinary skills that Bedouin have acquired through ages of habitation and experience in the wilderness." Say what you will about an Israeli-government policy that looks to push Bedouin into cities, ignoring hundreds of years of history. The army does just as Hobbs suggests—respecting the Bedouin's native skills and putting them to good use. Perhaps this is why the Bedouin I meet who are currently serving in the army seem so much happier than those who have already been released.

The Druze have had an easier time integrating into Israeli society, inside the military and out. At least, this is the conclusion one might draw from talking to Amal Nasser El Deen.

I go to see the former Knesset member, who is now eighty-three, in his office at the *Yad Labanim Druzim*, a memorial to Israel's 369 fallen Druze soldiers in the village of Daliyat al-Karmel. He sits behind a large wooden desk, with photographs of Prime Minister Binyamin Netanyahu and President Shimon Peres hanging over the Israeli flag on the wall behind him. Nasser El Deen is a Likudnik: a member of the right-wing party of Netanyahu, Menachem Begin, and Ariel Sharon. When I suggest that, as an Arab, his membership in this particular political organization sounds odd to Western ears, he laughs—when he was in parliament from 1979 to 1988, he says, half the party spoke Arabic. It was the political home of Jewish immigrants from Morocco and Yemen, from Iraq and Syria and Algeria. This isn't my point, and he knows it.

But Nasser El Deen wants to talk about his son. Lotfi Nasser El Deen was killed in action in 1969, while Amal was on the road between his home in Daliyat al-Karmel and a meeting in Tel Aviv.

"At the same hour Lotfi died, my body became paralyzed," he tells me. "I stopped my car and sat on the side of the road for half an hour. I couldn't go forward. I had no strength. So I turned around and headed back to my office in Haifa. After half an hour, the town major of Haifa and the Druze unit officer arrived, and they sat down across from me at my desk, and they just looked at me. And for several moments they didn't speak. I said to the unit commander, 'I know something happened. I have two brothers in the army, and I have a son. So tell me what happened.' He said to me, and he was crying, hard, 'Lotfi is no longer with us.' I said to him, 'What happened? I talked to him last night. He said he was coming home.'"

The day Lotfi Nasser El Deen died was to have been the day he was released from the army after five years of service. But while returning his equipment to a base near Tel Aviv, he got word that a terrorist cell had crossed the border from Jordan, near the Great Rift Valley. "He refused to return his equipment," Nasser El Deen tells me. "He told his commander, 'I'm getting a force together for an operation.' And he did. He went at the head of the force, and they got to a particular spot, and the infiltrators opened fire on him and he was killed. On the last day of his service. He was twenty-three."

Nasser El Deen unscrews the lid on an orange coffee pot and pours us each a small cup of what Israelis call *botz*, mud. After a few moments of contemplative quiet, he continues. "It was very hard to hear this," he says. "But I knew that if I was weak, I would damage the funeral and my son. You know, the next day at the funeral there were thirty thousand people—thirty thousand!—who came from all over the country. It was the first time that the minister of defense, Moshe Dayan, appeared at a soldier's funeral. His aide approached me and said, 'Excuse me, Amal, I'm very sorry. I need to bother you for a minute.' I said, 'Go ahead. What's happening?' He told me, 'On Syrian radio, they are singing and joyful because they say Moshe Dayan killed your son. And they're saying that this is the fate of any person who respects the Jews and stands together with them.'"

Nasser El Deen takes a sip of his coffee before he goes on. "Here's Amal Nasser El Deen, they were saying, Druze, former soldier, a well-known public figure. His son was killed at the hands of the Jewish defense minister. So I called over the Israeli radio and TV people and I gave an answer. I said to the Syrians, 'You can sell your lies on the street of Damascus. Your lies won't work with us. Moshe Dayan and I are brothers. Here he is, sitting at my side.' The whole world saw this."

"A lot of Druze will tell you, the Jewish people and us, we're partners, etc., etc."

Rafik Halabi, a well-known television journalist and an "utterly secular" Druze, sits in the high-ceilinged office just off the entrance to his attractive home, which is also in Daliyat al-Karmel. Behind him is a bookshelf stacked neatly with videos and DVDs of reports he's filed over the years—on politics, on religion, one on the transmigration of souls, a central tenet of Druze faith. Beside the shelf is an editing suite, and over his shoulder is a photograph of Halabi with Israel's first Druze combat navigator, a young man whose face is obscured by the tinted visor coming off his flight helmet. Halabi's house is just a few short blocks from Nasser El Deen's office, but when they talk politics, the ideological distance dividing them seems almost interplanetary.

For many years now, Halabi has been a vociferous critic of Israel's policies toward its Arab citizens. His complaints, issued in TV news reports, newspaper columns, books, and documentary films, are remarkably similar to those I hear from the Bedouin. *We are second-class citizens. They promise that military service will help us advance, and it doesn't. The state appropriates our land with impunity. And once we're done serving in the army, there are no jobs.*

In recent years, Halabi says, Road No. 6, a new north–south toll road; the Beersheba–Nahariya train line; and a gas pipeline have all been built on land taken from the Druze community. The same goes for the city of Yoqne'am, a center of Israel's thriving high-tech industry. "Yoqne'am?" he says. "It's fantastic. Congratulations. Now, ninety percent of that is built on the land of Daliyat al-Karmel." In the 1950s, Israel paid local Druze "peanuts" for that land, Halabi says, and proceeded to seed it with a series of military installations. Later, the army camps were razed to make way for Yoqne'am.

"They took down those camps and instead of giving the land back to the Druze, they gave it to the contractors," Halabi says. "I say to myself, 'So, you did that. Now give fifty percent of the municipal tax to Daliyat al-Karmel. Give twenty-five percent to Daliyat al-Karmel. And let's say you built a hundred factories there? Build ten factories in Daliyat al-Karmel. But the state doesn't even see you from half a meter away!"

Halabi believes that Israeli Arabs get shortchanged in these situations because many of the relevant land-use institutions are not government institutions at all—they're offices founded specifically to serve the Jewish people. "The Israel Land Administration, the Jewish Agency, the Moshav Movement, the Jewish National Fund," he says, ticking off the list of groups. "These are not institutions of the State of Israel!"

Daliyat al-Karmel's streets are narrow and labyrinthine, but they're clean and well paved. And Halabi, for his part, has reached the pinnacle of his profession, working as a reporter and editor at the top networks in this news-obsessed country. He holds a college degree, and was an officer in the army. It looks to me, I say, like he and his neighbors are faring pretty well for second-class citizens.

"That's true, in comparison to the Bedouin," he says. "But not compared to Timrat."

Timrat is the nearby Jewish town where I've been staying with family friends. Its residents are well-off high-tech entrepreneurs, businesspeople, air force pilots and other military officers. Ask Timrat's residents about how the Arabs in Israel are treated and, after telling you what a shame it is that their neighbors aren't treated better, they'll say: *Still, it's much better for them here than in Syria.* Or, *You know, I can't just put an addition on my house without permits. If I do, the city will come and knock it down.*

In many ways, these arguments are true. In January, for example, Civil Administration bulldozers, accompanied by officers from the Border Police, demolished three illegally built homes in the West Bank Jewish settlement of Havat Gilad. One of those homes belonged to an ultra-Orthodox soldier named Shimon Weisman. "Even in my worst nightmares, I never imagined that while I was putting my life at risk in order to defend the homeland, policemen and soldiers would sneak in and destroy my house," Weisman said afterward.

The quality-of-life argument is worth acknowledging, as well. A recent survey, taken before revolution spread across North Africa, ranks Israel's standard of living as the forty-seventh highest in the world; the nearest Arab nation on the list is a pre-revolution Tunisia, coming in at number seventy-seven. Arabs here vote for their leaders, which, as yet, citizens of many Arab nations cannot. Israel's health-care system is also far better than just about anything available elsewhere in the Middle East; Arab presidents have been known to sneak into Israel under assumed names for specialized medical treatments.

But that, Israel's Arabs say, is like comparing apples and oranges. Because Arab Israelis don't judge themselves against the rest of the Arab world. They judge themselves against their neighbors.

When Amal Nasser El Deen's second son was kidnapped by members of Hamas in 1996, the army, the Mossad, and Shabak went looking for him in the West Bank. Saleh Nasser El Deen had recently finished his military service, and, taking advantage of what felt like a new openness in the aftermath of the Oslo Accords, he headed off to the Palestinian territories for a short visit. The Israelis never found a trace of him after that.

When an Israeli is kidnapped, it is very, very big news. Stories about Gilad Shalit, the Israeli staff sergeant kidnapped by Hamas in 2006, appear in Israeli newspapers nearly every day. Signs proclaiming that GILAD IS STILL ALIVE adorn cities and towns across Israel. Shalit's parents have become national figures, permanently manning a tent in front of the prime minister's Jerusalem residence to keep their son's fate constantly in the government's sight lines. On Shalit's birthday, in August, I get caught in a traffic jam when hundreds of supporters descend on the tent to stand with the Shalit family in demanding that the prime minister trade hundreds of Palestinians currently held in

Israeli jails for Shalit's safe return. A few days later, while driving from Timrat to the nearby Memorial for Fallen Bedouin Soldiers, I hear the host of a pop-radio station go to commercial by announcing how many days Shalit has been imprisoned.

"So why do we hear so much about Gilad Shalit and nothing about your son?" I ask Nasser El Deen now.

"Because I'm certain that my son is no longer with us," he says. "Which is different from Shalit, who is alive."

"Why are you certain?"

"My son is Druze. And they don't like the Druze in the West Bank. Hamas is harsher in the case of a Druze. They don't like us. They say we're traitors. We say different. But I'm sure, almost sure, that they executed him."

Twelve years later, Amal Nasser El Deen's grandson was the first Israeli casualty of the 2008 war in Gaza, killed near Nahal Oz when a Palestinian rocket exploded beside him. His name was Lotfi, after his uncle, the first of Nasser El Deen's sons to die.

Rafik Halabi: "Let's talk for a minute about whether or not it's good for the Druze to get drafted. Maybe on the individual level it's good. Maybe it's even good for the community. But on a gut level, do the Druze get satisfaction from this thing? I'd say no. Really no. Now, many Druze will tell you: 'What are you talking about? We're Israelis! We're Zionists! This is our country!' Nationalist speeches. But I'll tell you about the youth. I'll tell you about my second son, who was in the army. What did it leave him with? Was it important to him? It's not important to him. He knows that the civilian problems of the Druze are so intense, so painful, so difficult—land problems, infrastructure problems, budget problems, relationship problems— that they raise questions about the draft. More than ninety percent of ultra-Orthodox Jews don't serve in the army, and their political power gives them more rights than anyone else in the country. The equation of obligations and rights is an equation that does not exist."

On July 27, 2010, the same day that Faisal abu Nadi invites me into his home and offers a debatable account of the destruction of his village's "clubhouse," I go to see El Arakib, the Bedouin village that the ILA has just demolished. Israel says the village is illegal; El Arakib's residents point to their nearby cemetery and say they've lived there for decades. The competing claims have been making their way through the courts, and a government source tells me that it was a court order that finally allowed the demolition to go forward. The residents of El Arakib, though, insist that the case was still being adjudicated at the time the bulldozers moved in. Either way, it bears noting that Israel didn't touch the cemetery, though presumably it, too, was illegal.

I spend the better part of an hour wandering around the ruins. Piles of corrugated metal, iron bars, and concrete rise like boils on the back of a dust-covered hill. Dozens of pigeons roost in the scattered remnants of their coop. Bulldozed trees lie on their sides, roots jutting into the air like a dead dog's legs. Piles of hay smolder.

Meanwhile, a few village men are hammering together a wooden frame for a new tent. Once they've covered it with a black tarp, I approach and ask where I can find the village sheikh. They point me to a small olive grove that remains standing near the foot of the hill, and I walk over and ask the sheikh, Sayah al-Touri, if we can talk.

He's in a gray robe, a white turban, white cotton pants, and dusty black loafers, and has an imposing white mustache. He displays none of the vaunted Bedouin hospitality when I appear, but then again, as of this morning he doesn't have a house. I crouch down next to him, trying, pathetically, to match his position: feet flat on the ground, knees bent, butt dangling an inch or two above the dirt.

"The Nazis that they talk about?" he says. "They didn't do the kinds of things that they did to us today. They say this place isn't suited for Arab settlement. It's our land! We will continue to build! We are already building!"

A group of local men begins to assemble, just listening at first, eventually launching into a little call-and-response exercise.

"This land is the land of our fathers and our grandfathers," al-Touri says. "Three hundred and fifty people live here. We have been living here for a hundred and ten years!"

I ask him if he or any of the men in his village served in the IDF.

"It's no honor for me to serve," he says. "This government is not a government that gives anyone respect. Do you think they wouldn't have destroyed this place if we served in the army? Is that what you think?"

I realize, after a long pause, that it's not a rhetorical question. I tell him I don't know.

"First of all, they destroy soldiers' homes," he says. "Even officers with two stripes!" The group of men starts getting animated.

"Paratroopers!" one yells.

"Trackers!" another shouts.

The sheikh, meanwhile, goes quiet. He just stays where he is, crouching, staring at the ground, while the men around me talk over each other. My thighs are on fire, shaking embarrassingly. I can't hold this position any longer, so I stand up. The sheikh stays where he is; he's been forced to move once today already.

A week after I visit El Arakib, Israel returns and destroys whatever the villagers have rebuilt, including the twice-demolished home of forty-six-year-old father of three Abu Madyam Kayid. When I return the next afternoon, I find Kayid sitting on a milk crate, smoking, in a tent he's just finished putting up. His wife comes by with a kettle of tea and wordlessly pours a paper cup for each of us.

"We started building after they left, in the evening," Kayid says. "As sure as we are that they'll destroy this again, we're sure of ourselves—we'll keep on building."

I tell him I was here the previous week, when the village was razed the first time. "I spoke to the sheikh," I say. "He told me that guys from this village don't serve in the army—that it's no honor to serve a country that would do this to its citizens."

Kayid thinks a minute, removes his leather cowboy hat, mops his brow with the back of his hand. "There were two guys," he says.

"What happened to them?" I ask.

"It wasn't pleasant for them to live here, so they left."

"Where did they go?"

"Rahat," he says. Rahat is one of the cities Israel established for the Negev Bedouin.

"And it wasn't pleasant for them why?" I ask. "Because the others here didn't approve?"

"Right," he says. Then he climbs onto a tractor and invites me over to see the rubble where his house once stood. El Arakib has since been destroyed, and rebuilt, nineteen more times.

There was no requirement, under the initial court order authorizing the destruction of El Arakib, that the Israel Land Administration return to raze rebuilt structures. Still, subsequent demolitions didn't actually require a court order—a more easily obtainable administrative order from the ILA sufficed. "That's a stupid act, to go destroying it back and forth," says a government source. "The government had to knock it down because the court ordered it. But after the first time, that's it.

They made El Arakib a symbol. I don't think it's smart."

It is one of many symbols that observers and the Bedouin themselves say may spark a third intifada—this time emanating not from Palestinians in the West Bank and Gaza, but from the Bedouin citizens of Israel proper, if not their fellow Israeli Arabs.

"There may be something that happens that ignites them," says Clinton Bailey, the Bedouin scholar. He notes that the First Intifada was sparked by a single car accident in Gaza, and the second erupted after a visit by Ariel Sharon to Jerusalem's Temple Mount. This time around, he says, it could be further home destructions, or even an unpopular decision from the panel working to bring the Goldberg Committee's findings in line with government thinking. "There's a very good chance that they're going to offer things to the Bedouin that the Bedouin can't accept," Bailey says. "All I can say right now is that the tinder is there."

Of course, it's also possible that the committee on the Goldberg Committee will produce a proposal that manages to satisfy all parties involved. In June 2011, this second panel, known as the Prawer Committee, issued its recommendations, which included relocating some thirty thousand Negev Bedouin to expanded authorized areas around existing government-planned towns such as Rahat and Hura, and offering these transplants compensation in the form of money and land. As soon as details of the plan were released, influential Bedouin came out against it. The cabinet was set to approve the recommendations in mid-June, but strong opposition forced a delay. At the time of this writing, intense behind-the-scenes wrangling is underway to forge some sort of consensus, but no one involved is overly optimistic.

Even among those who anticipate an outbreak of public opposition, though, the form it will take is another question. Will it be violent, like the October 2000 riots in which a dozen Israeli Arabs were killed in clashes with police? Will it resemble the protests that succeeded this year in Egypt and Tunisia, and may yet elsewhere in the Arab world? Or will the dimensions of an uprising be less clear?

"*Intifada*'s a generic term," says Moshe Arens, the former defense minister. "There's a lot of crime out there. A lot of stealing. A lot of poaching of the property of Israeli farmers. A lot of traffic accidents. If you want, you can call that intifada. It's a reflection of the social conditions of most of the Bedouin population here."

The Bedouin identify primarily on the basis of tribe and clan rather than as a larger community; they lack cohesiveness and a unified leadership. Further, desert life has made them patient sufferers, for better and for worse. If, however, they do rise up, the soldiers among them—charged with protecting the state from disturbances of this sort—may well find themselves in an untenable position.

A few weeks before leaving Israel I meet with Eli Atzmon, a longtime military-intelligence officer and onetime head of the Bedouin Authority, a position that put him in charge of enforcing house-destruction orders. Now a private consultant to Bedouin making land claims, Atzmon's views are frequently sought by Israel's political leadership. Like Arens, he believes that the army can be a great equalizer—but says the problem goes much deeper than anything the military can fix on its own.

"It's true that the minorities today can go to more places in the army than before, but that's not enough," he says. If Israel continues along its current course, Atzmon tells me, its growing Arab population will begin to see the Jewish state as inevitably set against them. "A little boy who is awakened at five in the morning and sees a large force next to him and sees that they've destroyed his house—he doesn't know how to do the math," he says. "Justified? Unjustified? The government? The law? It doesn't interest him. They destroyed his house. He'll remember that for the rest of his life."

Here Atzmon pauses for a moment and scans his tiny office, which is lined with maps of Bedouin settlements and file boxes labeled with the names of tribes and villages. These documents are the tools with which Israeli Arabs have attempted to lay claim to their homes; the tools Atzmon hopes to use to help repair a badly broken situation. Eight months after we first meet, the government approaches Atzmon in hopes that he will agree to persuade the Bedouin to get on board with the Prawer Committee's plan. He doesn't immediately sign on, insisting that the committee first give the Bedouin themselves a hearing. That doesn't happen. Instead, Atzmon is now pushing for significant changes based on what the Bedouin *would* have said, had they been invited to speak. Whether or not these changes will be made remains unknown; the latest effort to solve the Bedouin land problem is poised at the edge of a precipice. But the status quo, Atzmon says, will serve no one.

"You can't go around destroying houses and think that it will all pass quietly," he tells me. "The Islamic Movement is waiting in the wings. Everything together boils, boils, boils. And in the end it will explode. And whoever doesn't see that is either blind or doesn't want to see it."

THE NORTHEAST KINGDOM

by NATHANIEL RICH

1

E HAD ALWAYS BELIEVED that his immortality would take the form of the Aerojet. The two-stage, solid-fuel boost rocket had been, in its time, one of the crowning achievements of human technology—the first apparatus to collect data on the higher atmosphere. There were other worthy accomplishments—his long tenure as chairman of Aerobee International, for instance—but the Aerojet should have been sufficient to rate him an obituary in the national papers. The thought consoled him, though he had once hoped for more. He remembered, as a boy, dreaming about alien encounters, the exploration of new worlds, Martian colonies secured under prodigious glass domes, silent spaceships diving through orange canyons. Unfortunately he'd been born far too early for any of that. So as he slipped through the early decades of his retirement, swallowing his yogurt every morning and assembling his model airplanes in the afternoon, he cheered himself with the thought of the inevitable column of newsprint that would one day be dedicated to his memory.

Beneath the headline (SAUL WYNGARTEN, ENGINEER AND SPACE-AGE SEER) would appear his portrait and, next to it, a file photograph of the Aerojet, that thin column of propulsive energy, his gift to humanity.

Saul first began to wonder whether he might not be remembered for the Aerojet at his centennial party, when the body of his nephew, Joseph, was found in the bathroom. Joseph's death was not in itself surprising; at seventy-four years of age he was disturbingly unfit, reddish, and fat, with an advanced case of gout that required him to wear an oversized plastic boot on his left foot. No, it was what happened directly after the body was discovered that forced Saul to question the most basic assumptions he'd made about his fate.

Until then it had been a festive evening, and not just because loud, drunk Joseph was nowhere to be found. On the back lawn of Saul's Vermont home, seated around him at seven rented round tables, were his son and daughter, their children, thirteen great-grandchildren, and even little Saul Schapiro, his two-year-old great-great-grandchild. The sight of all his descendants gave Saul a ghostly sensation, as though he were looking back from the grave. There were toasts and polite laughter, and finally Saul himself stomped onto the stage. He braced himself against the sides of the podium, hard, and the tenacity of his grip prompted one of his grandsons to rush to his side for support. But Saul wasn't unsteady. He was overwhelmed.

He was remembering his own great-grandmother's centennial. Although he had been only eight at the time—less than a month before he left Vienna forever—the memory felt more real to him than the patient, upturned faces of the people who sat on his lawn in plastic folding chairs. He saw the cobwebs dangling from the sill of the high lacquered window in Gommie's drawing room; the long candles set at irregular intervals along the banquet table, dripping into pinkish pools of wax; and, most vividly of all, Gommie herself, her smiling, crenellated face perched like a stuffed animal above her evaporated body. Deaf and immobile, she had been far less fit at one hundred than Saul was today. But on that distant night ninety-two years earlier, as her quavering hand delivered half-thimbles of Slivovitz to her small, crooked mouth, he could tell that she had been happy.

At the podium Saul recalled Gommie's party, laughing at the memories. But as he stepped off the stage to benevolent applause, an unsettling thought occurred to him: Everyone at Gommie's house that day—Gommie herself, Saul's aunts and uncles and even his little cousins, his parents, his poor sister—they were all dead.

Who, then, are all these clapping people? These people who claim to be my family?

Then a shriek came from inside the house and Joseph's wife and daughter burst into sobs.

Saul was as disturbed as anyone to learn of the death of his favorite nephew. It was a gruesome display, the mountainous body twisted on the carpet. But what bothered him most deeply—what stayed with him in the days, years, and decades that followed—was the look that his guests gave him once the ambulance had removed the corpse.

"Are you all right, Grandfather?" asked one young woman whom he could not identify. Saul began to respond but was chastened by something cold and suspicious that flashed in her eyes. Old Art and Bethany Mossberger gave him the same look, as did his niece Janet and Janet's husband. He sensed something uneasy, also, in his own children's manner with him: the two of them refused to make eye contact, and Elon even dodged Saul's embrace. As if Saul were somehow responsible for Joseph's coronary!

When your parents are still living, they stand between you and death. When they die, you're next in line. These people in their white jackets and summer dresses were staring at Saul like he'd made a devil's bargain; like he had skipped his turn, and those behind him would now have to go in his place. Saul had violated some unwritten law. He had been gluttonous with life, he'd eaten too much. Where had his extra portion come from? It was as if they believed he was eating the life out of their bodies.

In the following years—101, 102, 103, 104, 105—both of Saul's children died and his grandchildren scattered. There were fewer phone calls. His most frequent visitors were a pair of representatives from the Gerontology Research Group, two women in their fifties—or sixties, maybe even early seventies, it was difficult for Saul to distinguish anymore. One woman was silent, an obsessive note-taker, with the large clinking bracelets of a Hapsburg madam. The other wore oversized glasses and was unusually tall—a poor indication of longevity, Saul had always believed, the excessive distance between heart and brain causing a dissipation of the vital energies. Saul was only sixty-five inches himself.

They visited his home in Hastings every six months, with their clipboards and questionnaires and hushed voices. They brought him a refrigerator magnet on which was printed, in childish writing, I'M A CENTENARIAN AND I FEEL ONEHUNDREDPERCENTENARIAN! Their attitude with him was more skeptical than curious. They observed closely his steady, strong hands, his clear, brownish skin, his erect posture, the nimble activity of his restless feet. The tall one asked the questions, while the small one stood ready with a pen.

To what do you attribute your longevity? What is your diet? How would you rate your average level of stress, on a scale of one to ten? What do you want from life?

"I want to see man explore new planets," said Saul.

The mousy woman wrote on her pad, nodding furiously.

"And what advice do you have for people who want to live long lives?"

"I don't know," Saul said. "Keep breathing, I guess."

They gave him patient smiles and waited for him to continue. But he had nothing to add. The silence quickly became uncomfortable.

"Did you ever read about the Aerojet?" he said finally. "It was the first apparatus to collect data on the higher atmosphere."

The women thanked him for his time.

When Saul's grandchildren did visit, their own children often found it difficult to understand who he was. They stared at him as they would a statue, and quickly grew bored. After a while they would wander off, playing with his model airplanes until their anxious parents screamed, *Put those down, they aren't toys.*

"But they are," Saul would say, encouraging the children. "They *are* my toys."

One person did stay behind: Jacob Wyngarten, Elon's oldest son. Jacob moved into his father's childhood bedroom. The state had refused to renew Saul's driver's license after his one-hundredth birthday, so he'd required an assistant to buy groceries and take care of the house until he could find professional help. Jacob had volunteered to work for a month, but the circumstances suited both men, so he stayed.

A quiet child, Jacob had expanded into a plump, gentle adult with a dry sense of humor and a slight nervous flutter around the corners of his thin mouth. He'd never married, and was now in his mid-fifties. He had mentioned in passing, once or twice, a certain friend—Saul suspected this friend was a man, but he did not pry.

Jacob had visited Saul and Esther for a weekend at the old house on Orchard Drive, once, when he was still in grade school; he had spent most of the day exploring the woods. When Esther went out to water the herb garden, she overheard him talking to himself. That evening, Saul remembered, she had expressed doubts about the boy's masculinity. "He just seems a tad ethereal," she had said to Saul. "He's in outer space." Saul defended his grandson, pointing out that, as a rocket engineer, he, too, spent most of his days in outer space. "You know what I mean," Esther had said. And Saul, though he didn't admit it to his wife, had agreed. The boy *was* a tad ethereal.

Jacob had traded currency at a Manhattan bank with such success that he had retired ten years earlier. He continued to trade for himself, but it was only for sport; he had all the money he could ever spend. He behaved genially around Saul, but in company he grew restless. When his sisters and cousins visited, Jacob made excuses to leave the house.

"I don't like the way they treat you," Jacob told him.

"How's that?"

"Have you noticed that they only come to see us when they're sick? Cousin Fred was here a week after being diagnosed with prostate cancer. Joseph's daughter showed up after she found out she had inherited his gout. Annabelle only brought her son after he was in the hospital with mono."

"Everyone has health problems."

"Not everyone."

"Eventually everyone. Or so I imagine."

"They just want to reassure themselves that they have your genes."

"So? I appreciate the company."

"They don't talk to you. Not really. They don't want to know about your accomplishments, your thoughts on life. They only want to know how closely they're related to you. Cousin Alan's kid wanted to know your blood type, for heaven's sake. Your blood type! You're a science experiment to them. It's repulsive."

"I don't think that's fair," said Saul, but his voice was quiet, almost inaudible, and his grandson didn't press it any further.

Jacob was happiest when they were alone together. He cleaned the house, bought groceries and cooked, ordered new model airplanes—

dozens, more than Saul imagined he'd ever need. The collection had grown enormous, unwieldy, the vessels arrayed across two ping-pong tables in the garage. Jacob had to park his car in the driveway, but he didn't complain. He even made a point of dusting the completed models once a week.

Only the Aerojet was granted a privileged perch. It sat on Saul's bureau, right beside the alarm clock. It was the first thing he saw when he woke up. On unclouded nights the moonlight reflected off its hull and the glow served as a kind of nightlight.

Though he never would have mentioned such a thing to Jacob, this light was important to him. As a young man, so many years ago, he had been told that when you grow old, you stop fearing death. You grow indifferent to it. The big things cease to bother you, while the small irritations become disproportionately vast. And when you reached an extreme age, when you passed a century as Gommie had, this irksomeness turns into disappointment and despair. Finally, you welcome death. Jacob had shown him a newspaper article about the world's oldest person, a little Japanese woman (Saul was mentioned in passing in the final paragraph, near the bottom of the list of oldest living Americans). She was quoted as saying, "I don't need to live a hundred more. I enjoy nothing but eating and sleeping."

This sentiment was foreign to him. A hundred and seven years into his life, whenever he thought of death, a hot panic overtook him, getting under his collar and into his brain—just as it had when he was seventy, forty-seven, twenty-seven, even seven years old. He remembered one night bursting out of the apartment and running, barefoot and breathless, down Kaiserstrasse, until the chill of the autumn wind in his face and the rough cobblestones against his feet sent the panic scurrying back to its cage. A century had passed, but the attacks still came. Only now it wasn't so easy to get out of bed in the middle of the night: he worried about knocking into something.

So he lay in bed, the Aerojet glowing beside him, and stared into the nothingness. Occasionally he had to push his hand over his mouth to stifle a gasp.

Several years later the little Japanese woman had a heart attack in her sleep and died. She was one hundred and fifteen years and forty-six days old. It was Jacob who answered the phone. When he turned to face Saul, the receiver pressed against his chest, the corner of his mouth was trembling. Saul knew what it was about. He rested his tube of airplane glue on his worktable and rose to take the phone.

"Congratulations," said Jacob. "You made it."

So the relatives began to come to Hastings again, though not immediately, and not before the thin-lipped adjudicator from Guinness, who presented Saul with a framed certificate and clapped him on the shoulder so forcefully that Jacob ordered the man to leave at once. The television reporters, too, descended with their moronic questions ("What was World War I like?" "What was the most depressing part of the Great Depression?"). The mayor of Hastings, only twenty-five years Saul's junior, stopped by with a formal certificate. "I hope I'll make it as far as you one day," said the mayor. "What would be the odds of that, two codgers from Hastings?" He wished he could stay longer, he said, but he was due at the hospital for his dialysis appointment.

The two women from the Gerontology Research Group—the Sickle Sisters, Jacob called them—arrived two days later in their rental car. They had just returned from Okinawa, where they had attended the former record-holder's cremation. They greeted Saul with false warmth.

"Please accept our congratulations, sir," said the tall one, wincing.

He couldn't fault them. They were like hospice nurses, or death-row wardens: the job demanded that they spend their days with the soon-to-be-dead. True emotional engagement would be detrimental to their work. Their purpose was to observe a unique and valuable scientific phenomenon. Saul, an aerospace engineer, knew what that was about.

A week later a dozen people wearing matching white T-shirts appeared at the doorstep. Jacob was at the store, so Saul greeted them himself. He took them at first for salesmen, and was about to slam the door when he noticed on their shirts a blown-up photograph of his own withered, frowning face. The lettering above it read OLDEST MAN IN THE UNIVERSE, OUR SAUL.

"Surprise!" the strangers yelled. Saul glanced uneasily between their faces and his own, staring back at him from their shirts. One man stepped forward and spoke in an excessively loud voice.

"Saul! It's me, your great-grandson! Max!"

Very well, so it was. He hadn't seen Max since the centennial. In the intervening years the man had narrowed unhealthily; his chest was flat, and his cheeks were like deflated tires. He didn't appear to have inherited any segment of Saul's genetic code. His teeth were uneven, and he was bald but for a few cobwebby hairs that gathered just above the ears. His nose, though, was distinctly patrician, a slender, fluted cylinder, no doubt a surgical flourish.

"It's been fifteen years," said Saul.

Max chuckled awkwardly. "Not that long, I don't think!" As if to distract Saul, he thrust forward a skinny child. The boy had unusually long eyelashes and a devious grin. "This is your great-*great* grandson. Saul, may I introduce you to Saul?"

"Ah, yes," said Saul senior, extending his hand. "We've met. At my centennial. You were a toddler then."

Saul Junior shook his ancestor's hand. "It's a real honor, sir."

Saul Senior laughed, and the other people standing outside laughed loudly in response. Saul stopped laughing.

"Who are all these people?" he asked Max.

"Descendants, Saul. Your blood. We're here to celebrate you."

But Saul did not believe that they were his descendants. He surely did not remember them from the centennial, and they barely resembled the younger Saul, or each other, let alone him. Nor did they seem even to know each other. He couldn't be certain, of course—by now there must have been born dozens, if not hundreds of Wyngartens he'd never met. But these people seemed very odd. And in his gut he felt the familiar scurrying beginning again.

"I'm afraid I'm quite busy at the moment," he said. He began to explain that he was in the middle of a new model—the Vought Cutlass, a Cold War jet fighter—that required immense concentration and sustained energy. But he was interrupted by another bout of laughter. He supposed that the idea of a one-hundred-and-fifteen-year-old man keeping busy must have amused them.

Max, still laughing, took the opportunity to shove Saul Junior through the door, and followed the boy into the house. Saul, fearful of being trampled, pulled to the side, and then the whole T-shirted coterie rushed in.

They filled the living room like moths, flapping about the furniture. To Saul's astonishment, they put their hands on everything: the miniature Etruscan figurines that Jacob had brought home from a yard sale; the green archival cases containing issues of *Aerospace* going back five decades; the stately, broken-down radio with its torn speaker overlaid by curved striplings of wood arranged in a floral pattern. They left no room for Saul, so he stood uneasily in front of the fireplace until a large woman roughly three times his size, sighing with consternation, made space for him on the couch.

Max had taken a seat across from him, in Jacob's armchair. Saul Junior knelt at his father's feet. Max stared at the elder Saul with great intensity and, it seemed, hunger.

"Saulie boy. Saulie, Saulie, Saulie. You're a hard man to get a hold of. With Jacob always answering the phone, and the door—"

"Max? I'm a little agitated. I have valuable things lying around—"

"What's the secret?"

"Excuse me?"

"The *secret*, Saulie. You know: the Philosopher's Stone, the Holy Grail, the Fountain of Youth. What is it? *Where* is it?"

"Well, Max," he said, clenching his jaw, "I'll tell you the same thing I've told the reporters. My only secret is: Keep breathing."

Max's smile froze on his face. He lowered his voice to a whisper. "I need to know, Saul."

There was a loud crash. The framed photograph of the Aerojet launch had dropped from its hook above the fireplace and fallen onto the stone mantel. Saul jerked around and saw a man of roughly eighty-five years, with corncob glasses and ginger hair, cradling the crooked frame with trembling hands. There was a desperation around his eyes and his twitching nose, an eagerness that looked out of place on a man of that age.

"What are you doing?" said Saul, his voice rising. "What is this?"

"I'm only readjusting," said the man with the ginger hair. "It looked askew."

"Who *are* you, anyway?"

The man was briefly speechless. He looked distractedly off into the distance, and then his eyes focused again on Saul.

"I'm Arnold," he said at last. "Your nephew. *Arnold.*" Arnold's lips pressed flat together, sheepish. His T-shirt billowed over his slender frame. It was easily three sizes too large for him.

Saul stood up. "Max, I don't like this. What is going on?"

"Wait," said Max, the smile beginning to curdle on his lips. "We need to talk. Let's be calm." He rose and rested his hand on Saul's shoulder. His voice grew quieter still. "I can tell the others to leave. How about that, Saul? Then it'll be just you and me. Like old times. Like when I was a boy. Remember? Remember that, when I was a boy?"

Saul tried. All he could come up with was a large-faced smudge running madly around the dining table at the house on Orchard Drive. His daughter was Julia. Julia had a son, Harold; this Max was Harold's son. And now Saul Junior. He suddenly regretted his shortness with Max. Maybe all of these people were his family after all.

"Tell me," said Saul. "How is your father? My grandson. Harold."

"That's why I'm here," said Max. His arm was becoming heavy on Saul's shoulder. "My father is dead. Mother too. They weren't seventy years old. Not even seventy!"

"Dead?" said Saul. "But when?"

Then Jacob backed in the front door, cradling a bag of groceries in his arms. When he turned and saw their visitors, the bag fell to the floor. Something cracked.

"Everyone out!" he cried. "Everybody get out!"

The descendants froze. They looked to Max, waiting for some cue.

"Hello, Jacob," said Max. "We wanted to pay Saul a visit. To celebrate his achievement. You're not his only family, you know."

"What did I tell you, Max?" said Jacob, glaring. "We don't want to see you."

"I know that *you* don't want to see me," said Max. "But Saul has said no such thing."

Jacob glared icily. Saul had never seen him so angry.

"It doesn't matter," said Max. "We were leaving anyway." He turned to Saul. "I'll look forward to continuing this sometime soon."

Max turned to walk to the door, taking Saul Junior by the hand. The others followed, gently setting down Saul's possessions, emerging from the bathrooms, the dining room, the cellar. The last person to leave, a sickly woman with pale yellow skin and whitish hair, appeared in the doorway to the garage. Saul had not noticed her before. She was holding his World War II Messerschmitt Bf-109 propeller airplane. It was only when Saul glared at her that she seemed to realize it was still in her hand. Seized by terror, she rested it on the kitchen table and hurried out. Jacob closed the door firmly behind her, and turned the lock.

"Sit down," said Jacob. "You don't look well."

"Harold is dead. No one told me."

"No one wanted to upset you."

"Do you know how many of my people have died? The balance on the ledger shifted decades ago. I can absorb one more."

Jacob sighed. "I should have told you. It's just... Max. There's something wrong with him. He's unstable."

"Unstable?"

"He's been calling. He thinks you can help."

"Why?"

"He thinks you know something."

"I don't know a damn thing, Jacob." Saul's voice cracked, and he paused before continuing. "Not a single damn thing."

Jacob shrugged. "That's what I told them."

"Is that what the others wanted? Were they all sick?"

"I don't know who they were," said Jacob. "But I don't like that they have our address."

The Hastings post office received such a large quantity of mail for Saul that Jacob had to register a special box. There were fan letters (*You're my favorite Super-C EVER*) and requests for autographs, but most of all, there were questions. Although they touched upon various subjects— diet, psychology, exercise—they could be reduced to a single one: How do I live longer?

Television crews from England, South Korea, and Denmark filmed him during his afternoon walk on the forest road. Neighbors brought over baskets with fresh fruit and vitamins. Saul could not drive with Jacob into town without being assaulted by well-wishers. Young girls wanted to touch his skin: so smooth, so thin, like tracing paper. "You're the best thing that's ever happened to Hastings," gushed Mrs. Cramble at the farmers' market. "The best thing that's ever happened to Vermont!"

It was unseemly the way Jacob, like a bodyguard, had to repel the townspeople. Saul decided not to go into Hastings anymore, and not to answer the door.

As it so happened, his great-grandson Max was the one person he did not have to worry about. Not two weeks after his visit, an envelope appeared on Saul's doorstep. It had no stamp, nor an address; it simply said *Great Great Poppy Saul.* Jacob handed it to Saul when he brought him his breakfast in bed—a scoop of plain yogurt under a tablespoon of olive oil, a slice of rye toast, and a small glass of freshly squeezed orange juice. After he finished the yogurt and drained the last of the juice, Saul opened the envelope. The letter was written in a messy, uneven hand:

> *Dear Great Great Poppy,*
>
> *My dad died six days after we came to see you. His heart was damaged. He didn't want to die.*
> *Do you really have a secret?*
> *If so, please write me at Saulthegreat323@gmail.com.*
>
> *Love,*
> *Saul (Jr.) Schapiro*

"But this is very distressing," said Saul, handing it over to Jacob.

"There's nothing you can do," said Jacob.

Saul nodded and rose from the bed. The note stayed in his head, but he couldn't think about it until he went through his morning exercises: ten laps around the house, ten waist-bends. On warmer days, such as this one, he could still touch his ankles. Then he sat down at his worktable, where a new project awaited him: the Focke-Wulf Fw-190.

"This was the pride of Marshal Goering," said Saul, laying out the pieces on the table, the curved segments of yellow balsa, the miniature propellers like crushed black flies, the rubber tires like slices of licorice.

He thought: *His heart was damaged.* He thought: *He didn't want to die.*

"It looks like a beauty," said Jacob.

"Oh?" Saul glanced over his spectacles. "Ah. Yes. It maintained superiority over the British Spitfire 5 for almost two years. It was faster, and it could carry more bombs."

"I'll let you to it."

"Wait," said Saul, picking up a plastic bomb. "Will there be more visitors?"

"I'm afraid there might be. You've become a kind of a celebrity. That's how it is with these things."

"I've done enough, damn it!"

Jacob looked up, alarmed by the tone of his grandfather's voice.

"I don't want to see them," Saul continued, heat rising in his chest. "I don't want people in our house. I don't want people walking beside me on the forest road."

Jacob nodded.

"I just want to work on my planes in peace. Is that too much to ask? I couldn't have helped Harold's son. I don't *know* anything!"

"I know," said Jacob, touching his grandfather's shoulder. "I know."

Saul's hands were shaking now. The plastic bomb in his hand fell to the table.

In the coming weeks the siege intensified. Visitors rang the doorbell all day; journalists from countries on the other side of the planet telephoned after midnight. Did Saul realize he was less than six months short of the official record for oldest living man ever, set by the Danish American Christian Mortensen, who was 115 years, 252 days old at the time of his death? (Yes, he did—the adjudicator from Guinness with the sandpaper lips had informed him.) How much longer did he think he would live? What was he living *for*?

"You want to know what most upsets me?" he asked Jacob one night. Jacob had just turned away a choir of young girls who had assembled on the front porch to sing "Edelweiss."

"The constant harassment?"

"It's not even that. I don't like to be reminded constantly of my own death. I don't *care* if I'm one hundred and fifteen years old. I didn't want to die when I was fifteen, when I was thirty, when I was eighty—and I don't want to die now. No one talks about this. But, damn it, it's true."

Jacob nodded. "All right, Saul. Don't get worked up. Besides, at the rate you're going, you'll live to two hundred."

"And then? And then? What happens *then*?"

His grandson rose and took the old man's light head into his chest.

"There now. There."

Jacob's sweater grew damp, but he held Saul, held him until the sobbing had come to an end. Saul's entire head fit into the palm of Jacob's hand.

Later, after Saul had said good night and the lamps were switched off, he cried out from his bed.

"Yes?" Jacob ran in, breathless. He was wearing only his boxers, and his gut wobbled like a gyroscope. The movements of his limbs were clumsy and frantic.

"The Aerojet!" said Saul.

"Sorry?"

"Would you give me the Aerojet?"

"The Aerojet? Yes. Of course. The Aerojet."

Jacob, calmer, picked up the model from the bureau and angled it on the bedside table until it reflected the light of the moon. The darkness dissipated. The room mellowed to a gray haze. Saul heard himself exhale.

"Saul," said Jacob, "how do you feel? Physically, I mean."

"Fine! I feel fine! Now you, too? You with these questions?"

"No, no. That's not what I mean. I was thinking. I had an idea about how to get rid of all these people. Once and for all."

"Yes? Let's hear it."

"We move."

"Nope." Saul shook his head. "The Sickle Sisters would stay after us with their clipboards and inquisitions. Same with Guinness. The newspapers and the rest wouldn't be far behind."

"That's just the thing. We'd have to get rid of them."

"And how might we do that? They never stop! They never will. It can only get worse once I pass the Mortensen fellow."

"As I see it, there's really only one option."

"I'm listening."

"It's quite simple," said Jacob. "You have to die."

2

On the way out of Hastings Jacob parked in the empty lot behind the post office and fed three envelopes into the mailbox. The first two were addressed to the Gerontology Research Group and Guinness World Records. The third, addressed to the Hastings mayor's office, included a large check and the deed to Saul's house. A letter, signed by Saul, bequeathed his house to the town. The single stipulation was that the garage, with its two hundred aviation models on display, was to be called the Aerojet Room; it should be open to the public, and admittance should remain free in perpetuity.

"I'm not sure this is a sharp idea," said Saul, as they accelerated past the Stardust Diner and over the Hastings Bridge. It was the 162nd day of Saul's 115th year, placing him exactly three months short of Christian Mortensen's record. Jacob's station wagon was filled to the roof with their possessions, including more than forty unopened boxes of new model airplanes and spaceships. Saul slumped in his seat like a bag of laundry, his head covered by a blue linen bedsheet so that he wouldn't be visible from the street. Wedged between the two front seats were four framed photographs—the Aerojet launch, the portrait of Esther that had stood on Saul's bedside table, and two portraits of Saul, one from his Aerobee retirement dinner, the other from the centennial party, with his children, Julia and Elon, at his side. They seemed like tokens from the life of a stranger.

"What if they find us out?" he asked Jacob. "Aren't we breaking some law?"

"Everyone in the world is waiting for you to die. They're more suspicious of you alive than dead."

Saul crinkled his nose. "Just make sure to get the obituaries, will you?"

"Sure," said Jacob, glancing anxiously at the small mass under the blue sheet.

"I sound grumpy, don't I?"

"You could say that."

"I'm sorry. I don't feel grumpy. Actually, I feel good. I haven't felt this good since my centennial."

"You can take the sheet off now. We're beyond the limits."

Saul pulled the sheet down. He blinked in the spray of light. "I'm not kidding," he exclaimed. "We're free! This is a new beginning, isn't it?"

Jacob laughed. "It sure is."

"Now give me the music player."

Jacob reached into the glove compartment and pulled out an iPod.

"This," said Saul, "is what I'm talking about." He moved his finger around the wheel, scrolling down to Count Basie. He found "It Won't Be Long" and pressed PLAY. As the brass reverberated in the car's tinny speakers, a ghostly smile cracked open Saul's soft face. His fingers begin thrumming on the dashboard.

"*No, no babe, it won't be long*," he sang in his small voice. "*No, bab-ee, it won't-a-be-long.*"

Jacob, shaking his head in disbelief, merged onto I-91.

Two hours later, a handmade sign welcomed them to WILSON'S GORE, POPULATION ~~TEN~~ ELEVEN.

"We're close," said Jacob.

Saul nodded. As he replaced the bedsheet over his head, he thought, How precious was this life! The falling sun making blue crystals on the blue fabric, the low trickle of a forest brook audible in the distance, the insistent tapping of flies against the windshield, the smell of burned leaves in the air. A new adventure beginning. The cold, crinkly dusk welcoming them to the Northeast Kingdom.

Four-hundred-and-sixty-six million years ago two landmasses collided in the northeastern corner of Vermont, forming a two-thousand-square-mile region bounded by the Green Mountains to the west and the Connecticut River Valley to the east, filled in by lakes and dense forest and divided from the rest of the world. The Northeast Kingdom has never known a housing shortage. Drive into any of the region's fifty-five towns and gores—or Newport, its single incorporated city—and you will find a person eager to sell you a home. There are inconveniences: few paved roads, fewer stores, a spotty electrical grid, extreme cold and blanket darkness during the winter months. But for pure isolation, few regions in this country can beat it.

Saul's favorite thing about the new house was that it was only ten minutes away from an abandoned movie theater. The theater had a giant parking lot, which was barren except for the yellow grasses that had begun to sprout through the seams of the cracked asphalt. Saul hadn't driven a car in fifteen years. Ever since they'd first passed the lot he'd begged Jacob to give him a lesson.

"The right pedal is the accelerator," said Jacob, clicking on his seat belt. "The left is the brake."

"Christ, Jacob. I'm not an amnesiac."

The car eased forward, then pulled up, hard. Their heads lurched forward, then back.

"Saul? Are you okay? Saul?"

"I'm fine," said Saul, flexing his neck. "Just forgot this was one of those new models. I tried to go into second gear."

"It's an automatic. Take your hand off the gearshift." Jacob's chin trembled. "I would like to go on record to say that I think this is a terrible idea."

"Jacob, I'm one hundred and fifteen years old. I can make decisions for myself."

"This is becoming a refrain with you."

"Are you getting crusty in your old age?" said Saul.

"Seventy-one is old to most people."

Saul pressed on the accelerator and the car stuttered forward. "Not to me."

After several loops around the parking lot Saul started laughing, a wheezing sound that emanated from deep in his chest.

"What is it?" said Jacob, his fingers white on the dashboard.

"I love this. I love this so much."

"Great. How much more?"

Saul, silent, kept circling. At the edge of the lot he spotted a dark shape disappearing behind the side of the building. He pushed down on the brake. Jacob again bounced forward.

"What is that?" said Saul. "Is there somebody?"

Jacob squinted but could not see anything. His vision was not good. It occurred to Saul that it probably wasn't very safe for Jacob to be driving so much himself.

"Don't move," said Jacob. His voice was strained, frantic. "Did he see us?"

The curiosity was too much. Against his better judgment, Saul inched forward until they could see around the side of the building.

No one was there; only two porcupines the size of piglets. They roamed lethargically across the asphalt. Saul laughed loudly. A sudden wave of elation passed through him.

He opened his door and stepped out, and Jacob hastened to follow him. At the sound of the car door the animals did not move any faster, but pricked up their needles, becoming nearly twice as large as before.

"Have you ever seen anything like that?" said Saul.

"They're porcupines."

"I know what they are. Aren't they incredible?"

"I suppose so," said Jacob. He coughed, shivering in the cold. "Shall I drive us back?"

Saul ignored him. "They say sexual desire fades away in old age. That's not exactly true."

Jacob looked back and forth between Saul and the waddling porcupines. "You don't mean..."

"Damn it, Jacob, I'm not saying that the porcupines make me hot. It's only that watching them hobble after one another, their crazy quills raised in the air—there's something exhilarating about that, don't you think? Tonight—tonight I will go to bed with a smile on my face."

"I'll have to take your word for it." Jacob went back to the car and settled behind the wheel. He waited for several minutes while Saul shuffled behind the porcupine procession, shadowing them to the edge of the forest until, under a fallen tree, they disappeared. Saul burst into laughter, raising his hands to the sky.

*   *   *

Saul was elated to have his time back. He ate his yogurt in bed every morning, assembled his models in his sunlit workshop, and discovered a new daily walk along a forest path that began in his backyard and advanced beside a meandering stream before looping back to the house. Every few days, Jacob drove thirty minutes to a supermarket in West Charleston and brought back the *Caledonian-Record* and whatever other newspapers happened to be in stock. Two weeks after their move, the obituaries started appearing: SAUL WYNGARTEN, 115, OLDEST MAN IN THE WORLD. Mrs. Victoria Cramble was quoted as praising the "remarkable agility" of Saul's mind and body until the last days of his life. There were no pictures of the Aerojet.

"These are for the fireplace," said Saul, handing the newspapers to Jacob. "No one cares about science anymore."

"Biology they care about. Longevity."

"If they really cared about longevity—about the longevity of the species—they wouldn't talk about me. They'd talk about investing in outer space. Nobody takes the long view."

Jacob spent most of his time working on the house. He had bought it from a grateful real estate agent in Barton, nearly fifty miles west. The place had been abandoned for years, and was in a state of decay; most of the floorboards on the porch had rotted, the kitchen pipes needed to be replaced, and water stains like brownish lakes spread across the second-floor ceiling. Shingles peeled off the exterior. A window in the upstairs bathroom was broken and two sparrows, their necks snapped, decomposed in the bathtub. A brown couch in the living room had sprouted into a grotesque sea anemone. The agent recommended a contractor to Jacob; on afternoons when workers came over, Saul hid in his bedroom. Jacob told them that a friend was visiting. They assumed it was a lover, and didn't pry.

After the first few months, when the major work on the house was finished and the excitement of their self-abduction began to cool, Saul noticed a change come over Jacob. He spent less time at his computer, trading equities. He woke later in the day, just before lunch, and retired directly after dinner. One afternoon, when Saul came down from his studio for a snack, he found Jacob lying in bed. The lights were out, but Jacob was awake.

"Tough going on the Rialto?" Saul asked him.

"It doesn't really matter," said Jacob, rotating ever so slightly toward Saul. An antiseptic odor filled the air. "I mean, it seems grotesque to care about making more money. We have more than we'd ever need. At least for the next century, say."

"That sounds like cause for celebration!"

Jacob didn't seem to hear him. He stared into the folds of his blankets.

"It's just strange," he said. "I've never lost like this before."

"I see."

"I mean, it's not so much in the scheme of things. It's just—my instincts must be off."

"There's no need to take it personal, Jacob."

Jacob looked up sharply, as if becoming aware of Saul's presence for the first time.

"You know how it is with veteran pitchers, when they lose velocity on their fastball? The good ones develop other strategies. They become crafty: they perfect their breaking pitches, they hone their command of the strike zone, and they rely on their knowledge, accumulated over the years, of the opposing hitters' weaknesses. But it's artificial—they're on borrowed time. And they know it. After another year, maybe two, the batters figure out their tricks. Then it's all over."

"But there are always new tricks." Saul was almost giddy in his effort to sound hopeful. He didn't like seeing Jacob like this. "That's the thing you need to understand. Always new tricks."

"Maybe. But I'm too old to learn them."

Saul didn't know what to say.

"It's okay, Saul. I'm just tired. I need to rest."

"Yes. That might be it."

"Can I ask you one thing?" said Jacob.

"Anything."

"Before you go, would you mind just closing the blinds? It's very difficult to sleep with the light coming in around the edges."

Saul's one hundred and sixteenth birthday passed without comment; they had long ago lost track of time. But one morning Saul read the date on a newspaper Jacob had brought back from the market. When he mentioned at dinner that they'd missed his birthday, Jacob apologized gratuitously and promised to buy him a cake.

"That's okay," said Saul. "I'll take a new carton of yogurt."

"You know you've beaten Christian Mortensen."

"Who?"

"The oldest man to ever live."

"Ah, him. It's funny—my life has become so small that the only names I ever need to remember are Jacob and Saul Wyngarten."

"Christian Mortensen never made it to one sixteen. That, if not your birthday, is reason for celebration."

They never had a party. The winter was hard on Jacob. No matter how many blankets he propped over himself on the couch, no matter how brightly the fireplace burned, he always complained of the cold. In March he developed a miserable cough and quarantined himself in his bedroom. Saul heard him every morning, hacking violently for nearly an hour. Finally he couldn't take it anymore. He knocked on the door.

No response. Saul knocked again, harder, and the door opened.

Jacob, deathly pale, stood in his boxers and a T-shirt with a yellow ring around the collar. He was shaking from his exertions. The blood vessels around his eyes had popped.

"You need to go to the hospital," said Saul.

"I'm not leaving you."

A bloody foam had formed on Jacob's chin. Saul stepped back. He found in his pocket a handkerchief and held it over his face.

"Well, you're not staying here. You're too sick."

"The closest hospital is in Colebrook. Over the New Hampshire border. That's nearly three hours round trip. Plus waiting rooms. And they might make me spend the night. No way, I—"

Jacob surprised himself with a violent cough. It crumpled him like a blow to the stomach. Blood spattered on the floor. He coughed more, then gagged slightly. Saul stepped farther away, until his back was pressed against the wall on the opposite side of the hallway.

"It's just my throat," said Jacob. "It hurts. My throat *hurts*. It really hurts. It hurts, it *hurts*, it *hurts*—"

He left in the car fifteen minutes later.

Saul had never felt more completely alone. He stood on the porch and listened to the chiming music of the frozen branches. They moved as if an animal, or person, were passing through them, but he was certain it was a trick of the wind. When he closed his eyes he saw his grandmother's teaspoons clinking against the inside of ceramic cups, stirring milk-clouded coffee. A single truck rumbled by on Route 105, eleven miles south. The sky was dull purple. He made a fire and fell asleep in front of it. He woke at dawn in time to watch the final embers burn to ash.

* * *

Jacob returned two afternoons later, wearing an entirely new set of clothing. The clothes he had worn the day of his departure had been mislaid at the hospital, he told Saul; he had dispatched a nurse to bring his measurements and his credit card to the nearest men's store.

"Your clothes were mislaid?" asked Saul. "I don't follow."

"How are you? Have you been eating?"

"The refrigerator still works."

Jacob clapped Saul on the back and removed a full bag of groceries from the backseat of the car. He flinched under the weight and let out a light, shallow cough before righting himself. Jacob's new polo shirt, Saul saw now, hung loosely from his shoulders; the belt was notched in the last hole, but still his pants billowed around his upper legs. If these items were indeed his size, his size had changed.

"What did they say?" asked Saul.

"Who?"

"About the cough."

"Oh, that?" said Jacob, backing cautiously through the front door. "It's perfectly fine."

"Why were you there for two days?"

"Small-town inefficiency. Plain sloppiness. I was really beside myself." He rested the groceries on the kitchen table and turned to Saul with a strange grin. "Some people, you know? Some people. You just can't account for it."

Saul nodded. Thin trickles of sweat descended from Jacob's hairline down the side of his face and onto his collar. Jacob seemed not to notice.

"Are you okay?"

"Sure," said Jacob. "Just a long drive. I'm going to take a little rest. I'll be back in a few to put all this away and make dinner."

But Saul could see that he wouldn't be coming out again that day.

* * *

Saul tried to peek inside Jacob's window at least once a day, when he went on his afternoon walk, but the blinds never lifted. "Just riding out the winter," Jacob would call from the depths of his room, when Saul knocked. One morning, while Jacob was out on one of his final supermarket runs, Saul entered Jacob's bathroom and opened the medicine cabinet. He found eight different pill bottles affixed with stickers from the hospital. The pills were very small, and there were hundreds of them. Saul said nothing that night, but the next day he volunteered to do the grocery runs himself. His driving was flawless now, and if you drove in the mid-afternoon and kept to the country roads you could usually avoid encountering other cars.

"No way," said Jacob. "If you got pulled over, I'd go to prison. This whole thing would end. You'd be committed to some kind of an elderly ward."

"I can pass for ninety, maybe even eighty-five. I still have my posture. If anyone asks, I'll say I'm visiting my grandkids."

"Don't be absurd. I'll go. After my nap."

Jacob escaped into his room, but not before leaving the car keys on the dining-room table. Whether this was intentional or not, Saul could only guess, but that afternoon, when he returned from the supermarket, Jacob didn't comment. He eyed Saul backing through the front door with a bag of groceries in his arms and shook his head in awe. Then he withdrew into the darkness of the room and closed the door.

Toward the end of the next week, just as the streams began again to trickle through the forest, Saul awoke to a muffled thump. At first he thought he'd dreamed it. But then he heard the squeak of wood on wood, another thud, and a moan. Saul kicked his legs out of bed and stood up. He steadied himself on the bureau, the evacuation of blood from his brain making him dizzy, and made for Jacob's room.

He found Jacob sprawled on the floor, halfway between his bed and his bathroom. One leg had been lassoed by the bedsheet; the poor man lay on his side, his head twisted awkwardly around, his wide, dry mouth gaping like a carp's. His eyes rotated up and fixed on Saul's.

"I fell," he said at last. "I was trying…"

"That's okay," said Saul. He stepped slowly toward his grandson.

Jacob blinked and seemed to gain focus, but no part of his body moved.

"Don't worry," he said. "You can't catch this."

"You know what it is?"

Jacob nodded. "It's not contagious."

Saul lowered himself to the floor and began unraveling the sheets. He pushed the body until Jacob flopped onto his back, his head flat on the ground.

"You can't move. Is that right?"

Jacob turned his head a millimeter to one side and back again. Saul caressed his forehead. Jacob closed his eyes.

"I'll drive you to the hospital," said Saul. "Once you regain your energy."

"I feel funny asking this," said Jacob, looking up in Saul's general direction. "But… I need to."

"You can ask me anything. You know this."

Jacob blinked again. Saul dabbed Jacob's watering eye with his pajama sleeve.

"Is there a secret?" said Jacob.

"A secret for what?"

"Why?" His voice was a whisper. "Why are you still alive?"

"I don't know, Jacob."

"You can tell me. You know me. I'm not like the rest—the rest of them."

"I wish I could." Saul's voice was soothing, a kind of lullaby. "I don't know. I just want life. I want it so much."

"But so do I." A garbled, choking noise came from deep in Jacob's throat. "I guess I thought that over the years I might, I don't know—*learn* it from you. Or that I would catch it somehow. What's the opposite of a disease—an immunity?" He coughed again. "We could be a comfort to each other. Forever."

At his grandson's words Saul withdrew slightly, as if to dodge a foul odor. "You'll be okay, Jacob," he said. "You'll be okay."

"I won't," said Jacob. "But you will."

And then a thick curtain fell over his eyes. It was the same expression Saul had seen in the face of Jacob's father, and the others at his centennial, after Joseph was found dead. He couldn't believe it—not Jacob too, not after all their years together. It was too cruel. Jacob had loved him. Saul believed that. But then the hardness set like a plaster cast. Jacob's features became rigid, and Saul realized what transformation was taking place. The skull, pressing against the thinning flesh, was making its true shape known.

Gently, but not without revulsion, Saul let Jacob's head drop to the floor.

3

The next day, Jacob's door still shut, Saul woke up early and drove the thirty-eight miles to Newport. Turning off of Main Street to Railroad Square, he found what he was looking for: a wooden sign, hanging from the eave of a large Victorian house, advertising the services of one Dr. Marshall Habersham M.D., General Practitioner. He parked in the circular driveway and walked up the stairs. The front foyer led into a study that had been transformed into a reception area. A bell chimed, and immediately a man entered from the opposite side of the room. He was young—forty, Saul thought, maybe fifty; perhaps sixty—freshly shaven, with thin-rimmed spectacles resting loosely on a wide nose, beneath a puff of damp reddish hair. A towel was folded over one arm.

"Can I help you?" said Dr. Habersham.

"I'd like a checkup," said Saul. "My name is Joseph Wicker." He didn't know where the name came from; it just fell out of his mouth. He explained that he lived abroad and was visiting a nephew over in Island Pond for several months. He didn't feel sick, but he was due for a physical and did not want to wait until he returned home. At his age, and so on. He could pay in cash.

Dr. Habersham nodded and shook Saul's hand. "And what is your age, might I ask?"

"Ninety-one," said Saul. "I'm ninety-one years old."

"Well," said the doctor, smiling. "Congratulations on that."

He led Saul into a converted dining room, in which there stood an examination table covered by a sheet of wax paper. Photographs of New York City in winter, behind gaudy bronze frames, decorated the wall. Saul removed all of his clothes except for his white boxer briefs. Dr. Habersham palpated the thin, bluish skin of his chest, arms, neck, and back. Saul coughed on command and stared into the light of the otoscope. The doctor shined the light into Saul's ears. He slipped the cuff of the sphygmomanometer around Saul's scarecrow arm. The doctor nodded to himself, and then began to shake his head. Finally he left the room, having told Saul to get dressed. When he returned, his lips were arranged in an inquisitive curl.

"Where did you say you were from?" asked the doctor.

"Austria," said Saul. "But I didn't say."

"You got a high diet of fish and vegetables there?"

"I suppose I do."

"And you said you're ninety-one?"

"That's what I said."

"Because I have to say," said the doctor, "with all respect, I can't believe that."

Saul tensed. "I'm sorry?"

"Based on these tests, I wouldn't put you a week over eighty-five. Eighty-five maximum."

"They came out well?"

"Clean bill of health. I'm impressed."

"How about the blood pressure? The spine? The stomach?"

"Nothing I can see. You might live to one ten, keep going this way, Mr. Wicker."

"I see. You're sure?"

"Listen—what's your secret? What do you do to stay in this kind of shape? For a man in his nineties it's astonishing. Is it Austria? Do you live in the mountains or something?"

"I have just one piece of advice," said Saul, sighing. "Keep breathing."

"Keep breathing!" Dr. Habersham laughed loudly. He took off his spectacles and wiped his eyes. "That's good. Keep breathing!"

Saul gave him two one-hundred-dollar bills and left without saying another word.

He had once read that when an elderly person loses their spouse, they tend to die shortly thereafter. Jacob wasn't a spouse, but he was Saul's only friend, only family. So was this finally it? From some dark passageway fear waited to lurch at him, but for now he wasn't afraid.

He stood outside Jacob's bedroom door. If he called the police, they'd figure out who he was. He'd become a scientific experiment. They wouldn't allow him to live. But how to bury the body? Jacob was a large man, even at the end, and Saul wasn't strong enough to carry the corpse, let alone dig a hole in the ground. Yet if he didn't act soon the body would begin to decompose.

But he couldn't resolve this now—it was 3 p.m., time for his walk. The routine could not be disrupted. He had to keep moving. This was essential. As horrible as Jacob's death was, he needed badly to keep moving.

He stepped into the overgrown backyard and turned in to the forest, dodging a branch that came at him like a beckoning, arthritic finger. Lost in thoughts of Jacob, the Aerojet, his obituaries burning in the fireplace, he shuffled along the dirt path, enclosed by the familiar density of the old trees. Squirrels, in their perpetual state of mortal terror, darted through the underbrush. The leaves vibrated with insect life. Saul absorbed all this and felt as if he were, in some deeper sense, merging with the forest—that his heart shared the pulse of the life around him, that he was a distant appendage of some vast organism. But then the foliage rustled more purposefully, urgently, and it seemed as if something—or someone—was coming through the woods for him.

Of course that was impossible. It was probably just a pair of porcupines.

Yet when he turned a corner he found himself face-to-face with a man of about one-hundred-and-ten years. This man was even shorter than Saul, with a long, healthy face and a straight back. He wore hiking clothes: a plaid cotton shirt, brown leather boots, and khaki shorts that bore robust, wiry legs.

He looked familiar. This was alarming. To be discovered by someone from his previous life would be ruinous. It'd all be over for him. With irrational determination, Saul turned and began walking back to the house.

"Hey there," said the man.

Saul moved more quickly, his knees grinding in their joints with every step.

"Don't be stupid," said the voice. "You're going to fall." He seemed to be closing the distance.

Saul was almost running now. His lungs burned. His left arm, unaccountably, throbbed. He misjudged a stone in the path, his foot landing awkwardly on it, and he tripped. For a horrible moment, as the ground suddenly started to rush up at him, he was certain that he was going to fall on his face. But he managed to land his other foot and, after stumbling for several steps, he grabbed on to a tree, hugging it. Branches cut into his fingers; his forehead knocked gently against the bark.

"Hello, Saul."

The voice was directly behind him. He turned.

The man was watching Saul with a look of concern. "Are you all right there?"

"Do I know you?" said Saul, his chest still heaving.

"You might," said the man, with a crooked smile. "But we've never met."

"I don't understand."

"Christian," said the man, extending his arm. "Christian Mortensen."

He knew the name, he thought. But from where? Then it came to him.

"Christian Mortensen? But—you're dead. You died before your hundred-and-sixteenth birthday."

"That's what the paper said," said Mortensen, his eyes bright and flinty.

Saul straightened his back. "Explain yourself. What is this?"

"Like you, I was exhausted by the attention—the scientists, the journalists, the family members. What could I tell them that they didn't already know?"

"Keep breathing."

"Exactly. Just keep breathing."

Saul nodded to himself; he tried to arrange his thoughts.

"What do you want?" he asked. "You can have the record from Guinness. I have no use for it."

Mortensen threw his head back and laughed.

"I don't want the record. Besides, it's not mine. There's a Japanese man among us, Kyozo. When I was born, he was already married with children."

"Kyozo?"

"There are others like you and me," said Mortensen. "You are not alone."

"How did you find me? How did you come here?"

"We keep better records than those idiots at the Gerontology Research Group. We always want to increase our numbers. We learn from each other."

"How many of you are there?"

"Many. They look forward to meeting you, Saul. You won't be a freak anymore. You'll just be one of us. No one will care about your age. No one will ask you imbecilic questions."

Around him Saul saw columns of sunlight descending through the canopy, the wide branches of spruce needles waving like fans in the breeze, a file of ants lumbering along the crease of a dead brown leaf. He shut his eyelids, hard, and when he opened them again he half-expected that Mortensen would be gone. But the man was still there in his silly hiking boots.

"So you know the secret," said Saul.

"You mean, why we've made it so far?"

"Yes," said Saul, bracing himself up. "Why we're still here."

Mortensen shrugged. "I'm afraid I don't know. None of us do."

"Ah. That's what I figured."

"I do have a theory, though. It goes like this: Most people think they want to live forever, but in fact they don't. They want to give up. They're tired, they're in pain, they've lost the ones closest to them. Their bodies don't want to go on. Their minds reject themselves. Their spirits are ready to pass on to the next place."

"And you and me—we're different?"

"Of course. We want to stay. Badly. Even after everyone we've known and loved has left. That makes us strange."

"Go on."

"Of course, it's nice to live together. We can help each other out. I can help you move your grandson's body, for instance."

Saul blanched. "You know about Jacob?"

"We wouldn't have intruded while he was still alive. But we thought you needed some help."

"Yes," said Saul. "I do. I need a little help."

"Very well. Let's head back."

Saul felt faint. But he followed when Mortensen began to walk back to the house.

"After this, after the burial," said Saul. "I'm still not clear. What do we do?"

"You join us. If you like."

"Where?"

"We have some property not far from here. In the Northeast Kingdom. You'll like it."

"What do we do there?"

"Anything. You can bring your airplanes, if you want."

"I see. I think I would like that."

They walked in silence.

"Is that it?" said Saul. "We just sit around?"

"Mostly we do the same thing we've always done. We live."

"That's it? Just live?"

"That's all there is."

The path ended and the white house emerged from the bramble.

"And hope?"

"Yes," said Christian. "We hope. We hope everything will turn out all right."

"Well," said Saul, bounding up the stairs to his back porch, "that is something I know how to do."

And so Saul, with a spring in his step, went inside to retrieve his grandson's decomposing corpse.

THE HENS

by RODDY DOYLE

CHAPTER ONE

THE PHONE CALL was a surprise.

—Hello?

Not the call itself. Felicja received perhaps five calls a day, from her boyfriend and her other friends, and she made as many calls herself. And texting was the punctuation of her life. *On bus*, *In Q*, *Luv u*. Every event and feeling was recorded.

But this particular call was a surprise.

—Hello?

It was a woman's voice.

—Hi, said Felicja.

—Am I talking to Felicja?

—Yes, you are.

—I have hens.

—Yes?

—I need someone to look after them, said the woman. —Do you do that kind of thing?

—Yes, said Felicja, immediately, although she wasn't sure what a hen was, or if she'd heard the woman properly. She thought a hen might be a chicken, but, just now, she didn't care. If a hen turned out to be a wart-covered oaf with green teeth, she'd still look after it and tickle it under its chin.

She texted her boyfriend.

Job!

He texted back.

?

And Felicja answered: *baby sit chik hens.*

A week before, Felicja had walked through a fancy neighborhood of large houses near the sea and also close to her home in Dublin, putting a small slip of paper through each letterbox. MY NAME IS FELICJA. I DO ALL JOBS. 086-577432. She did this for two days, until she received her first call, as she walked away from one of the houses. The caller, a man, told her to turn around. She did, and saw a man in the window. He was smiling, skinny, and naked. He held his phone in one hand and his penis in the other.

—I will tell the police! Felicja shouted, before she had time to feel stupid. This naked man had her phone number; hundreds of people now had her number. It was too late to print a new slip. MY NAME IS FELICJA. I DO SOME JOBS.

But there were no more calls. She sat at home and waited. *Bored.* Nothing happened. The recession had hit the big houses. ALL JOBS had already been done.

Then the hen woman called.

And now Felicja stood in the woman's garden and looked at the hens. They *were* like chickens. Felicja was delighted. She herself ate chicken all the time.

—I eat them, she said.

—No, said the woman. —You mind them. You look after them.

Felicja saw that the woman was staring at her.

—Do you understand?

—Of course, said Felicja.

—Are you Polish?

—Yes.

—Do you have your references with you?

—Of course, said Felicja, again.

She handed copies of two letters to the woman, and then moved closer to the hens. There were four of them. Was this the job? she wondered. Counting the chickens—making sure that the four did not become three, or two, or five?

—Jesus, said the woman. —You're an architect.

—Yes, said Felicja.

—But why are you doing this? the woman asked.

Felicja shrugged.

—Recession, she said.

She could see the excitement on the woman's face. What a story she had! An architect babysitting her chickens! Felicja decided to change the subject.

—Why do you have these chickens? she asked.

—Why?

—Yes. Why?

—Same as you, said the woman. —The recession.

—These chickens are also architects?

—No, said the woman.

They both started to laugh.

—I like them, said Felicja. —You sell the eggs?

—No, said the woman. —We eat them ourselves. We're self-sufficient.

—You eat only eggs?

—No, no, said the woman. —I actually got them for the children. As an example, you know. To economize.

—I do not understand, said Felicja, although she understood perfectly. This woman was going to hire her so that she could economize on eggs.

The woman stopped smiling. She looked at her watch.

—You don't have to understand, she said. —You just have to *mind* them.

—For how long?

—Three hours, said the woman. —Every weekday.

—At what time?

—Lunchtime.

—Lunch equals three hours? said Felicja.

The woman stared at Felicja.

—Minimum wage, she said. —Okay?

—How much is this minimum wage? Felicja asked, although she knew.

—€7.65, said the woman.

—Not enough.

—Ten.

—Three hours, said Felicja. —At that time of day. This means I am not free for other possible work.

—Fifteen.

—A total of €45 each day?

—God. But all right.

—Five times a week, makes €225, said Felicja.

—All right.

—I don't clean the house or wash the clothes?

—No, said the woman. —That's already—done.

—Cool, said Felicja. —And PRSI?

—Well, Jesus, said the woman. —Let's make it €250. It'll be handier.

—Cool.

The woman picked up her bag.

—I've to dash, she said. —A meeting. Later.

She walked across the lawn, into the kitchen. Felicja stood and looked at the hens. There were still four. She went to the kitchen door; she thought she'd make some tea. But it was locked.

CHAPTER TWO

The woman returned to the house at about three. She didn't come out to the garden, where she'd left Felicja. Felicja sat in a damp deck chair and texted her boyfriend—*BoredX*—and occasionally counted the chickens. Then she looked up and saw the woman at the kitchen window. She was at the sink, filling a large pot with water.

Felicja went and tried to open the door, but it was still locked. She knocked. She heard a key being turned, and the door opened. The woman had changed her clothes; she was wearing jeans and a plaid shirt.

—There are still four chickens, said Felicja.

—What? said the woman. —Oh, good.

—You locked the door, said Felicja.

—Habit, answered the woman.

—You will pay me now?

—What? said the woman. —No. I mean, sorry. Come in.

She stepped back, and Felicja stepped in.

—I do not know your name, said Felicja.

—I'm sorry, said the woman. —I'm Dee. I've been rude, I'm sorry. I'm just putting some pasta on for the monsters before they get in from school.

She picked up the pot and brought it to the cooker. Felicja followed her.

—So, Dee, she said. —My salary?

—End of the week. Okay?

—This is the end of the week, Dee, said Felicja. —Today is Friday.

Dee's smile dropped off her face.

—Well, fine, she said. —You've come through your probationary period. With flying colors. I'll start paying you next week.

She turned on the gas beneath the pot.

—I wasn't always a stay-at-home mum, Felicja, she said. —Don't try to exploit me. Don't even think about it.

The woman was insane. But Felicja wanted her money. And she quite liked the hens.

—Okay, she said. —But you will not exploit *me*, Dee.

—We speak the same language, said Dee. —See you on Monday.

Felicja's boyfriend, Darren, still had a job. He was Irish, and very respectful of his country's culture and traditions. So it was after midnight and he hadn't come home. But Felicja didn't mind, not very much. He'd texted to tell her where he was—*Pravda!* He'd invited her to join him—*Save me!* But she stayed in. She was broke, and she wanted to work on her blog, *Polegirl-in-Ireland*—although she was thinking of changing the name.

It had started as a diary, a what-I-did-today. But she got bored with that. Living her full day, then coming home to write about it— it seemed to make less of the day. There was no comparison between sex and writing *I then had some sex with Darren.* Sex won, every time. Even boring sex was much better than writing *I then had some sex with Darren.*

After a week, writing *I went to work this morning* or *I then had some sex with Darren* became unpleasant, even dishonest. She'd tried to write *Today, Peter told me that I no longer had a job*, but she really didn't want to. And she didn't want to write *I think Darren is in love with another girl, called Heineken.*

Someone had once told Felicja that she spoke English as if she was telling a fairy tale. So Felicja started to write fairy tales. And she enjoyed it. Writing about ogres was probably much better than having sex with them.

The NAMA walked the land, eating all the builders and the fat cats.

She wrote satirical fairy tales.

The NAMA had come from a land far off called Poland. But there were no builders left in Poland—he had eaten many and the rest had fled to Ireland. And there was no such thing as a fat Polish cat. So the NAMA followed the builders.

She wrote, and people read. She'd been stunned when she discovered that more than two hundred people had read her most recent chapter. Stunned, delighted, and terrified—*OMG!* Her empty days began to fill again.

But she couldn't write all day, and no one paid her to do it. So she continued to babysit Dee's chickens.

The following Monday, Dee did not lock the back door when she left. She knocked on the window, and waved, and was gone. Felicja spoke to the hens.

—How are *we* today?

Not one chicken answered.

—Should I call you chickens or hens?

The chickens fussed around as if they felt insulted.

Felicja waited some more minutes, then went into the kitchen. She sat at the table and wrote in her Moleskine notebook.

The NAMA did not travel to Ireland in the belly of the Ryanair. He moved through many lands, and over wide rivers and seas. But he ate nothing as he moved, through many summers and harsh winters.

She went to the window and checked on the chickens. They were clucking and scratching, doing what they always did.

Except one of them was missing.

CHAPTER THREE

Felicja pressed her face to the window. She tried to see the missing hen. She looked again at the remaining three and hoped that the fourth would step out from behind her sisters or brothers or whatever they were. But this did not happen. The three remained three.

It seemed the right time to use a word she'd learned since arriving in Ireland.

—Shite, she said.

She went outside, still hoping. There was the shed—the coop. The chicken could be in there. But, she saw now, its door was closed. The coop was on legs—stilts. She bent down to look underneath it, her head almost touching the wet ground. But Felicja knew she wouldn't see the chicken.

There were no more hiding places. The garden walls were bare—no hedge or bushes. She even looked up at the roof of the house. Chickens, she knew, couldn't fly; their wings were useless. There was a seagull up there, on the chimney. But he, or she, was alone.

The remaining three chickens looked unperturbed. They weren't pining for their friend. That was probably a good sign. There were no feathers on the grass, no blood. No fox or wolf had carried the chicken away. There were no wolves in Ireland. But as her boyfriend, Darren, had said, there'd been no Poles in Ireland, either, and now the place was full of them.

What would Felicja do? Phone the police? Tell them that a chicken had been kidnapped? This was not a good idea.

She could buy a replacement. But where? In the nearest Centra or Spar? She could place the new chicken, plucked and headless and wrapped in cling-film, beside the other three and hope that no one noticed.

It was ridiculous.

She could phone Dee, the woman who would be paying her for

looking after *four* chickens. *One chicken has departed*, she could say. *You may reduce my salary by one quarter.*

But she wouldn't phone Dee. It was pointless, and too late. Dee was standing in the kitchen, looking out at Felicja. Dee's mouth was opening and closing, very slightly. Felicja knew: Dee was counting chickens.

—Where's Biffo? Dee asked when she came out to the garden.

—Biffo?

—The rooster, said Dee.

—Rooster?

—The man, said Dee. —The one that doesn't lay eggs.

—Ah, said Felicja. —The man appears to be gone, Dee.

It was Dee's turn to ask the one-word questions.

—Gone?

—I think, perhaps, a fox took him.

—Fox?

—Yes, said Felicja. —I have no other explanation at the moment.

—Oh Christ, said Dee. —He's gone over the wall.

—This is true?

—He's after Monica's Rhode Island Reds.

—Over this wall? said Felicja. —But he cannot fly.

—That's right, said Dee. —But he can jump. The bastard. Come on.

An hour later, Felicja sat with Dee in the kitchen.

—So, Felicja, said Dee. —Tell me why I shouldn't sack you.

Felicja was watching Dee's two sons, handsome boys who looked as if they had been made from frozen milk, as they silently ate slices of pizza—goat's cheese and chorizo—and thumped each other.

She looked at their mother.

—Because I have learned from my mistakes, Dee, she said.

They had climbed over the wall with the help of a stepladder, and had dropped—fallen—into the garden that belonged to the mysterious Monica. But Monica had not stayed mysterious for long. She had stepped out of her kitchen holding Biffo in one hand and a bread knife in the other.

—I told you, Dee! she shouted—actually, she screamed.

"Dressed to kill" was a phrase that Felicja had heard many times, and now she knew what it meant. Monica had been wearing a black leather skirt and red Manolo pumps. She held the knife to Biffo's neck.

—Your crow is never going to *rape* my birds again!

It was the pumps that saved Biffo. They sank into the grass, and Monica began to fall backward.

—Shit!

She let go of the rooster as she fell. Dee grabbed him before he landed and threw him back over the wall. Then she turned her attention to Monica, who was lying on her back, still clutching the knife.

—On your back again, Monica? said Dee. —You must be expecting company!

Back in the kitchen, Dee looked at Felicja.

—So, said Dee. —Tell me why I shouldn't sack you.

Felicja watched *The Apprentice* most Monday nights.

—Because I have learned from my mistakes, Bill—I mean, Dee, she said. —I know I am the right person for you.

—It's war, said Dee.

Felicja wanted this job. She wanted to write about these mad middle-class women at war.

—The Chicken War, she suggested.

—That's it, said Dee, and she smiled. —Are you ready for battle?

—Yes, Dee, said Felicja. —I am prepared to die for Biffo.

—That's the girl.

CHAPTER FOUR

Dee wanted Felicja to come to the house immediately. It was two in the morning. Felicja checked. Yes, the clock read 2 a.m. exactly. Less than a week in the job and Felicja was already working overtime.

—Wear dark clothes, said Dee, just before she hung up.

Felicja opened the curtains and dressed in the light of the moon. She put on black jeans and a black shirt while the owner of the shirt slept and snored and mumbled something that, to Felicja's ears, sounded like Irish poetry. She looked at her boyfriend, stretched out in the moonlight.

—I will in me bollix, he said in his sleep.

Felicja rode Darren's bike to Dee's house. She stayed on the empty footpaths because the bicycle had no light. Dee opened the door before Felicja had time to ring the bell.

—In, in!

Felicja followed Dee into the kitchen. Dee was also dressed in black, and Felicja saw a price tag hanging from the back of her neck. Dee had paid €230 for her camouflage.

—Oh-kay! said Dee. —Ready for action?

She threw something black at Felicja. Felicja caught it and saw that she was now holding a hood—a balaclava. Dee had already put hers on.

—How do I look?

Even with the balaclava over her head, Dee looked like Dee. It was something about the way she stood, and her mouth—it was the mouth of a much younger woman than Dee. In fact, it seemed as if Dee had somehow borrowed the mouth from one of her sons.

—You look very nice, said Felicja. Then she slipped her own hood over her head.

—I am ready for action, Dee, she said.

She remembered her favorite line from *The Apprentice*.

—I will hit the ground running.

The balaclava tickled her top lip. She wanted to laugh. Dee unlocked the back door.

—What about your husband, Dee?

Dee turned.

—What about him?

—He will not be assisting us?

—No, said Dee. —He doesn't actually live here.

—No?

—No. He's moved in with a slut half his age.

—Yes?

—Yes.

—What age is he, Dee?

—You're a tonic, Felicja. Let's go.

—We are not bringing some knives, Dee?

—Not this time, said Dee.

They ran, crouched, to the back of the garden. There was a plastic bucket, upside down, against the wall. Dee stepped onto the bucket and was soon over the top, into the mysterious Monica's garden.

Felicja would have been quite happy to return to the kitchen; she'd had a most enjoyable time already. But Dee obviously expected her to follow. She landed beside Dee, in the flowerbed. Dee ran across the garden, past the chicken coop. Again, Felicja followed.

They stopped at the far side, crouched in against the wall. They looked at the upstairs windows. The lights were off.

—Monica sleeps, Felicja whispered.

—I doubt it.

They went over the second wall, into the next garden.

—This house belongs to?

—Shhh! Maeve.

—And she is?

—A bitch.

Felicja saw yet another chicken coop. Dee headed straight for it. And Felicja followed.

—No lock, Dee whispered. —Fab. Tell me if a light goes on.

Felicja heard the door scrape when Dee opened it. It was unbearably, hilariously loud. Then she heard scrabbling—and a squawk.

—Let's go!

Yet again, she followed Dee, back across the garden. She began to wonder why Dee wanted her there, when she saw the chicken—and she understood.

Dee was holding a chicken upside down, close to her body.

—Hold him till I get over, she whispered.

—Him? said Felicja.

—Maeve's cock.

They both laughed, and tried not to—and that made it better and worse.

When Dee reached the top of the wall Felicja handed the man-hen up to her. Then Felicja climbed the wall. She scraped her hand as she jumped, but she made it over.

—Open the door, Dee whispered.

Felicja pulled the bolt of Monica's coop. The noise filled the world for a very long second. They both looked at the windows. No lights came on. Dee threw in the man-hen. She bolted the door and they ran.

—He's a Leghorn, Dee explained, back in her kitchen. —Monica's Rhode Island Reds won't know what hit them.

Dee sipped her gin and tonic.

—But Monica will.

She lifted her glass.

—To victory.

Felicja lifted her own glass and clinked it against Dee's.

—Why did we do that, Dee? she asked.

—I hate them, said Dee.

—The chickens?

—The neighbors, said Dee. —They were my idea.

—The neighbors?

—No. The hens.

Felicja brought the balaclava home. She stood beside the bed and looked at Darren. He hadn't moved. She put on the balaclava. She leaned down to his face and thumped his chest.

CHAPTER FIVE

—Good morning.

—Godddd!

Darren looked up at the black woolen face and screamed.

—This excites you? Felicja asked.

He screamed again.

Then stopped.

—Felicja?

—No, said Felicja.

—It is.

—Okay, said Felicja. —It is Felicja.

By now she felt quite foolish.

—Who took your face? Darren asked.

—It is still here.

—I can't see it, said Darren.

She could have removed the balaclava. But she didn't. She chose to hide behind it. She watched him as he got up from the bed, making sure he didn't touch her, and went—*scurried*—to the bathroom. She listened as he vomited, then urinated, then brushed his teeth. She removed the balaclava.

Darren came back.

—Where's the hood? he asked.

—I took it off, said Felicja. —I will put it back on?

—Eh… yeah.

Eight hours later—it was midday—Felicja brought her blog up to date. *I had some successful sex with Darren.* She immediately deleted that sentence, but not because it wasn't true. She had had very successful sex with Darren, but only after they had swapped heads.

—You like sex this way? she'd asked Darren.

—Yeah, said Darren. —Outstanding.

—You think my face is so very unattractive?

—No way.

So Darren had put on the balaclava.

—It's an itchy ol' thing, he'd said when they'd let go of each other and he'd pulled the balaclava off again. But he'd folded it, afterward, like he was an altar boy and it was a sacred garment, and put it under his pillow.

Felicja looked at her empty screen. Then she started to write about Dee.

I work for a madwoman.

She liked that. It was dramatic and true.

I look after her chickens.

Happy with her work so far, Felicja looked out the window. It was snowing. She hoped that the chickens were warm in their coop.

I do not work on a farm and there are only four chickens. But, as part of my job, I also accompany my employer at midnight as she kidnaps the chickens of her neighbors.

She looked; it was still snowing.

My employer's name is Dee.

Felicja looked at the name on the screen. She thought about changing it.

She walked through the snow to work. She bought coffee on the way. She took the lid off the cup, so she could watch the rising steam attack the falling snow. It was a very pleasant walk. She saw children making a little snowman. She also saw a very minor car crash.

She rang Dee's bell, and waited. She rang again, and watched the snow. She heard the door being opened, and turned. It was not Dee.

—Hi, said Felicja.

—Like, you're to go into the garden, said one of Dee's two sons. Or perhaps both of them had spoken; they were identical, these milky-faced boys, in their skinny jeans and big slippers.

—You are not at school?

—Sent home.

—Why?

—Snow.

—That is a reason to be sent home?

They shrugged, together, as if they had rehearsed the gesture many times. Then they stepped back, like two doors opening in front of Felicja. She walked past—through—them.

—Mum's waiting for you, he—*they*—said.

They were quite stupid boys, Felicja thought. She could see the snow through the glass of the kitchen door. She'd find a place for snow in the story; the snow would fall all day.

She forgot about the snow when she saw Dee.

Dee was covered in feathers. She had, in fact, become a chicken.

—Dee?

—The bitch, said the chicken.

—What has happened? Felicja asked.

The snow fell on the chicken. The flakes fell on the feathers.

—The bitch you refer to, said Felicja. —Is it Monica?

—No, said Dee the chicken.

—Is it Maeve?

Dee nodded. *Snow and feathers danced around her.*

—What did she do? Felicja asked.

—She plucked Biffo, said Dee.

—Ohmygod!

Only now, Felicja saw the rooster. It was standing beside Dee, almost covered in the snow. It was half its usual size, without its feathers.

—She pulled out these feathers while he was still alive?

—Yup, said Dee.

The Chicken War had started.

CHAPTER SIX

—You're Polish, aren't you? said Dee.

—Yes, Dee, said Felicja. —I am Polish.

—So you don't mind killing animals.

Felicja shrugged.

—I'm easy with that, Dee, she said. —It's cool.

Although she wasn't sure if it was, in fact, cool. Felicja had never killed an animal, had never even thought about it. But she'd delivered the answer she knew Dee wanted.

Biffo's feathers had been washed from Dee's hair in the shower, but the hot water had done nothing to remove the anger that made Dee's face look so sharp and lethal. And so very beautiful.

Looking now at Dee, Felicja was quite confident that Dee would need no help when the time came to kill. Dee's eyes said one clear thing: slaughter. Felicja was glad she was not one of the neighbors' chickens, or even one of the neighbors' children. Chicken blood alone would never satisfy her mad employer's lust for vengeance. Nothing with lungs was safe.

It was still snowing, quite heavily. It fell like plucked feathers past the kitchen window.

—Ready? said Dee.

—We are not waiting until tonight?

Dee pulled two knives from the wooden block beside the microwave. She tested their sharpness with an apple. Peel and pips hopped along the counter. Then she threw one of the knives at me.

—There's no point in waiting, said Dee. —Let's cut some throats. Boys?!

Two voices delivered one word.

—What?

—How's Biffo? Dee shouted.

She had wrapped the featherless rooster in a duvet and put him in a cardboard box in front of the plasma television. Biffo was watching *Scrubs* with Dee's two sons.

—He's cool, the sons shouted back.

—He isn't bored, is he?

—No, he's well into it.

—Good. We'll be back in a minute.

Felicja had picked the knife up off the floor. She didn't know where to put it. But Dee was already at the door, opening it, and gone.

I followed Dee into the snow. The knife in my hand felt good.

They followed the same, simple route they had followed the night before, over the wall, made magical by the snow, and into mad Monica's enchanted garden. They wore no camouflage this time, and no masks. As she climbed, Dee held her knife between her teeth. Felicja wanted to do this too, but worried that she'd slip and slice off some of her face. Instead she dropped her knife over the wall and found it quite easily on the other side. The soft crunch of their boots as they ran across the snow was, perhaps, the most beautiful, exciting sound that Felicja had ever heard.

This is so cool, I thought. This is the sound of silence.

Dee had stopped in front of Monica's coop.

—We kill *these* chickens, Dee? Felicja said.

—We do, said Dee.

—But these are Monica's chickens, said Felicja. —You said it was Maeve who plucked the Biffo.

—This is war, girlfriend, said Dee. —There are no neutrals.

—You will not wait until Monica actually does something wrong?

—She *will* do something, don't worry.

Dee opened the door of the coop.

—This is preemptive, she said. —Like Bush going into Iraq.

She stood up and looked at Felicja.

—It's not fashionable to say it. But he was fucking right.

She bent down.

—Come to Mammy, little red hens.

Felicja was in love with Dee. *Or, perhaps, just overwhelmed.* She'd never witnessed such decisiveness, such calm and elegant savagery. Dee swung a Rhode Island Red into the air in front of her face, then stabbed it, once, and twice—and dropped it. *Blood jumped from the hen, onto the snow.* The chicken ran in a silent circle around Dee, as if thanking her. Then it stopped its charge, and fell, and died.

Dee already had the next one in her hands.

—Let me help, Dee, said Felicja.

"It's my turn," I said.

—Go to it, girl, Dee said. She held the hen in front of Felicja. —This one is a Red, a Russian. Now's the time.

Ohmygod, I thought. I am doing this.

The blood shot over Felicja's shoulder.

I was so happy. Perhaps I was becoming Irish.

Dee put the blade back in her mouth and jumped at the next wall. Felicja, happily—oh, so happily—followed.

Maeve's hens were hacked and dead in less than a minute. For a second inside that minute, Felicja wondered at the fact that she had never seen or met Maeve. This was about to change.

As they ran at the wall, laughing and blood-covered, a woman with a lot of hair and a baseball bat jumped—*jumped!*—out the kitchen window. But she was too late. They scrambled over the wall—they could hear Maeve's quick feet on the snow—and fell into Monica's garden. Where Monica, mad, magnificent Monica, was waiting.

Ohmygod.

CHAPTER SEVEN

Looking back, a few hours later, Felicja wondered if she had actually witnessed what she knew she had witnessed. A bloodbath.

—You bitch!

Quite a small bloodbath—four women, three knives, and a baseball bat.

—You copied my kitchen!

—Fuck you, Monica! I went retro years before you!

—Retro?! Hah! That's called middle age!

A war with resentments as deep and as dark as any that had fueled a Balkan conflict, with causes that went back to a time before the current recession and the purchase of hens. A time long before Felicja left Poland.

She had never seen mothers fight with knives before. Yet she'd been in the middle of it. She had the evidence; she had the stitches, and the bruise on her cheek.

—He left me because of you!

—He was leaving you anyway, coke-nose!

Felicja sat in her bed now, exhausted and elated, still shaking, and tried to type. But her fingers slid from the keys or just missed them. Her arms were shaking so badly—as if she had been carrying heavy items for many hours.

I saw Monica staring at Dee, and I knew that this was not a new fight. They stared, and then they attacked.

Felicja did not know if Monica was still alive. Maeve, she felt certain, was dead. Dee had promised to text Felicja, but Dee was, perhaps, also dead. There'd been so much blood, so much noise, at least one life must have ceased. No other conclusion was possible.

Yet Felicja, so recently the witness of such Shakespearean violence, sat in her bed and laughed quietly. *I am alive*, she thought—she did not write this. *I am alive.* The police would be calling in the morning, to interview her. Felicja, after all, had stabbed Monica the second time. And yet she laughed.

—I got the Aga before you!

—And you fucked my husband on it!

Maeve fell off the wall and pushed me into Monica. But Monica was already bleeding to death before my knife entered her. I turned in time to see Dee bite Maeve's neck.

Dee had snarled as she bit, like a fox—or a wolf—attacking one of her hens. But Maeve must have sensed that war was imminent when she'd dressed that morning, because her neck was protected by two high collars and a scarf that had cost what Maeve had recently come to think of as a fortune. The baseball bat was a present from her ex-husband, his parting gift to her. "It'll keep you company through the dark, dangerous nights," he'd said. These words Maeve had repeated to Dee, in friendlier times, and Dee had repeated them to Felicja.

But now Maeve calmly choked Dee with the baseball bat.

—Take the angora out of your mouth, Dee!

Dee obeyed, so she could free her tongue.

—Marks and Sparks do angora, do they?

She pushed the bat away as she spoke, and stepped back, which allowed Maeve a clean swing. It hit Dee's shoulder and caught Felicja's cheek on its way back. Now, in bed, Felicja felt the bruise. It was not so very bad; she quite liked it. The police would also like it, she thought. Evidence—*I was provoked.*

Felicja hit Maeve twice, with the butt of her knife, when she saw

Maeve preparing to swing again at Dee. She wasn't happy with the first knock; Maeve hardly seemed to notice it. So she'd grabbed Maeve's head with one hand and knocked her senseless with the knife butt in the other. Dee—beautiful, crazy Dee—slashed at the woman with her knife as she fell. Felicja was certain—but perhaps not so very certain—that Maeve's head was no longer part of Maeve by the time Maeve's body landed in the snow.

I watched calmly as Maeve fell. I also watched calmly as Monica's knife cut through the lining of my jacket, through my sweater and my skin.

Felicja was not frightened. She had murdered—or, she had helped to murder—a woman only hours before. She might spend many years in prison. But Dee would be there too. Felicja had already checked on Google: there was no death sentence in Ireland.

Infidelity and furniture—these were the true causes of The Chicken War. Husbands and retro lamps, Aga ranges, the collapse of the Irish economy. And the chickens too, of course.

In 1939, the Germans invaded Poland. In 2010, the chickens invaded Dublin.

Felicja stopped typing. She lay back on the bed. Her arm hurt, and her cheek. She'd never felt happier.

CHAPTER EIGHT

She slipped the balaclava over her head. She had just heard the door downstairs being opened. Darren, her boyfriend, was on his way up. Felicja counted his steps. He was very close now to their apartment. Felicja placed the knife in her mouth; she held it lightly between her teeth.

Darren entered and saw Felicja.

—Nice one.

Felicja watched his eyes. She lay back against her pillows—and then her phone buzzed.

She jumped.

—Shit! she said, or something like that—the knife was still in her mouth. She took it out and stared at Darren. Her face was hidden but Darren could still detect the anger.

—Don't look at me, he said.

She knew she wasn't bleeding, because she'd made sure the sharp edge had been facing away from her mouth. But she put her fingers to her lips, and looked.

Darren had gone into the kitchen.

—I did this for you, Darren! she shouted.

—Back in a sec! he shouted back.

She heard him open the fridge door, and remembered the text that had made her jump. It was from Dee.

Cme.

Felicja texted back.

Whre?

Darren was still in the kitchen.

Hse.

Felicja answered.

Wil hit grnd runng.

When Darren came back with a can of Heineken and a cheese string, Felicja was putting on her jacket and searching for her notebook.

—You're not going again?

—Yes, said Felicja. —I am going.

Getting into the jacket was difficult. The stitches in her arm hurt quite badly. She gave up the search for the notebook; she'd find it later.

—What happened to your jacket?

Darren pointed at the bloodstains, and at the white padding that seemed to be pouring out of the slit in Felicja's sleeve, where Monica's knife had torn it.

—Oh, that? said Felicja. —It is not so very important. A bitch did it.

—A bitch?

—A bitch with a knife. Goodbye. Enjoy your beer.

Darren's bike was locked in the hall, but Felicja didn't want to go back upstairs to ask for the key and face more questions. So she walked. She ran—she tried to run. She slid on the ice and laughed and almost fell.

Dee's strange sons stood at the door to her house, like very skinny versions of the two fat boys in *Alice in Wonderland*. They stared, terrified, at Felicja. She removed the balaclava and walked past them, into the house.

—Dee? she called. —You are here?

She found Dee in the kitchen, reading her notebook. Felicja's notebook.

Dee looked up at Felicja. Her face was neither bruised nor scarred. She stared at Felicja for quite some time.

—Dee—

—Shut up.

Dee looked back down at the page.

—Listen, she said.

Then she started to read.

—*Biffo's feathers had been washed from Dee's hair in the shower, but the hot water had done nothing to remove the anger that made Dee's face look so sharp and lethal. And so very beautiful.*

Dee stopped reading.

—You wrote this?

—Yes, said Felicja. —I was—

—And I'm mad too, am I?

—I did not—

—Have you any idea how this makes me feel?

—I am sorry.

—Sorry?

—Yes, Dee. I am very sorry. I do not—

—Oh, shut up.

Dee shut the notebook with a small bang. She stared at it as if she was deciding where to throw it.

Felicja understood it now: this was why she'd climbed the walls, why she'd followed Dee and murdered her neighbors. So she could write about it. She would get the notebook back. Her knife was in her jacket pocket.

Dee looked at her.

—So.

—Yes, Dee?

Dee held up the notebook.

—There's more of this?

—Yes, Dee.

—Christ.

—I have a blog.

—It's fucking fantastic.

—I am—what did you say?

—I read this, said Dee. —And I felt, wow.

—You felt wow?

—I felt very fucking wow, said Dee. —I felt, I don't know, vindicated. And—

She whispered.

—Cool.

She laughed.

—And sexy. Again. God.

She laughed again.

—But we can do better than a fucking blog, Felicja.

—I do not understand, said Felicja.

—A book, said Dee. —Come on. A movie. *My* story.

She sat at the table.

—Let's get started.

—But Dee, said Felicja. —Are Maeve and Monica still alive?

—Who cares? said Dee. —Yeah, they're fine.

She patted the notebook.

—They'll love this, she said.

—You think so?

—I know so, said Dee. —I'll call them. They can come over and help us.

—I do not understand, said Felicja.

—I know you don't, said Dee.

She smiled.

—That's why you're so perfect.

RAPUNZEL

by STEVEN MILLHAUSER

CLIMBING

HAND OVER HAND, each foot lifting above the other and pressing against the rough stone, his back tense, his neck arched, the braided hair tightening in his fists: the Prince is strong, but it's no easy task to make his way up the face of the tower. The adventure excites him. He thrives on obstacles, perils, impediments of every kind. He is filled with such exhilaration that he would cry out for joy, except that his teeth are clenched and his lips stretched wide in a grimace of exertion. He remembers his first glimpse of her: the window high above, the dark figure below, the hair coming down like a shower of fire. Now he's climbing that burning hair, which, in the summer dusk, in the shadows of the high pines and firs, is not golden, as he always remembers it, but the color of a bale of hay in the shade of a stable. There is danger in the climb, since at any moment he might fall and crack his neck, break his back. And even if his hold is sure, a second danger threatens from the forest: the sudden return of the sorceress, who will see him trying to reach the forbidden place. The Prince welcomes danger, exults in it, for it's danger that makes him feel his life. In the late dusk the tower lies in darkness, but up above, where the sky is still pale, the casement window catches the last light. The Prince thinks: If only it could be this way forever!—the pull in his arms, the thrill of the ascent, the scrape of branches against his neck. An owl calls in the forest. The Prince pauses, slaps at an insect, continues climbing. From his upthrust hip, his sword hangs straight down, as if it has stopped suddenly in the act of falling.

THE MIRROR

As the Prince climbs the tower, the sorceress returns through the forest to her cottage at the edge of the darkening village. The cottage is surrounded by a high wall; the sorceress has no use for neighbors. Inside, she walks past the table and the cupboard and goes at once to her dressing table, where she picks up an oval mirror with an ivory handle. It is always like that: after the tower, the mirror. In the glass she sees her reflection staring at her with a familiar look of revulsion. She glares back with fascinated loathing, with a kind of eager bitterness. She detests the thick eyebrows, the small eyes set too close together, the thrusting ridge of the nose, as if drawn by a village caricaturist sketching a witch. Her lips are a knife-slash, her chin juts out like a knuckle. From a wart in her chin-cleft, three hairs stick out like tubers sprouting from an old potato. Her skin is yellow. Her black hair hangs in her face like bush-branches over a fence. Her herbs, her roots, her medicinal salves, even her spells, which can raise towers out of thin air—all useless. She thrusts the mirror aside. The cruelty is that she has always loved beautiful things. At once she thinks of Rapunzel. And her heart lifts: the golden hair, skin like the down of a swan, the graceful slope of the nose. Rapunzel is safe in the tower, asleep under her coverlet. She will visit her darling when night is done.

HAIR

In the tower chamber, Rapunzel lies waiting for the Prince. Sometimes she waits by the window, but this evening she is lying on her bed, on the other side of the small room. Her braided hair stretches across the coverlet and over the wooden table to the hook in the ledge. She's proud of her hair, which is much longer than she is, and comes pouring out of her like rain from the sky, though it takes up a lot of room and can be a nuisance as it drags around the floor picking up dust. Sometimes she wishes she could cut it all off with a sharp *snip-snip* and watch it lie there nice and dead without it slithering along after her all the time. At sunset, as soon as the sorceress let herself down, Rapunzel drew up the thick braid, waved good night from the window, and stood watching as the sorceress disappeared into the dark trees. Not long after, the Prince appeared in the small clearing at the base of the tower. Rapunzel tied her braid again around the hook in the ledge, then let down her hair hand over hand, as if she were lowering a bucket into a well. When the last handful was over the sill, she returned to the bed and lay down. Even though her braid is tied to a hook, she can feel the tug of the Prince as he climbs. He's like a boy, her Prince, teasing her by pulling her hair. Through the window she sees the darkening sky. She knows that he loves the difficult climb, but she herself does not love it; she worries every second about the return of the sorceress, she's afraid that even the slightest movement on her part will cause him to lose his grip and plunge to his death, and she dislikes the perpetual tugging at her scalp. She wishes they could find another way. But the tower has no door, there is no stairway, even the sorceress can't reach the top without climbing the rope of hair. Of course, there's the half-finished silk ladder hidden under the mattress, but the thought of it fills her with anxiety. Rapunzel turns her mind to more pleasant things: the moment the Prince will appear in the window, the leap of her heart, his hand on her face. She can hear the squeak of her hair on the hook, the sound of his foot, far down, against the stone.

BEAUTIFUL WOMEN

As the Prince climbs toward the top of the tower, he thinks suddenly of the palace, which lies on the other side of the forest. Rapunzel is so unlike the ladies of the court that he sometimes finds it difficult to account for what draws him to her, night after night. The ladies of the court are so beautiful that they are dangerous to behold. Sometimes a courtier, catching a stray glance, is stricken as by a bite in the throat; such a man sickens with love as with a wasting disease. The Prince, who has never been sick in his life, admires the ladies of the court and is by no means indifferent to their amorous glances. He has had many opportunities for clandestine adventure and, for so young a man, is already an experienced lover. But although there are many varieties of physical loveliness at court, he's aware of a note of sameness, for the ladies who surround him are remarkable above all for something high and severe in their beauty: the tightness of their pulled-back hair reveals the fine lines of their cheeks and foreheads, the narrowness of their nostrils, the exquisite modeling of their lips. Sometimes a courtier, bored by such abundance of perfection, seeks out the opposite: a coarse-featured peasant girl, a plump merchant's wife with a crooked tooth. The Prince, too, has had adventures in the country villages and farms, though he looks not for coarseness but for the unexpected burst of beauty in a gesture or a look. Always, in his love adventures, he has felt pleasure and something else: a remoteness, a lack of conviction, as though he were sitting nearby, observing the antics of the young Prince performing a seduction. It is never that way with Rapunzel. It's as though she has slipped inside him and moves when he moves. What he sees, when he looks at her, is harder to say. The court ladies would find her wanting in beauty. There is nothing proud and haughty in her face, nothing lofty in the cut of her bones. Sometimes, turning to look at her as she lies beside him, he is startled by something childish and unformed in her features; it's as if he has never seen her before, doesn't know what she looks like. At other times, when the Prince is alone and tries to summon her to mind, he can't see her with any certainty; he sees only what she is not. What he remembers, always, is the first sight of her hair, falling from the tower like fire. She seems to exist only in the realm of dream. Is that why he returns to her, night after night? To assure himself that he isn't dreaming? And suppose she finds the courage to leave the dream-tower, as he wants her to do. Will she dissolve in the hard light of the sun? The Prince's thoughts irritate him like gnats; he shakes them away. Reaching up, he grips the hair, lifts a foot and slaps it higher on the wall. He looks up at the evening sky. Somewhere up there, an invisible woman is waiting.

WAITING

The sorceress, too, is waiting. She is waiting for the long night to begin, so that it can come to an end. In the first light of dawn, she will return to her Rapunzel. She can, at any moment, leave her cottage and make her way through the forest to the tower, but she resists what she recognizes to be no longer a real temptation. After all, she spends the entire day with Rapunzel; the night is for herself. It is better that way. She doesn't want Rapunzel to tire of her—lately there have been troubling signs—and besides, there are things that need to be done at home. Because she hates the sharp light of the sun, which draws attention to her witch's face, her demon's hair, she works in the dark. As soon as the moon is up, she will step outside and tend her vegetable garden, cut dead twigs from her pear and plum trees, water her shrubs and flowers. Then she will carry her clothes in a basket to the stream that runs along the edge of the village. She will wash her clothes under the moon and carry them home to hang on a line to dry. She will bake bread in the oven for Rapunzel, she will fetch water from the well. Only then will she prepare for bed. In the dark she'll remove her long black dress and slip on her night-dress, which no one has ever seen. She will lie down in her bitter bed and think of Rapunzel, white and gold in her tower. Standing at her dressing table, the sorceress glances again at the mirror. She reaches for it, snatches away her hand. She begins to pace up and down with her hands behind her back, the top of her body leaning forward, as if she is walking uphill.

HELPLESS

As she waits for the Prince to reach the window, Rapunzel feels the sensation she always feels when he's partway up the tower: she is trapped, she can't move, she wants to cry out in anguish. She understands that her feeling of helplessness is provoked by the long climb, by her refusal to stir for fear that she'll cause the Prince to lose his grip, by the continual tugging at her scalp. What's taking so long? She reminds herself that only during the climb itself does she feel this way. The Prince's descent takes place swiftly, nothing could be easier, no sooner has he dropped below the sill than he's standing at the foot of the tower far below, looking up. The sorceress herself climbs the tower as if she's walking across a room, even though she carries a sack on her back filled with vegetables and bread. Why oh why does the Prince take so long? He must enjoy making her miserable. Or is it possible that he isn't taking as long as she imagines, that he's actually rushing up to her like a great wind, and that only the eagerness of her desire makes his progress seem so slow? Through the open window Rapunzel can see the top of the hook, the little jumps of yanked hair. Will he never arrive?

DISAPPOINTMENT

The window is just above his head, with another pull his face will rise over the sill, but as the Prince grips the window ledge he feels the familiar burst of disappointment. He is disappointed because the climb is about to end, the victory is within reach, already he longs for a new difficulty, a stronger danger—a beast in the forest, an assassin in the chamber. He would like to battle a dragon at the mouth of a cave night after night, as he fights his way to Rapunzel. He is happy of course at the thought that he'll soon be reunited with his beloved, whom he has imagined exhaustively during the long hours of the tedious day, but he knows that, in the instant of seeing her, he will be startled by the many small ways in which she fails to resemble his memory of her, before the living Rapunzel replaces the imaginary one. As he pulls himself up to the window ledge, he wishes that he were at the bottom of the tower, climbing fiercely toward his beloved.

SUSPICION

As the Prince rises above the window ledge, the sorceress pauses in the act of pacing in the dark cottage. Rapunzel has seemed changed lately—or is she only imagining things? Sometimes, when the sorceress looks up from the table in the tower to watch Rapunzel sitting across from her, bent over her needlework, she sees the girl staring off with parted lips. If she asks her what she's thinking, Rapunzel laughs gaily and replies that she isn't thinking anything at all. Sometimes the girl sighs, in the manner of someone releasing an inward pressure. The sorceress, whose unhappiness has sharpened her alertness to signs of discontent, is alarmed by these evidences of a secret life. She speaks gently to Rapunzel, asks her if she is feeling tired, reaches into the pocket of her dress and draws forth a piece of marzipan. The sorceress is well aware that she has placed Rapunzel at the top of an inaccessible tower in the middle of a dark forest, but she also knows that her sole desire is to shield the beautiful girl from the world's harm. If Rapunzel should become dissatisfied, if she should ever grow restless and unhappy, she would begin to imagine a different life. She will ask questions, open herself up to impossible desires, dream of walking on the ground below. The tower will begin to seem a prison. It is not a prison. It is a refuge, a place of peace. The world, as the sorceress knows deep in her blood, is full of pain. She vows to be more attentive to her daughter, to satisfy Rapunzel's slightest desire, to watch for the faintest signs of unrest.

AT LAST!

Rapunzel watches as the Prince swings gracefully into the chamber, stares at her as if spellbound, and at once turns to unfasten her hair from the hook in the ledge. Everything about the Prince moves her heart, but she is always disappointed by the way he looks at her at the moment when he arrives. He seems bewildered in some way, as if he's surprised to find her there, at the top of the tower, or as if he can't quite figure out who exactly she is, this stranger whose hair he has just been climbing. With his back to her he begins pulling up her hair from below, setting the coils of her braid on the table, pulling faster and faster as the slippery heap of hair slides from the table and drops to the floor, where it quivers and shakes like a long animal. When the Prince turns toward her with his hands still holding her braid, as if he has come to her bearing a gift of her own hair, he no longer wears a look of bafflement but one of tender recognition, and as she rises to meet him she feels her release flowing through her like desire.

SHAMELESS

The Prince lies back languorously on the rumpled bed, watching Rapunzel move about the chamber in her night-dress of unbound, shimmering hair, and reflects again on her absence of shame. He knows many court ladies who are without shame in matters of love, but their shamelessness is aggressive and defiant: the revelation of nakedness is, for them, an invitation to enjoy the forbidden. One lady insists that he stand aside and watch as she undresses herself slowly, pausing for him to admire each part as she caresses herself with her hands; at the very end she holds before her a transparent silk scarf, which she then lets fall to the ground. In their desire to outrage modesty, to cast off the constraints of decorum, the Prince sees an allegiance to the very forces they wish to overcome. Sometimes a peasant girl in a haystack reveals a sensual frankness for which the Prince is grateful, but that same girl will carry herself primly to church on a Sunday. Rapunzel is without shame and without an overcoming of shame. She walks in her nakedness as if nakedness were a form of clothing. The innocence of her wantonness disarms the Prince. There is nothing she won't do, nothing she feels she should resist. Sometimes the Prince wishes that she would tease him with a sly look, that she would cover her breasts with an outspread fan of peacock feathers, that she would lie on her stomach and look at him mischievously over her shoulder, as if to say: Do you dare? The Prince is a fearless lover, but there are times when he feels shy before her. At such moments he longs for her to resist him violently, so that he might force her into submission. Instead he bends down, far down, and kisses, very slowly, each of her toes.

INTO THE FOREST

Rapunzel watches from the window as the Prince descends quickly, hand over hand, and leaps to the ground. He looks up, calls her name. So far down, he seems no Prince, but a small creature of the forest, a fox or a weasel. He turns, vanishes into the trees. The dark sky is breaking up with dawn. A sudden desire comes: to leap from the tower, to fall down, down; her hair lifting above her like a column of smoke; the wind rushing up at her; the world's weight gone; lovely falling; blissful dying.

BRUSHING

In the brightening chamber, the sorceress sits at the table by the window, brushing Rapunzel's unbraided hair. Rapunzel sits across from her, sipping an herbal brew. Her needlework lies to one side; she looks a little tired. The sorceress fears she isn't sleeping well, or perhaps is coming down with something; the herbal remedy should restore her. Because the hair is so long, the sorceress doesn't begin at the top and brush down. Instead, she begins at the bottom, holding an armful of hair on her lap and brushing it free of tangles. The brush is of pear wood, with dark boar bristles; the sorceress received it from an old woman in the village as payment for curing an ache in the back. When she finishes with one lapful of hair she reaches down for another, gently pushing aside the brushed portion, which spills puffily over her legs to the floor. From a distance the hair is blond, but up close she can see many colors: wheat, fawn, red gold, butter yellow, honey brown. The hair on her lap is a warm cat, asleep in the sun. When she is done combing, the sorceress will plait the hair patiently into a single thick braid. The soft folds will gradually become heavy as rope, a sunshiny snake slithering along the floor. Again she looks at Rapunzel; she never tires of looking at Rapunzel. The girl's head is turned toward the window but she is not gazing out. Her eyes are half-closed; morning light strikes her neck and lower cheek; she is not blinking; she is gazing in. A penny for your thoughts! the sorceress wants to cry, but she continues brushing the hair in her lap. Suddenly she bends forward, buries her face in the hair, breathes it in, covers it with kisses. She looks up guiltily, but Rapunzel dreams away.

THE LADDER

The Prince, riding home through the forest in slants of dawn-light, reproaches himself for his weakness. Once again he hasn't asked about the ladder. Each night he brings Rapunzel a cord of silk, which she's supposed to weave into the lengthening silk ladder concealed beneath her mattress. He might easily have presented her with a fully formed ladder, when the idea first came to him, but he wants her to engage fully in the act of escape. The Prince fears that she may not be ready to leave her sheltered life for the public life of a Princess; lately, indeed, she has avoided all mention of the ladder. This ought to disturb him more than it does, but he himself is not without doubts. Instead of asking her about her progress, he hands her the silken cord in silence. She slips it under the mattress. They do not speak of it.

SECRETS

As the sorceress continues to braid her hair, Rapunzel is relieved to be spared another of those piercing looks. Can the sorceress suspect something? Rapunzel understands that by concealing the existence of the Prince, she's cruelly deceiving the sorceress, who is also her godmother. The thought pains her like a splinter burning in a finger. She'd love to tell her all about the Prince, since the sorceress would be sure to like him if only she knew him; often Rapunzel imagines the three of them living together in the sunny chamber. An instinct tells her to keep it to herself. She knows that the sorceress adores her, spoils her, sees to her every need, but it's precisely the intensity of her devotion that warns Rapunzel not to speak. She is everything to the sorceress; but everything leaves room for nothing else. Sometimes, at a sudden sound, the sorceress will leap up and go to the window. Then her eyes, searching the forest, grow hard and cold; her body, bent forward, seems crooked and ancient. At such moments Rapunzel looks away and waits for the change to pass. She knows that the sorceress craves continual signs of strong affection, which for that matter Rapunzel has always felt for her; the nightly visits of the Prince can be taken only as acts of betrayal. It's also true that the Prince, while not attacking the sorceress directly, disapproves of what he calls Rapunzel's imprisonment, and wants her to escape with him from the tower to the court. There they will be married and live in happiness all the days of their lives. Rapunzel glances at the mattress, under which the latest cord of silk lies beneath the half-finished ladder, and then at the sorceress, who is bending over and pressing her face against the folds of Rapunzel's hair.

THE PLAN

The Prince's plan is composed of two parts, the escape and the destination. He has revealed both parts to Rapunzel up to a point, but only up to a point, since each part includes complex secondary calculations that he hasn't yet found time to discuss with her in the detail they deserve. The escape will be difficult, without a doubt. The tower is forbiddingly high—to jump is out of the question. But the Prince has thought of two ways. The first is the ladder, which requires her full participation, demonstrated over the course of many weeks. They no longer discuss the ladder, which lies hidden under the mattress like an old love-letter buried in a drawer. But there's a second way, one that acknowledges the impulsive in human nature and invites Rapunzel to risk all at a moment's notice. When he judges the mood to be right, the Prince will reveal this second method. They will spring into action. He'll fasten her braid to the hook and lower himself to the bottom. Immediately Rapunzel will draw up her hair, unfasten it from the hook, and fasten it a second time, using the very end of the braid. In this manner she'll be able to descend by means of her own hair. At the bottom, the Prince will cut the braid with a pair of gold scissors borrowed from his mother's seamstress, and they will escape into the forest, where two horses will be waiting. They will ride off to—where, exactly? For the destination, like the escape, is no simple matter, and here too the Prince has not been entirely forthright with Rapunzel. He has told her that he wants to bring her to the court, and this is true enough. But he hasn't confessed to her his fear that she might find it difficult to live as a Princess among courtiers and ladies, all of whom have a style and manner that might seem to her impossible to emulate. They themselves, and in particular the court ladies, will observe her closely and judge her according to their code. Rapunzel is not familiar with the fashions of the court. She lacks the court wit, the court polish, the court gift for concise and allusive speech. Even her name will draw amused attention. The Prince is not ashamed of Rapunzel, but he knows that the pressure of polite disapproval is likely to make him impatient with her shortcomings. Even if she should make an initial impression of freshness and innocence, such qualities might, in the long run, come to seem wearisome to the court. It might therefore be better to avoid the court altogether and flee with Rapunzel to a royal residence in the remote countryside. Such residences, it is true, are supplied with a large contingent of servants, many of whom wield great power within the household and are accustomed to high-born masters with an instinct for command. Gentle Rapunzel, who has no experience of public life, will immediately be seen as weak. Wouldn't it be better, in every way, to choose a humble cabin on a wooded mountainside, far from the haunts of man? There they can live alone, without a care in the world. They will eat wild berries plucked from the vine, drink water from clear streams, and wander hand in hand in the paradise of Nature. In his mind, the Prince hears the phrase "paradise of Nature," which pleases him, but which also makes him uneasy. The Prince knows himself; he knows that he grows restless when he's away from court for more than a few days, for he misses the repartee, the rich feasts, the continual arrival of messengers bearing reports of wars, the sense of being at the center of a vital world. Mightn't it be better, all things considered, simply to move with Rapunzel from place to place, staying no more than a few weeks in a single dwelling? The thought of a wandering life does not please him. It's as if he can never imagine a settled existence for himself and his beloved. It's as if he himself is imprisoned in the tower, and can see nothing beyond the familiar chamber, which he carries in imagination from region to region—a restless and unhappy solitude.

NIGHT WORRIES

In the cottage, in the middle of the night, the sorceress walks around and around the table with her hands behind her back, the top of her body leaning forward. Ah, she is sure of it: Rapunzel is concealing something. The girl flicked her eyes away more than once during the day, as if to avoid scrutiny. At other times she sat staring off with her eyes half-closed, like someone fallen into a trance. The sorceress senses danger. Has someone discovered the tower? Has Rapunzel been seen in the window? She imagines the worst: a stranger scaling the tower, entering the chamber. Rage flames in her; she must calm herself. After all, the tower is well hidden, surrounded by massive trees in the middle of an immense forest. It can't be seen at a distance, since the top does not reach above the highest branches. Even in the unlikely event that someone should discover it, there is simply no way for him to reach the top: the tower is too high, the walls are without purchase for foot or hand, and no ladder in the world is long enough to reach the window. Even if such a ladder should be fashioned in the workshop of a master craftsman, it could never be carried through the dense forest, with its irregular growth of vast, mossy trees. Even if a method should somehow be contrived to carry it through the trees, the ladder could not by any stretch of the imagination be set upright in the small space between the tower and the thick branches, which come almost to the tower walls. Even if, for the sake of argument, it should be granted that a way might be found to stand the ladder against the high tower, the sheer impossibility of drawing it up into the little chamber would immediately become apparent. Even if, by a suspension of the laws of Nature, the ladder should miraculously be drawn up into the chamber, it would leave highly visible traces of its presence in the tangle of thorn-bushes that grow around the tower's base. No, the turned-away looks, the half-closed eyes, the drift of attention, must have some other cause. Has Rapunzel caught an illness? It might have been transmitted by one of the crows that sometimes land on the windowsill and sit gleaming there like wet tar in sunlight. She's told her time and time again to stay away from that windowsill. But Rapunzel's appetite remains unchanged; in fact, she has been growing plumper of late. There must be another explanation. Something is wrong, the sorceress can feel it like a change in the weather. As she continues pacing around and around the table, she thinks of secret causes, hidden reasons, dark possibilities. In the night that does not end, in the circle of floorboards that creak like animals in pain, she pledges herself to new intensities of vigilance.

UNREAL

Because the Prince knows about the sorceress, but the sorceress does not know about the Prince, Rapunzel reproaches herself for behaving dishonestly toward the sorceress; but she knows that she has been dishonest toward the Prince as well. It isn't simply that she's stopped working on the silken ladder concealed beneath the mattress. It is far worse than that. The Prince has often spoken to her of his life outside the tower. He has described the court, the jeweled ladies, the circular stairways, the unicorn tapestries, the feasts at the high table, the bed with rich hangings, and she has listened as though he were reading to her from a book of wondrous tales. But when she tries to imagine herself stepping into the story, a nervousness comes over her, an anxious shudder. The images frighten her, as if they possess a power to do harm. The ladies, in particular, fill her with a vague dread. But there is something else. The court, the King, the handmaidens, the flagons, the hounds—she can't really grasp them, can't take hold of them with the hands of her mind. What she knows is the table, the window, the bed: only that. The Prince has burst into her world from some other realm, bringing with him a scent of far-off places; at dawn, when he vanishes, she wakes from the dream to the table, the window, the bed. And even if she were able to believe in the dream-court, she knows that she herself can be no more than an outlandish visitor there, an intruder from the land of faerie. Under the stern gaze of the King, the Queen, the courtiers, the jeweled ladies, she would turn into mist, she would disappear. If only things could stay as they are! Now the sun has set. The sorceress has vanished into the forest, the Prince has not yet come. It is cool at the window. Rapunzel feels a burst of gratitude for this moment, when the calm of dusk comes dropping down like rain.

1812 AND 1819

In the 1812 edition of the *Kinder- und Hausmärchen*, the discovery of Rapunzel's secret comes when she innocently reveals her pregnancy by asking the sorceress why her dresses are growing tight. In the second edition, of 1819, Wilhelm Grimm, in an effort to make the stories more suitable for children, altered this passage. The discovery now comes when Rapunzel thoughtlessly asks the sorceress why she is harder to pull up than the Prince.

DISCOVERY

It happens suddenly, as these things do: a careless word, a moment's lapse of caution. Everything changes in an instant. Now the sorceress, hideous with rage, stands leaning over Rapunzel, who is falling backward in her chair as she lifts one forearm before her face. The sorceress holds a large pair of scissors wide open—like a beast's jaws—over Rapunzel's braid. The braid hangs over the girl's shoulder and trails along the floor. The sorceress's nose, like another dangerous instrument, thrusts violently from her face, as if she's trying to slash Rapunzel's cheek with it. From the wart on her chin, three stiff hairs spring forward like wires. Her eyes look hot to the touch. Rapunzel's eyes, above her forearm, are so wide that they look like screaming mouths. Her eyebrows are raised nearly to the hairline. An immense shadow of scissor blades is visible on the bodice of her flowing dress.

DUSK

It never palls: the feel of the hair in his fists, the sheer wall soaring, the pull of the earth, the ache in his arms, the push of his feet against stone. No palace behind him, no dream-room above him, but only the immediate fact: hardness of stone, twist of hair, thrust of knee. He is young, he is strong, he is happy, he is alive. The world is good.

WILDERNESS

With a crunching squeeze of the scissors the sorceress has cut off Rapunzel's hair, her treacherous hair, and has banished her to a wilderness. It is a place of rocks and brambles, of weed-grown heaths; prickly bushes and twisted trees rise from the parched earth. Sunken paths of bone-dry streambeds hold clumps of thistle. The sun is so hot that toads lie dead in the shadows of rocks. The night will be bitter cold. Rapunzel crouches in the hollow of a boulder. She presses the heels of her hands against her eyes until she sees points of light. She drops her hands, stares out. It is no dream.

AT THE WINDOW

He's there, the evil one, the usurper. The sorceress watches the look of horror come over his face like a shaking of leaves in a wind. She sees that he's handsome, a Prince, a young god; the beauty of his face is like needles stabbing her skin. She howls out her hate. Never see her! Never! Her words scorch her throat, burn his eyes. He has all the world, the handsome one, the god-man, he is rich, he is happy, he needs nothing, and yet he has climbed the tower and stolen away her one happiness. Even as black hate bursts from her like smoke, she feels the power of his face, she is stirred. She wants to scratch out his eyes with her claws. The Prince stares at her with eyes that are changing, eyes that are no longer young, then leaps from the tower.

FALLING

As he falls, the Prince knows that this is the secret buried in the heart of climbing, climbing's dark twin. Everything he loves is annihilated in this savage mockery of striving, this climbing-in-reverse. As a child he dropped a ball into a well and watched it fall. Now he is that ball. He's rushing away from the dream-chamber, which without him is rising higher and higher—soon it will soar above the clouds and be lost forever. And yet this falling, this soft surrender, fills him with such hardness of not-yielding that he can feel a swell of refusal, an upsurge of protest, and in an ecstasy of overcoming he embraces the last adventure: the rush of wind in his eyes, his hair streaming up over him, the sharp scent of green in his nostrils.

RAPUNZEL'S FATHER

On the other side of the high wall, which separates his property from that of the sorceress, Rapunzel's father is tending his garden. Since the death of his wife two years ago, he spends more and more time pulling out weeds, straightening the vine poles, watering the soil. The garden grows right up to the high wall, which he has crossed only three times in his life: once when his wife begged him to steal a head of lettuce from his neighbor's garden; once when he returned to steal a second head of lettuce and was caught by the sorceress, who made him promise to give her his child on the day it was born; and once after a year had passed, when he longed to catch a glimpse of his daughter, but found only the sorceress, who shrieked out her rage and told him that if he ever tried to see his daughter again, she'd tear out his eyes and strike his wife blind. Much time has passed since then. Sometimes he thinks of her, the daughter that he gave away, but it is like thinking of his own childhood: it's all so long ago that it doesn't seem part of him. As the Prince falls from the tower, Rapunzel's father bends over a weed that has sprung up at the side of a string-bean vine.

EYES

And the Prince falls into a thornbush. And the thorns scratch out his eyes.

TIME

Time passed. Two words, a breath: time passed. Days rush by like wind in your face, weeks are devoured by months, years are gone in the space of two syllables. Time passed. Time passed, and a great thornbush grew up around the tower. Now the stone was entirely hidden, bristling with thorns as sharp as daggers. The casement window, too, was no longer visible behind twisting branches. Every morning, before the sun rose over the forest, a dark figure appears at the foot of the tower. She seizes a thorn branch, which cuts deep into her hand. As she climbs, lines of blood run along her fingers and arms. The thorns rip her dress, catch her hair, slash at her face and throat. The pain eases her a little. At the top she pushes through the thorn-window into the dark chamber. There she washes herself at the basin, sits at the table, and begins to unbraid Rapunzel's hair. When the hair lies in soft folds on her lap, she brushes it, very slowly. When she is done brushing, she braids the hair carefully, then lays it in winding, ropy lines on the bed. All day she sits and gazes at Rapunzel's hair. Sometimes she unbraids it and brushes it again. The sorceress seeks relief, but there is no relief. There is only the fading light behind the window of thorns. When the chamber begins to grow dark she pushes herself through the sharp branches and makes her way down the tower, tearing her body on the long thorns, gripping them with her bloody hands.

THE CHAMBER AND THE WILDERNESS

In the days of the tower chamber, Rapunzel would sometimes dream of another world, an open world, without walls that stopped her at every point. Now, in the wilderness that stretches away in every direction, she seeks only shelter: the walls of a hollow rock, an opening in a rise of ground, the low space under a bramble bush. She listens for the sounds of hungry animals. She wraps her two babies in coverings of branches and dry leaves.

DARK

As Rapunzel roams in the wilderness, the Prince wanders in darkness. He has learned which fruits he can eat and which fruits will twist inside him like sharp metal. Sometimes he's so weak with hunger that he chews on pieces of bark, swallows them down. He has learned to listen for the sounds of creatures who might bite his legs, learned to strike out with his sword and feel the warm blood on the blade. He sleeps wherever he can in the forest, seeking out hollow places behind branches that hang to the ground or feeling his way to shallow openings in hillslopes. Once, waking, he feels a tongue licking his face. His skin is hatched with dried blood, his branch-ripped clothes are smeared with smashed berries and leaf-slime. Bits of leaves cling to his hair. Around his waist he wears a girdle of woven vines. Though he's still young, a streak of white cuts like a gash through his tangled beard.

THE SECOND RAPUNZEL

In the long nights the sorceress is busy. She draws on her deepest powers, snatches visions out of the dark. Sometimes she wakes to find herself on the hard floor. In the mirror her eyes are wild. She neglects her garden, shuts herself up in the shed behind her cottage. One morning at daybreak she climbs the tower with a bundle on her back. At the top she takes a knife from her pocket and cuts a hole in the branches that cover the casement window. Now she can pass her bundle through without catching it on the thorn-points. In the chamber she unwraps the bundle, lays the figure on the bed. Skillfully she attaches the hair. She slips the night-dress over the figure and steps away. A narrow ray of sunlight strikes the faintly flushed cheek, the closed eyes. The forearm is bared to the elbow. The image of wax and blood is so exact that it seems to be the living and breathing girl. A dark joy floods the heart of the sorceress. She sits watching over the sleeping girl. No harm must ever come to her.

SONG

Time passes in the wilderness, where the infants have grown into children, but for the Prince there is no time, only a darkness that is always. In the nothing of his days he comes to a place of rock and brambles.

Here, there is sun like flakes of fire. Here, there is hot shade that presses up against him like wool. In the dry ground he digs up roots, sucks their bitter juice. At night the air is cold as snow. He sleeps against stone. When something strikes at his leg, he beats it with a rock. The holes of his eyes hurt. One day, resting among spiky bushes that clutch at his arms, he hears a song. He is shivering with fever. He doesn't know whether the song is within him or without. He is back at the tower, the hair coming down like fire. He rises shakily. The song touches his face. He stumbles forward as though pulled by a hand.

TEARS

In the shadow of her rock she looks up and sees him. His arms hang like broken branches. His eyes are dead, his lips a bitter wound. His wild hair, his beard. From the depths of dream he has come to her, the lost one. He looks like a dying tree. She is standing before him, the stranger. She tries to remember the tower, the braided hair. Now her hair is ragged and full of thistles. The children have sucked at the breasts where he has sucked. Tears scratch at her eyes like thorns. They drop onto the stones of his eyes. In the wilderness, water is rushing between rocks, blossoms are bursting from thorns. Slowly the Prince opens his eyes.

HOMECOMING

Banners fly from the corner towers. Streamers hang from every window. As the Prince enters the main courtyard with his bride-to-be and their two children, voices of welcome fill the air. The Prince sees the faces of dear friends, lovers, companions of the hunt, but he is curiously unmoved. He wonders whether it's because, as they cross the courtyard, he can think only of her. It's as if he fears that at any moment he might lose her again in the dark. But as he moves among the courtiers and ladies, who part before the steps that lead to the Great Hall, he understands that his estrangement will not be temporary. Between him and the faces that welcome him lies the darkness. His wounds are healed, his beard is short and cut to fashion, his cloak is trimmed with ermine, but he is no longer of their world. He turns to look at Rapunzel. He tries to remember the girl in the tower, the hair coming down like a shower of fire, his feet against stone—it's all a story in a book. The woman beside him is marked with a fierce beauty of suffering that makes the court faces seem childlike. As they approach the high steps, he touches her arm. The day has tired him a little. He looks forward to the end of the long celebration, when he and she can be quiet for a time.

IN THE TOWER

In the thorn-tower, where Rapunzel lies sleeping, the sorceress sits brushing the hair in her lap. Rapunzel has been tired lately; it is good for her to sleep. A ray of sunlight slants through the space in the thorn-crossed window. It strikes the back of a wooden chair, runs across the stone floor, climbs the bedside, lies across the coverlet. When she is done combing the hair until it shines, she will braid it slowly and carefully, feeling the weight of it in her lap. From time to time she looks up at her darling, who sleeps peacefully, safe from harm. Suddenly the sorceress stiffens with alertness. She lays aside the hair, goes to the window, and looks out between branches of thorns. It was only a crow, landing on a pine branch. She returns to the chair and continues brushing. Later she will get up and smooth the coverlet, plump the pillow. When Rapunzel wakes, the sorceress will prepare an herbal drink. She will feel her daughter's forehead, she will ask if there is any soreness in her throat. But for now she will let her sleep. There's no hurry. They have all the time in the world.

RAPUNZEL

Walking beside the Prince along the courtyard, toward the steps leading to the Great Hall, Rapunzel is aware of the glitter of many jewels.
The costumes are richly colored and catch the sun. On a gallery above
the courtyard, men bearing shields look down. Voices cry out in welcome. She tries to recall her childish fear of these faces, but it is like
trying to recall the pictures in an old book. Long ago she lived in a
tower, in the middle of a great forest. The sorceress, the high window,
her hair falling toward the bottom of the tower, all of it is fading away.
In the sunlit courtyard she sees flashes of bright hair, high-arched eyebrows, earlobes with rings. She will study them, she will learn what she
needs to learn. The Prince no longer doubts her, as he did in the time
before the wilderness. Night after night he came to her in the tower.
She can feel his eyes on her face. She turns, sees that he is tired. Soon
he can rest. She understands that he is done with trials and challenges,
with perilous adventures. She understands one more thing: she is stronger than the Prince. It is good. She will laugh again, she will grow out
her hair, she will play. But for the moment, as they approach the steps,
she will walk beside her Prince among the courtiers and the ladies,
inviting their attention, meeting their glances, looking calmly at them
as they observe their Princess.

THE JUNGLE

BY JACK TEAGLE

THE JUNGLE

PERFECT!

LOOKS LIKE A GOOD FISH POOL.

THERE'S ENOUGH TO MAKE SUPPER.

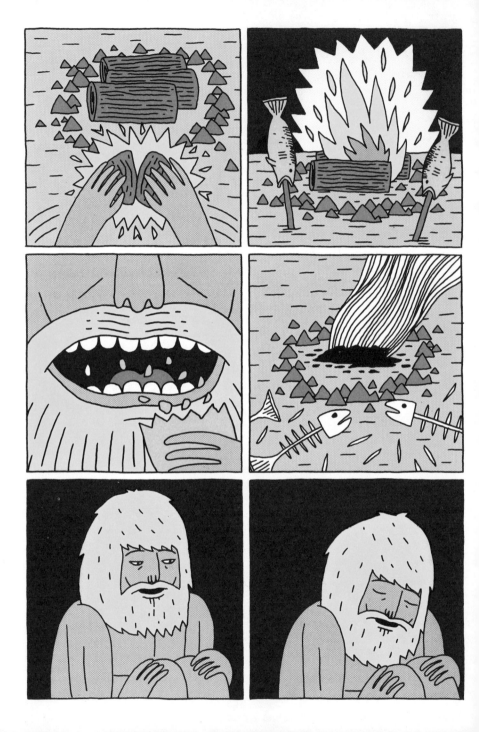

STOP!

I JUST WANT TO TALK WITH YOU!

CRED

by ADAM LEVIN

THE FUNNY THING about Kelly's body was the way it appeared to weirdly bulge above the puss area whenever she wore clothes, but then was fine (flat, smooth) once she got naked. (This might more accurately be described as the funny thing about Kelly's *pants*, seeing as it had to be the pants that caused the bulge. And yet the pants were normal, Levi's five-oh-whatevers, so it wouldn't be the way the pants were made that was funny, but the way the pants fit her body. Unless it was a funny way she *wore* the pants, i.e., maybe they would have fit just fine if she didn't pull the waist so high or low, or—it didn't matter. What mattered was that the way her overpuss area bulged or *seemed to bulge* when she was clothed, but then didn't bulge or seem to when she was naked, was… funny.) Cort didn't know whether to think of this as a gift or a curse, though. On the one hand, the bulging overpuss area was off-putting, and that kept, he assumed, any number of other dudes from hitting on Kelly, which, for Cort, meant (most likely) a more grateful girlfriend in terms of how she fucked, not to mention less competition. But on the other hand, was

Kelly THE ONE? Because if Kelly *was* THE ONE, then hey, great: no downside to a seemingly bulging overpuss whatsoever. If Kelly was *not* THE ONE, though, and Cort would, eventually, be moving on, then couldn't dating her hurt his chances with other girls later? Might not other girls, later, remember him as the guy who'd settled for that girl with the overpuss out to there, and thereby fail to feel flattered enough by his interest in them to give him a shot? And even if, with his native charm (he had a way with words), Cort could overcome that particular hurdle, might not a longer-term girlfriend, at some point further along in their relationship, find herself incapable—upon recalling Kelly's (seemingly) bulging overpuss—of accepting Cort's assurances that she was as attractive as she wanted to be? ("He says I'm not fat, but what does he know? His last girlfriend weirdly bulged above the puss area!") Or, worse, might not the new girlfriend choose to let herself go (split ends, rough knees, dimpled cellulite, etc.), believing that Cort, who had, after all, dated someone with a (seemingly) bulging overpuss, *wouldn't mind?* Well... sure. Of course. Sure. All kinds of retarded stuff *could* happen, thought Cort, but that was only the scratched-up lousy side of a coin whose shiny nice side was all the cred he'd get from girls for going out with Kelly despite her unfortunate overpuss bulge. And if it *did* turn out that Kelly wasn't THE ONE, and that Cort had been suffering the overpuss bulge for a smaller payout than real true love, not only would that land him in the black, karmically, but these cred-giving girls would be all over him, knowing he would never say anything, or even *think* anything, about their bodies to cause them any feelings of insecurity, because, as he'd have demonstrated by dating that girl with the weird bulge above the puss area, Cort wasn't shallow.

OF WOMEN AND FROGS

by BISI ADJAPON

*M*Y FRIEND ELISHA *says I should watch out for frogs after it rains. She says, "If a frog jumps on you, you'll turn into a man." I don't want to be a man and have hair growing around my mouth— that's the worst thing that can happen to a girl. Elisha is eleven, so she knows more things. And she's named after a prophet in the Bible. I am only nine, with an ordinary name. Esi.*

1

Today Papa and I are spending the night in a hotel room in Accra because I have to see the ear specialist tomorrow. I'll never tickle my ears again with rolled-up papers and sticks of grass. It's just that my ears kept itching ever since the day I got sick and Papa drove me up the mountain to the medicine woman with half a lip who ground up wet leaves and squeezed the drops into my ears. Now my ear is swollen and the pain feels as if someone is hammering a nail inside it. I think Papa is confused. He says educated people should stay away from juju men and women with their potions, yet he took me to see that woman with the leaves instead of taking me to the hospital. He says sometimes the black person's medicine is better than the white person's.

The hotel has lovely little houses sitting around a circular lawn. We have a room with a bed that Papa calls king-size. We don't need a sitting room or kitchen because we can sit at tables on the marble floor around the lawn, and men and women in white uniforms bring us anything we want to eat or drink. The jollof rice and fried-fish stew were so delicious I nearly chewed my tongue.

I'm in bed alone now but I don't mind, because I can hear Papa sitting on the veranda talking to a woman. I want to stay awake and wait for him but the night is warm and he and the woman speak in low voices that hum me to sleep.

Papa is the person I love most. At home he opens his accordion and music pours out and he laughs when I dance. He makes me a cup of Milo every night before I sleep, and then we lie on his bed and read the Uncle Ben's bedtime stories that come in big boxes from England.

The bed is making *shweequaw shweequaw shweequaw* sounds. I open my eyes. The moon is shining and Papa is a shadow on top of a woman who is also a shadow. The *shweequaw shweequaw* is because of the way they are moving. Something tells me I shouldn't be watching, but my eyes won't close. The bed rocks harder than before. Papa is groaning and twisting like something is poking him everywhere. Then he falls down beside me. I can see his white teeth and hear his lips smack. He is whispering Thank you, thank you, so I know he's happy. How can he be groaning when he's happy?

It's not so dark now. Papa's nose sounds like a car engine. The woman's copper-colored skin is light against Papa's very black skin. When I sit up, she lifts her head and looks directly at me. I have to cover my mouth with both hands because it is the woman who served us our supper.

"She's awake," she whispers, shaking my father. I lie back down immediately and pretend to be asleep.

"She's asleep, she's asleep," Papa mutters.

"No, she's awake, I swear."

"She's asleep, I tell you." Papa sounds awake now. "I gave her the medicine. She can't be awake."

I remember the tablet he gave me to swallow when we were eating our supper by the fountain. The way he looked around him and blinked made me think of someone telling a lie. So I brought the glass of water to my mouth, and when he looked away I threw the tablet under the table. Now I understand. The medicine would have made me sleep and I wouldn't have heard any *shweequaw shweequaw*.

The woman props herself up on her elbow and clutches the sheet to her chest. "But I saw her sit up!" she says.

Papa laughs. "I'll prove to you that she's asleep. Her ear is very painful. If she's awake, she'll scream the moment I pull it."

I quickly make my body go hard so that it won't hurt so much. Papa reaches over and yanks my ear. The pain is like a knife cutting me but I stay quiet. When he lets go, I swallow my sobs because I don't want him to be angry with me for not sleeping. I don't want him to find out I didn't swallow the tablet.

Papa heaves away. "See? I told you she was asleep."

"But—"

"Shh! Come here."

"No." Giggles.

"Do you have a baby in your stomach?"

"No—please... aaah."

"If you have a baby in your stomach, tell me."

"My stomach is empty. Please... do it."

The bed is squeaking again. They bounce me up and down and groan and weep and then Papa is off snoring. I feel like running the way ants do when something falls on their line.

Once, when I saw two dogs stuck together outside the house and pointed them out to Papa, he got angry and told me to get away from the window. So why is he doing the same with a woman? I can't ask my stepmother Auntie, because she'll wave me away and say that only a bad child asks so many questions. I can't ask my mother, because she disappeared when I was four.

Before my mother vanished, we used to live in Lagos, Nigeria, with my brother Kwabena. Just the four of us: Papa, Mother, me, and my brother. It was fun when Papa danced with Mother and they laughed, and when they let me sleep in their bed. There was no bouncing or groaning that I remember. But one night I went to sleep and woke up in Ghana without my mother. It makes my chest hurt that I can't remember what happened.

Now we live in a town called Kumawu. It is not like Lagos where the streets were clogged with squeaking cars and hawkers yelling while music poured from every store. Kumawu is a forest. Nothing but plantain trees and insect noises. My friend Elisha who warned me against frogs said the town got its name from a fetish priest. He planted a kuma tree in the town but the tree died. That's where Kumawu comes from. *Wu* means death, which to me is the loneliest thing of all. Because that's the way I feel when I want my mother.

When I woke up in Ghana without my mother, I found myself with a new family, as if a witch had made her disappear and replaced her with them. Five sisters and four brothers with names that took me forever to get straight. Most of them are away in boarding schools, so they only come home during the holidays. I don't understand how come my sisters and brothers are so old when they are also Papa's children. When I ask Papa, he just smiles and his newspaper goes higher to hide his face.

At night I don't like it when Auntie sleeps in Papa's bed, because I suspect she is the witch that made my mother vanish. It feels good when I slither between her and Papa and I dig my feet into her abdomen till she goes to sleep in the study where she belongs. When she's gone I can cuddle up to Papa and wiggle my little finger in the hole of his navel until I fall asleep. Next to him I am happier than an egg under a hen. His loud snoring doesn't bother me at all. When I sleep with Papa I don't dream of the black giant with wings spread wide swooping down on me and screeching.

2

I'm almost eleven now but I still watch out for frogs. It would be terrifying to wake up with a deep voice and bushy armpit hair and new things hanging off me. I'd rather be like Sister Mansa, who sings with such a sweet voice that everyone sighs. We live at Kibi now, and my siblings aren't strangers anymore.

It's Saturday, hair-plaiting time. It will not do to go to church on Sunday with untidy hair. Auntie attends the tiny Methodist church but we children love the Presbyterian church, which is bigger. The choir sings sweet songs and I get to wear a dress with a bow at the back and white socks with my shoes, which shows how civilized I am, even if my feet sweat. Papa never goes with us—he says the pastors devour the collection money. He would rather stay at home and read the Bible and give his money to the poor than let the pastors grow fat on it. I don't think Papa wants to tell God about what he did with Hotel Woman.

Today Papa has gone into town to have drinks with his friends because a man shouldn't spend too much time in the house, unless he wants to be called a woman. He is probably sitting at the bar sipping urine-colored beer, laughing loud enough to shake the walls, which is fine by me. Once, before Hotel Woman had her baby, Papa drove us both all the way across the border into Togo, where people speak French. All I understood was *wee* and *non*. He took me to a bar, sat me at a wooden table, placed a sweating bottle of Fanta in front of me, and told me to enjoy myself. He and Hotel Woman would be back really soon, he said. The afternoon air felt heavy, and I let the orangey liquid slide sweet and cool down my throat until two men at the counter lunged at each other with broken bottles.

By the time Papa and Hotel Woman returned, I had backed my chair into a corner and pulled my knees to my chest. I was nearly a statue. *She* was all teeth, clutching bags filled with new clothes he had bought for her. *Oh, we bought so many things, Esi. What a good girl you are for waiting.* I wanted to break the Fanta bottle on her head. Now I let him go to the bar without me.

I am cooking in the kitchen with Auntie when Sister Yaa yells, "Esi! Where are you? Come here at once!" I don't understand why she barks my name like that every time she wants me to do something, which is nearly all the time. I run out of the kitchen into the cobbled yard, where she is getting ready to plait Sister Mansa's hair. Sister Mansa's hair has been divided into several puffs that Sister Yaa will wind with black thread and gather on top of Sister Mansa's head like a stiff basket turned upside down. Sister Mansa is sitting on a low wooden stool. Her whole face bunches up when Sister Yaa brings the comb down and pulls. Sister Yaa couldn't be gentle if the Baby Jesus himself sat before her. I'm glad she's not plaiting my hair.

When she sees me, she says, "Look at you, insolent girl! Go to the room and bring me the hair oil." She sucks her teeth. God blessed her with the voice of a dog and the jaws of a crocodile. That's how quickly she can snap off your head. It would take witchcraft to figure out the reason for her anger. Sister Yaa never needs a reason to bite or hit. When I close my eyes I can still see the pink-red rectangles her teeth left in Sister Mansa's shoulder one night.

I have felt the sting of her palm on my back myself. When you know someone is about to punch you, you can make your body hard so it doesn't hurt too much, but Sister Yaa likes to sneak up behind me. I'll be examining a hibiscus flower or a caterpillar in my hand and then *wham*! No one hits like she does. When I turn, afterward, her eyes narrow like a snake's and she says, "*Alata ni aboa, wo n nim na wo ka a, me ku wo bi a!*" My Twi is good now, so I know what she's saying: "Nigerian animal, if you tell, I'll kill you well!" But she's pretty. Deadly pretty, that's what I think.

Anyway, I never tell. What is the use? Older sisters are allowed to knock you on the head to make you behave. That's why they have titles like the Roman Catholics: Sister This or Sister That. Besides, I'm sure it's my fault. I just have to try harder to find the reason. But why does she call me a Nigerian animal? We have the same skin and feel the same mosquito bites, so why is a Nigerian an animal?

This time, when she yells at me to fetch the hair oil, I am not upset. It's nice to escape from the kitchen where Auntie has me helping with the palm-nut soup. Auntie says, "You're a girl, so you have to learn how to cook." I have already pounded the orange-red nuts using a wooden pestle and mortar. I was careful to bruise only the skins and not crush the hard shells inside. After Auntie poured hot water on the mixture and the red juice came out, I pounded the roughness again and again and again. I don't understand what is wonderful about having blisters on your palm.

I dash into the bedroom I now share with my sisters because I'm too old to sleep in Papa's bed. An invisible cloud of smoked fish and palm-nut follows me. I love it when my sisters send me to our bedroom—when I am there alone I can loiter in front of the mirror. Anyone can get me to fetch something from the bedroom just by adding, "You can admire yourself in the mirror while you're there." My body is changing and I watch it any chance I get.

The mirror is the height of a woman and stands between two sets of drawers. I stand in front of it, frowning at my short hair. It's too soft, unlike my sisters', which stands upright like a hedge. I pick up the wooden brush with stiff black bristles and punish my hair, beating it away from my forehead until it slants backward. Much better. I turn sideways and stick out my chest to see if my breasts have grown bigger. They have not.

I pull the straps of my dress off my shoulders and examine the two little hills. Sister Mansa told me once that they would grow bigger if I allowed a termite to bite the tips. I rolled up my blouse while she held a struggling termite to each one. The termite stung the tips until I had welts all over and felt like plantains roasting on fire. I still don't see any change. I don't know why I listened to her when she had already made me cut off my eyelashes. She told me they would grow twice as long and they didn't.

I flatten my dress around me. I'm as straight as a sugar cane. I wonder what it feels like to have a body shaped like a guitar, like my sisters. Sometimes my new friend Gertrude and I crumple paper into balls and add them to the lumps on our chests. Then we walk on our toes, pretending to wear high-heel shoes. We play birthing games in which I have to crawl under her dress to be born.

Hotel Woman has a baby now, because of what she did with Papa. Papa put a baby in her stomach. I'm the only one who knows about it. When Papa took me to see them, he didn't say I shouldn't tell anyone, but I won't. If I don't tell then I can pretend the baby doesn't exist. I don't mind sharing cups of Milo and stories with my brother Kwabena, but I want Hotel Woman's baby to stay away.

Anyway, how can a baby come out of a place so tiny? I've never seen the spot. I can only feel it. Now I really want to see.

The only way to see between my legs is to lie down, but there's not enough room between the dressing mirror and the bed for me to use it. I pick up the small mirror. It's lying next to the yellow jar of hair oil Sister Yaa is waiting for, but surely she can wait a bit longer. Then I lower my back onto the cool vinyl floor and remove my drawers.

I draw up my knees and slip the mirror in between my thighs. I gape at the pawpaw color. I must be careful how I touch it, because everything seems so delicate. The door snaps open. Sister Yaa rears up. My hands attempt a quick cover-up.

"You bad child!" Sister Yaa says. My face is hot. I pray she won't raise her voice for everybody to hear but she does. "Is this what I sent you to do? I've been waiting for the oil forever! Get up!"

My bottom is cold when I pull up my drawers. My hands are shaking. Sister Yaa snatches the hair oil from the top of the drawer. "Go to the kitchen and help, instead of being a bad child!" she says. She jabs at my spine with her fingers and slaps me. My eyes feel peppery but the tears won't come.

In the kitchen, Auntie is bent over the palm-nut soup foaming on the coal pot.

"She was putting her fingers in her down-there!" Sister Yaa says. "Her under-canoe!"

Auntie drops the ladle into the soup and stares at me. She slaps her hands together like she is getting rid of dust. I want to sink into the earth like a beach crab.

"*Ei*, small child like you, whatever will happen when you grow up?"

Sister Yaa knows. She sticks her finger in her nose and says, "One day, the men will put it here." I don't know what *it* is but I don't want anyone putting *it* in my nose. I don't want *it* anywhere in my body.

"Fan the fire," Auntie says.

I drop onto the wooden stool beside her. I pick up the palm-frond fan and begin. We have a modern stove but Auntie prefers the coal pot. How I hate sitting in front of the fire flapping my wrist from side to side like a dog wagging its tail! But I fan until the coal crackles and tongues of flames lick the pot. If Auntie is happy she won't punish me.

"The fire is flaming, Auntie," I say. I scratch my head, wondering how to steal away and play outside with my brother.

"Prepare the snails," Auntie says.

I press my lips together to prevent the angry words from falling out. Kwabena doesn't have to fan the coal pot or grind onions that make him cry. He is outside while I have to stay in the kitchen and learn to cook. He has the burden of amusing himself and eating. But when I think of him with his ugly friends at school with their chewed collars, spitting and smelling funny, I'm happy I'm a girl.

After lunch I think Auntie is happy. I didn't complain once while I was working in the kitchen, even though my sisters did little more than plait their hair. Surely she isn't going to punish me after I prepared the snails and chopped off crab claws for the soup?

I am wrong. When I see Auntie sitting on a stool behind the grinding stone, my legs turn to mashed yam. She's got ginger in her hand. I should have gone with Papa to the bar.

The first time Auntie burned the evil out of me, I was seven. She had told me to empty the chamber pots, and I said no and called her a bloody fool. Papa always called her a bloody fool, so why not me? Well, I shouldn't have done that. She made sure I understood that only grown-ups had the right to use bad words.

But no one can do anything about what I store in my head.

I'd like to use the words now as I watch Auntie, sweat pouring down her neck. She has put the ginger on the flat grinding stone. Her fingers curl around a smaller stone and bang it on the knobby ginger root. Small stone scrapes against stone, crushing, crushing, crushing. Sharp smells. *Iya mi*, Mother, where are you?

Auntie raises her eyes to where I'm standing with my fists in my mouth, breathing fast.

"Esi, come here," she says.

My head and legs aren't working together. I don't want to go to her, but I go. The smell of ginger stings my nose. Yellow juice runs down the sides of the jagged gray stone. In the middle, the ginger forms a soggy yellow mound. My body goes hard. Sister Mansa and Sister Yaa appear from nowhere. Or have they been standing there the whole time?

"Take off your drawers," Auntie says.

I pull them down slowly, staring at the ginger.

"Turn around and bend over."

I feel screwed to the ground.

"I'll help," Sister Yaa says. She grabs my shoulders and spins me around. I shove her and she says, "Mansa, help!"

Sister Mansa puts her hands on my back and pushes until my head hangs down and my bottom points to the sky. They press my chest against my knees. I feel a cold, hard finger dig into my bottom. The ginger stings and runs into my pawpaw. Auntie feeds more and more ginger in until it feels like live coal inside me. I howl and howl. I wish Mother could rise up from wherever she is and strike down Auntie and flatten Sister Yaa into skin I can stomp on. I want to pop air from my bottom into their faces.

When they let me go, I can't stop shaking and crying. I waddle to the bathroom to wash myself, and Auntie calls after me, "I hope you'll remember how it burns the next time you're tempted to touch your under-canoe, you bad girl!"

Ginger is a steady burn, so the cold water does little to cool me. Auntie says the punishment will help me close my legs until a man chooses me for a wife. She's just like the wicked stepmothers in *Cinderella* and *Snow White*. I think she wants to kill me. This is why I never eat the *kenkey* she gives me when she makes it herself, instead of buying it like we usually do—I'm sure the lumpy corn dough contains poison she has put in it.

I want my mother. There's a pain crushing my chest and a fire in my throat. If she were here, she could explain about boys and girls and my secret places. I have no one to help me understand. When I ask Papa the words come out wrong and his jaws clench and his bottom lip rolls out. When I keep at him, he asks me if I want a cup of Milo or money to buy peppermint.

3

I don't like to keep sad thoughts in my head so in a week I forget all my problems. I find Papa in his study jingling his car keys and start peppering him with questions about my mother. He digs into his pocket and says, "Here, do you want to buy fried yam and fish?" That's all it takes for me to drop the questions. Then he drives off to visit an old man—the man Papa bought clothes from when Papa was a poor university student. I want to go too, but fried yam calls.

On the way to the yam-seller's house, I can see myself carrying the hot yam in a big leaf and eating it with the freshly ground red pepper that the woman will put on it. The fish is always so crisp I can eat the crunchy head as well. After that, I will visit my friend Sam so we can race old car tires. I don't want to be a man but I like playing with boys.

The woman who sells the yam has a nephew called Yaw. He is fourteen but he does not mind playing with me if there are so many other customers that I have to wait. When I arrive, the queue is a long snake over the dusty yard, so I ask the girl before me to hold my place. She agrees and I skip up and pull the rickety wooden door.

Yaw is sitting slanted back on a chair in the small sitting room, listening to music from a record player.

"Hello, Esi," he says. "Come in!"

I sit in the chair next to him and admire the record player, marveling at how the music comes from the pin moving through the circles on the disk.

"My uncle just brought this record," Yaw says. "Do you like it?"

"Yes!" I spring up and start dancing. Yaw's eyes follow me with a sleepy smile, snapping his fingers to the beat. When the record ends, I plop down on the linoleum floor while he puts on another one. I hum to myself and roll about, touching the legs of the chairs. I roll near the one Yaw is sitting on and find myself looking up at his legs. It's lovely how white his shorts are against his coal-colored skin, how the hair on his legs is so curly I want to straighten it. I reach up and pull a strand.

"Hey," he says, which makes me laugh and pull more hairs. It's fun teasing him. And I really like his hair.

Suddenly he is breathing fast like a person running. Then he is bent over me, sliding his fingers into my drawers. When I say nothing, he opens his trousers and lies on me. It makes me think of what Papa did with Hotel Woman. I want to say Thank you, thank you like Papa said but it hurts the way Yaw is stretching my skin. I tell him to stop and I roll away.

"Sorry." His smile is funny when he gets up.

I get up from the floor and pull down my dress.

"I'm going home now," I say, and forget about the fried yam.

A couple of days later, after lunch, Sister Mansa watches me walking in the yard and gives me a questioning look. When I move away from her I feel a pain where my left leg joins my abdomen. Out of the corner of my eye I see her point at me and exchange whispers with Auntie.

"What is the matter with you?" Auntie calls after me in a voice made drowsy from a heavy meal of fufu and groundnut soup. Sister Mansa gives me that look again.

"Nothing."

"Then why are you walking that way?"

"It's rheumatism," I say, because that is what Papa once said when a man asked him why he was limping.

Auntie says nothing else till after dinner, when Papa drives off to visit friends and she calls my name. I open the door to their bedroom and stand there cracking my knuckles. She is sitting at the edge of the big bed wearing nothing but a cloth wrapped around her waist.

"Come in," she says. "And close the door."

I take a couple of steps inside and pull the door shut behind me. Even from where I stand, I can smell the sharp mint of the dusting powder she dabs into her armpits after every shower. Her naked breasts are like rolled-out dough; they are so flat that I'm sure she can take one and sling it around her shoulders. She raises her arm and crooks her finger at me. I don't move. Although she doesn't have any ginger at hand, I sense trouble. I don't want to cross the black-and-white vinyl chessboard tiles stretching between me and the bed.

She says in a hard voice, "Come here."

I make my feet go to her.

"Lie on the bed and take off your drawers."

My fingers shake as I do as I am told. My knees are up and clamped together. She stands and gathers my dress to my stomach.

"No," I say.

She pries my knees apart and rears back. "Aaah! Esi, what happened down there? Someone has spread you. Who did this to you?"

I don't know what to say. I don't know if spreading has anything to do with what Yaw did, and if it does I don't want to get him in trouble. He's my friend, and I fear for him the way Auntie is shouting.

"I don't know what you mean," I say.

She shakes her head. "Get up, get up. Come with me." She sounds so disgusted I don't know what to say. She drags me into the kitchen, where Sister Crocodile Jaws has joined Sister Sweet Voice. I know I'm dead for sure.

"Did you find out what is wrong with her?" Sister Sweet Voice asks.

"Her down-there is sore. Someone has spread her."

Sister Sweet Voice giggles. Sister Crocodile Jaws says, "No wonder she's so thin! The boys have been feeding from her!"

"Ah, Esi, why did you let that happen?" Sister Sweet Voice says.

I feel as if I am covered with earthworms. I want to run into the bathroom and scrub, scrub, scrub my skin off until I grow a new one, the way a snake does.

Sister Sweet Voice starts singing, only her voice isn't sweet anymore.

School boys on a march
They found a girl
A stupid, stupid girl
They suckled, they fed
They fed from her

Sister Crocodile Jaws says, "Disgusting girl!"

Sister Sweet Voice says, "Shame on you!"

"And your mother is the daughter of a chief? *Twea kai*!" Crocodile Jaws spits. "Nigerian animal!"

"I'll have to treat her," Auntie says.

She puts a kettle on the coal pot. When it begins to boil she picks it up and tells me to follow her. My face feels heavy. I don't know how to cry anymore. I remember my grandfather's rambling house in Lagos, men bowing to him and women kneeling. How come in Ghana we are animals, *Iya mi*? I have no more words in my head.

In the bathroom, Auntie pulls out the larger chamber pot, the one painted white on the inside and green on the outside. White clouds swirl up as she pours the water into it.

"Take off your drawers."

Slowly, I pull down my drawers once again. It seems I am always taking off my drawers for one thing or another and it is never pleasant.

"Sit on the chamber pot. The heat will heal your wound."

I sit on it but I have to jump up shouting. My bottom is so small it slipped into the scalding water.

"Sit down!" Auntie says again. "The steam is good for you. It will heal you."

"It burns, Auntie!"

She settles onto a stool in front of me. "Just sit on it."

I lower my bottom as slowly as possible, but I have to jump up again. My bottom is on fire. Auntie grabs the chamber pot with both hands and dumps some of the water into the tub. She must have realized the water was too close to the top. The heaving in my chest lessens when I sit back down, but now my throat has started to hurt.

I sit for a long time watching my skin glisten. The ceramic tiles look like they are sweating, or crying large teardrops. An odd scent like steam from meat rises to my nostrils. I wonder what is cooking and if Auntie smells it too. But she sits in front of me with her lips pressed together, holding the words in because you don't explain things to a child.

I nod off until Papa opens the door and I jerk up. I didn't hear his Mercedes rumble into the garage.

"What is wrong?" he asks.

"She has been spread open," Auntie says. I look at Papa. His lips are tight. I know he's angry with Auntie for torturing me. He's going to yell at her, tell her what an evil woman she is.

"You stupid girl! You good-for-nothing tramp!"

The words fly from his mouth like knives, straight at me. I slump over. I don't know what a tramp is, but I know it's an awful thing. There is wood in my chest. He storms out and slams the door.

At bedtime, the sisters tell me they don't want disgusting me in their bed, so I curl up on the floor with a blanket between my body and the tiles. There is a burning between my legs. Small dots of red glow where the cocoa skin has come off. Papa didn't give me a cup of Milo, didn't play his accordion. Now the rain is pounding the roof. Even the sky seems angry, knocking things about—*boom! boom! boom!*

I want to ask God: What have I done? If a boy did something bad to me, why is it my fault? I remember the time Kwabena sat on a stool wearing shorts without drawers and his thing peeped through one leg. Sister Yaa noticed it and pointed it out, poking Sister Mansa in the shoulder. Sister Mansa laughed and said, "Perhaps he has used it to eat some girl!" They slapped their thighs as if to say, "Well done, boy." But when a boy does something to me, I am punished.

The rain is less angry now and I can hear the frogs. They sound as if they are gargling on stones. I've stayed away from them ever since Elisha told me they could turn me into a man. I'd rather be a girl in my own skin, but I don't understand why women are meanest to girls. Why is it that when Hotel Woman lies under Papa she makes him so happy he thanks her, but I get called a tramp for wanting to do the same with Yaw? Why does Hotel Woman get rewarded with trips to Togo and new clothes while I get ginger and a cold floor? Why do I have to keep the words in and not tell Auntie about the baby she should know about? God, tear my skin open, let my mouth hang in a scream loud enough to wake dead people!

In the morning, Auntie sends me to collect Papa's breakfast plates. He eats alone while everyone else eats in the kitchen. When I go to him, he looks at me with a sad smile. Then he opens his arms and says, "Come here." I run and bury my head in his chest. He says it's okay and gives me a spoonful of honey. Every drop is as sweet as Papa's smile, but my mind is made up.

The wet grass brushes against my legs as I walk to the edge of the forest. The frogs are gargling madly. I take off my clothes except for my drawers. Then I stretch out in the mud and wait for them to change me.

THE JPEG

by RACHEL B. GLASER

AT THE END of the third week of April, Anna looked to her calendar and felt nothing for the retriever who'd started off the month with such vivacity. It had excessive hair, as usual, billowing in the wind, but the dog's smile felt forced. Anna flipped the page and stabbed May to the wall with a thumbtack. Oh! The May dog was beautiful! Sniffing at a handful of flowers, eyes wet with life; Anna would have given a month's rent to be that dog, jobless and loved by everyone.

Mid-May, the weather became brilliant. Walking around South Philly with her ex-boyfriend, Anna noticed that the homeless people looked happier. One of them had a mattress set up under an overhang, and was playing music from a boom box.

Anna's cell phone started shaking in her pocket. It was a Rhode Island number; she quickly imagined a postgraduate award she could have won. She accepted the call.

"Hi, Anna, my name is Janine! I'm a sophomore at Rhode Island School of Design. How are you today?"

"Good, but—"

"That's great. I was wondering if you had a few minutes while I explain some new additions to the school you might be unfamiliar with?"

"Actually, I don't really." Anna rolled her eyes at her ex-boyfriend.

"Oh, I'm sorry to hear that."

"Yeah. I don't have any money to give either, unfortunately." Even art schools sounded so corporate over the phone. If anyone ever donated money, it probably went toward a new panini press.

"Well, can I at least check that we have your correct address?"

Three laughing Hispanic boys rode by on bikes. Anna felt sure that they were laughing at her. She picked at her pants and hung up the phone. Her ex-boyfriend looked at her, amused.

She desperately wanted to sleep with him, but he left her at his door. He said he was busy, and he'd had fun, and maybe they could hang out again sometime. Anna opened her phone as if someone had called, and then stared at the screen as if it held a long, intimate message. Her ex-boyfriend closed the door.

Their relationship had been a constant swap of power. Early on, Anna held the power. She forwarded his flirtatious emails to her friends, criticizing his overwritten prose style. Eventually, he wore her down and she fell in love, but by then he was sleeping with her friend. Later, Anna won him back, but a few months later he broke up with her, and she crumpled. She spent time with the school's terrible, but free, psychologist.

*   *   *

Anna was an unsuccessful glass artist. She worked part-time at a glassblowing studio, making giant, insanely colorful marbles that were then sold in old-lady stores. In June, she got one of her glass sculptures into a show, but it wasn't the usual kind of show; it was a show in an online world, for an online community. It wasn't her actual piece, just a JPEG of the piece.

Anna had to sign up for the online community to see the JPEG displayed in the show. She gave them all her info, but unchecked the box allowing them to send her weekly updates. She felt sly, unchecking the box. Then she had to design herself. It was fun, but Anna pretended that it was a drag. Pretended to no one. She made herself have a unicorn horn and crazy green hair. Then she regretted it, but there was no back button, so she continued.

In the online world, she teleported to the gallery. There were other JPEGs hung around her—paintings and drawings, nothing that impressed Anna. She glanced at them quickly, as she would have done in a real gallery, and then she saw another online person. *Excuse me,* she typed, *how do I walk?* The online woman told her to use her arrow keys. Anna tried to write back, but her character was walking very quickly away.

Anna searched for her JPEG, but her character kept walking into walls. The computer's view would switch, so that it would seem like she was inside the wall. Then she would bust out and try to walk up the stairs to the gallery's other floor, but she didn't know how to make herself use the staircase. She tried pressing the up arrow, and her character began to fly. She flew through the roof and into the air. Anna pressed no button. On and on her character soared. Farther and farther away from the JPEG. Arrow keys did not control her. Below her, the online world was beautiful and small.

* * *

The people who had been her friends in college had a potluck, but Anna didn't make anything. Instead she brought paper plates and put them anonymously on top of a stack of real plates.

When Anna spotted her ex-boyfriend it felt like all her breaths were being held in a small box in her chest. She had to remember to take each one out and breathe. When she breathed, another breath would be put into the box.

Most of the people at the party worked in the warehouse of an egotistical male art star. All day the girls painted photorealist versions of paintings that he had designed in Photoshop. For lunch, the girls ate in a massive cafeteria Anna had heard about many times. It made her sick to keep track of who was who. Of who had what personality. She took a breath from the box. She stood there in her fog.

While her ex-boyfriend talked to a pretty girl, Anna took out her phone and deleted his number. There, he's dead, she thought. He's vanished, over, irretrievable. Anna positioned herself next to female acquaintances. The girls were beautiful if she looked at them long enough. If only she could kiss *them*!

"It's hard with an ex-boyfriend," said a tall, stunning one whose name Anna couldn't remember. "You always want to jump in the time machine."

"Yeah," said Anna. "Wait, what?"

"You want to go back in time to how you felt about him and how you felt about yourself. You want to be younger even if it's only a few months younger."

"Yeah," said Anna.

The party was missing some magic party ingredient. Anna met a girl who couldn't find any cute guys. "Spring has sprung and my blossoming pussy needs to be deflowered," the girl said. "It's like all the bees are gone and I'm eager to bloom but nothing will pollinate me." Anna agreed with this girl. What if there weren't any more good relationships? What if glass art became really popular after she died?

"Yo, Party People!" A popular boy whom Anna had never seen before announced himself, and the party resumed. He wore crazy tie-dyed sweatpants and a telephone cord tied around his forehead. Her ex-boyfriend was now flirting easily with the blooming-pussy girl. Anna scanned her phone for a text message to save herself. She texted a coworker on a whim, then aggressively dug her coat out from a pile of other coats. Anna didn't know whether she was supposed to take the leftover paper plates home. She didn't know what was polite. As she hovered over them, uncertain, her ex-boyfriend approached her.

When Anna had first fallen in love with him, she'd felt that his face had been designed exclusively to get her attention. His cheeks had a little red to them, the way Anna imagined the cheeks of a Russian nobleman. His jaw was firm, and disregarding. She'd thought it was fate that drew her to him, and him to her, and kept her writing diary entries in her Google drafts; now, she was less romantic and knew she was just addicted to his face. After a person memorizes someone's face, they can become enslaved to that face. To feel comfortable, they need to witness the face. But the face wanders, the face dates other faces.

They stared at each other and her breasts ached. She wanted to slap him, but she wanted the slap to make his clothes fall off.

"You should call me tomorrow," he said offhandedly. "We could hang out."

The next day, Anna went to call her ex-boyfriend but his number was gone. She sent him an email and waited. She ignored a call from her coworker. She decided to join a lot of free dating sites. All morning she filled out forms. For each site she chose a different user name: *glass_animal*, *ghost_world24*, *bright_fires*. Her identity felt like a slender, shifting thing.

Her ex-boyfriend texted her to come over and she rejoiced. She did the enthusiastic bathing of someone who hopes to be slept with. After fussing with gel and bobby pins, she used cover-up to conceal her blemishes. She smiled in the mirror at this better version of herself. She felt like a witch, but a harmless and kind witch.

At her ex-boyfriend's, they talked and ate cold pizza. They watched some old *Arrested Development* reruns on his laptop. "You're like a rerun," she said to him. "But like a rerun I really like. Like I want to watch you."

She wanted to kiss him, but if he had wanted to kiss her he would have done it by now, right? Or maybe he wanted her to make the first move? She stared at a *Fight Club* poster she had never noticed before. "I should go, right?" she asked him.

"Yeah."

"Okay. Fine." Anna frantically tied her shoes. She got her coat and dropped her keys, then picked up her keys and went to the door. Just get out, she told herself; once you're outside you'll feel better. The air will soothe you. Her ex-boyfriend looked at her in the doorway and she felt a slow wave of anxiety collide with a fast wave of anxiety. "What?" she said.

"Nothing," he said. Get out, she thought. Just get out. Anna's brain hurt. She took a big breath. She would always feel like this! If she left the house she would feel even worse!

The ex-boyfriend offered her a hug. Sex would clear all this up. Sex could make people relaxed and happy. It was the best thing to do. It was a creative way to express yourself. Anna turned back. The ex-boyfriend sighed and the sigh sent bolts of hatred and desire through Anna. Her phone vibrated and she answered without looking.

"What?"

"Hi, Anna, my name is Janine, I'm a sophomore at Rhode Island School of Design, how are you today?"

Anna looked at the ex-boyfriend and pretended she was talking to someone interesting. "I'm okay. How are you?"

"Good! I was wondering if you had a few minutes to hear about some new additions to the school you might be unfamiliar with?"

Anna gave her ex-boyfriend a casual wave. She tried to look feminine.

"Sure," she said into her phone, and walked out the door.

"Well, the new library is almost complete, along with a new cafeteria in the new dorm building."

"Oh, cool. The building downtown?" The night air hit Anna in a very accepting way.

"That's right. And the library is just one of many new elements. However, RISD needs more help. Would you like to donate a small sum? There would be a plaque with your name on the library wall."

Anna reached her house, but saw that no one was home to distract her.

"What major are you, Janine?"

"I'm Illustration, but switching to Printmaking."

"Good. Printmaking is much better. Plus the boys are more socialized."

"Totally."

Anna went to her room and relaxed on her bed like a real person. Just talking to a friend, she thought to herself. She refocused on Janine. "Got any cool weekend plans?"

"Not so much. But Sonic Youth played last night."

"Lupo's?"

"No, Lupo's is over."

"Oh. I love Sonic Youth. In high school I didn't like them because I thought they were too noisy. But now I like them."

"I've always liked them," said Janine.

Anna played with her hair and put it on her face. She hummed a made-up tune into the phone. "You know, it's really crazy when you graduate. Like, crazy in the most boring way possible."

"Yeah, well, I'm not going to freak out about it now," Janine said.

"Well." Anna blew the hair off her face. She stared up at her ceiling fan. "You should maybe move to New York City. You'll need something exciting to make up for post-college depression."

There was a noise like Janine was eating something, or talking to someone else. Anna continued anyway. "Yeah, I don't know. There's a lot of boys in New York, a lot of art. You can probably live with your old college roommates if you like them. The degree won't get you that far, but maybe you have connections."

"I have no connections," Janine said.

"Maybe you could use your friends' connections." Anna shifted her weight. "The bars won't be as fun as the house parties in Providence."

"I just hope I make enough money to get a studio, or else I'll just be working in my room."

"Yeah. It's good to do something like music, too, to open up other parts of your brain. Like read some history. A lot of the bands you liked in high school will sound different to you. Same with movies. It might have been long enough to re-watch most of them."

"I might move to London or somewhere."

"Well, if you don't, then see if New York works for you. Or try and understand why it doesn't work."

Again there was the noise, like Janine was talking to someone. Anna pictured Janine, hanging out with the Printmaking boys while they took naked-punk pictures of each other.

"You'll be tempted to get back with your ex-boyfriend," she said, "but try not to bend to that temptation. Life has to be lived in order."

There was a long pause on the other end. "I hear it's like, impossible to get anyone to look at your work," Janine said.

"Take a look at me. I have a sculpture in a show."

"What gallery?"

"Just a small one in Philly. You probably haven't heard of it." Anna unfocused her eyes, looking at her wallpaper.

"Do they have a website?"

"No."

Janine was quiet. Then she said, "All right, I'm going to make my other calls now."

"Hey, great talking to you," Anna said. "Good luck in your life!"

She listened as Janine hung up the phone. Poor Janine. She would come out of college clueless.

At an opening for the egotistical male art-star, Anna wore a funny sweatshirt she had of horses running through lightning. "That is intense!" the blossoming-pussy girl said to Anna. "I am intense!" Anna said back. They had smoked weed in the gallery's bathroom and Anna felt amazed and correct. "I am basically a digital god," Anna told Blossoming Pussy. "There are digital copies of me on the internet!" Blossoming Pussy laughed uncontrollably. Anna's ex-boyfriend walked up and Anna flashed him a radiant smile. "It's you, the fifth love of my life and not my last!" she said. The photorealist-painter girls laughed. Anna's ex-boyfriend took her over to the corner.

"You are totally high!" he told her.

"You're just saying that because I'm saying incredible things," she said distractedly. He steered her over to a painting of flowers, paper clips, and cats.

"What do you think?" he said.

Anna laughed flirtatiously. Laughing is like showing everyone what your orgasm sounds like, thought Anna. She looked for Blossoming Pussy, but the other girls had reclaimed her. Anna saw the egotistical artist; he looked handsome and rich. She wanted a job from him, too, but a better one. A job where she sat on a cushion and made up jokes.

Her ex-boyfriend took her to another opening, one with dull

adults. The art was minimalist and there was no food. Anna looked at her ex-boyfriend and they were young together. "I wish I had met you through a dating site," Anna said, "so I could rate you in front of the world." Her ex-boyfriend laughed. It was like he had taken his personality out of a jar and it was trailing a sweet cloud behind it.

The night left Anna sucking his dick with feigned interest. During the most boring parts, Anna felt as though she were completing a farm chore. She laughed to herself and her ex-boyfriend got self-conscious. Afterward they lay in her skinny bed and he quickly fell asleep. She watched him, and he bored her.

She took her cell phone from beside the bed and down-clicked through her entire address book. She imagined all her friends and family members and bosses and landlords standing in a line like that, in alphabetical order. She could walk down the line, greeting everyone. She would stop, puzzled, in front of a stranger, and then he would explain that he was the pharmacist at CVS. And he'd be standing next to her best friend!

There would be a strange-looking woman somewhere in the middle. "Who are you?" Anna would ask.

"Leslie Futon," the woman would say quietly, and Anna would finally meet the woman with the online futon.

"The futon is no longer available," Leslie would say.

"I got a different one," Anna would say.

Then she would see Jessica Therapist. She would run past Jessica Therapist!

Jason, her ex-boyfriend from high school, would be making out with her cousin Jackie, but only because they were next to each other. Anna strolled down the line disgusted, fascinated. She came across another stranger. "I'm Anna," Anna said. "Who are you?"

"I live in your grandfather's old apartment," the woman said. "I guess you haven't deleted his number yet."

Anna snuck past an old boss who had fired her for no reason. With horror, she saw her mother talking animatedly to Anna's college friend Molly, who was completely drunk. She searched for someone she actually wanted to talk to. A good number of people were busy on their own phones. There were a lot of people she would avoid if she saw them on the street.

Her sister was next to her gynecologist. They looked indifferently at one another. Anna deleted a boring old friend she'd been guilted into being friends with. And a troubled, flirtatious boy who'd once told her she had "animal eyes." She deleted a number of doctors who had deceived her and worsened her health. Beyond them were many interesting-seeming people she had hit it off with, but never become close to. Anna deleted more and more of them. She watched the line jerk forward until her list was short and pure.

TALAT HAMDANI

an oral history recorded and edited by ALIA MALEK

Patriot Acts: Narratives of Post-9/11 Injustice, *the next book in the Voice of Witness series, will focus on the experiences of the innocent men and women swept up in the United States' War on Terror in the years since 9/11. Within the U.S. itself, countless individuals have been harassed by state actors and wrongfully detained, implicated in questionable terrorism prosecutions, and, in some cases, even sent to other countries to be tortured. To this day, the U.S. government continues to pursue policies that have been widely criticized by civil-rights and civil-liberties advocates.*

Among the narrators in Pariot Acts *is Talat Hamdani, a Pakistani woman who immigrated to New York City in 1979. Salman, the eldest of her three sons, an EMT and a police cadet, disappeared on 9/11. A month later, the* New York Post *published an article suggesting that Salman was still alive, in hiding, and that he might have been involved in the attacks. No evidence for any such involvement was ever produced, and Salman's body was ultimately identified in March 2002. Mayor Bloomberg, Rep. Gary Ackerman, and members of the NYPD honored him at his funeral service.*

SALMAN WAS A REGULAR KID

I WAS BORN in Karachi, Pakistan, in 1951. I am the sixth in a family of eight siblings. My father's dream was that all four daughters would be doctors. My three sisters, they are all medical doctors. So when I didn't make it into medical school—I studied English literature in college—he said, "Oh, you must do your PhD and put *Doctor* in front of your name!"

My husband, Saleem, was a family friend. He was eighteen and I was fourteen when we started talking to each other. He was very dashing and very handsome. We fell in love a few years later and got married in August 1975. I was twenty-four. We became really good friends; we understood each other.

Salman was born December 28, 1977. He was the first grandson on his father's side of the family. His birth was happiness.

About six months later, my brother told me that American visas were open. I had no desire ever to leave Pakistan, because I was happy. At that time, I was teaching high school in Karachi, I was close to my family, and I had a new baby. I was content with what I had. But my husband always wanted to move out of Pakistan. In spite of me being an educator, and him the manager of Three Star Battery (a company like Duracell), we couldn't save. Our income was very nominal, and he wanted to have a nice standard of living.

So he applied for a visa, and he got it. He came to New York City in July of 1978, and I came in February of 1979 with Salman.

My sons Adnaan and Zeshan were born in '81 and '83. In 1986, my husband bought a partnership in this convenience store, a bodega, in Greenpoint, Brooklyn, and I joined him in his business. I also took classes at Queens College, because I had to have some intellectual activity, some stimulation. In 1989 we moved to Bayside, Queens, and I got my teaching license in 1992. I became a full-time teacher at Middle School 72, in South Jamaica, Queens.

Salman was a regular kid. He was a *Star Wars* fan, and he especially liked Luke Skywalker. Once, I asked him, "What is this *Star Wars?*" and he said, "If you don't know the saga of *Star Wars*, then you are not an American, Mama!" He had all the movies and T-shirts, and he read the books. When he bought his car in 2001, the license plate read YUNG JEDI.

I still have the license plate. I still have the T-shirts.

Growing up, the boys were into everything—baseball, basketball, swimming, skiing, rollerblading. They played on teams at the Greenpoint Y, and Salman was the coach for the basketball team there the year after he graduated from high school. He wanted to do so many things, whatever he came across.

He studied biochemistry at Queens College and graduated in June of 2001. He wanted to become a doctor. That summer, he started working as a DNA lab analyst at the Howard Hughes Medical Institute. He was also in his last year of NYPD cadet training. Not only did it help bolster his application for medical school, but also it was something he would have been interested in pursuing if he didn't get accepted into medical schools. After the training, he would have been able to join the NYPD as an officer and go into NYPD forensics.

The night before 9/11, Salman was going over his application for medical school. That night, my husband, Saleem, wasn't feeling well. He was all flushed, so he called Salman to take his blood pressure. It was fine, but Salman said, "If you feel bad, if you feel something wrong, just call me again." That was the last time I saw him.

WE JUST WAITED FOR HIM

On 9/11, I left for work early. I was in my classroom from about 8 a.m. to 10:20 a.m; when I came out, there were teachers huddled up in the hallway outside the assistant principal's office. At first I thought, Let me go see, maybe the superintendent has come in for an inspection. But then I could sense that something was wrong.

I heard the teachers saying that the Twin Towers had been hit, that one had fallen down and the other one was burning. I called my husband. He was crying profusely, and he said, "You know, Salman is there!" He knew it. I don't know how, but he knew it.

I was trying to convince him Salman wasn't down there, that he was at work. His lab was at 65th Street and York Avenue—far away from the World Trade Center. But Saleem believed our son had gone down to the World Trade Center to help, because he would have seen the towers burning on his commute to Manhattan. Saleem knew he would have gone down there. That's all I can say. I said to him, "Don't worry, he'll call. He'll come."

At school, we carried on teaching. At one point during the day, I went into the school's media room, where some of the other teachers were watching the news on television. I found a seat up front so I could see what was happening on TV. It was so surreal. I just didn't know what to believe or what not to believe. One of the teachers said, "It must be some crazy Muslim, you know." Another teacher who knew I was there nudged her, and then she kept quiet. But I got up and left.

I got home at around 4:30 p.m. My youngest son, Zeshan, was home. He was trying to reach Salman. We called Salman's office, we called his cell, but nobody was answering. This whole time I was thinking, Salman is safe.

Still, I called up the police department and the ambulance company to ask if they'd sent him down there as an EMT. They said, "No, we did not send him." They had not seen Salman at all that day.

I told Saleem, "Don't worry. He'll be home." That night, we just waited for him. Nothing. He didn't come home. When the telephone systems were up and running and a call still hadn't come in all night, then we got really worried.

We never discussed the attack. I didn't think it had anything to do with his disappearance—wars happen in the world. We were definitely just focused on finding Salman.

THAT HE WAS DEAD NEVER CROSSED MY MIND

The next day my husband and I went to Salman's office. The staff there said that he'd never shown up the day before. The security guard went and got Salman's cell phone for us; Salman had left it there the night before 9/11. We asked the security guard what to do, and he said, "Maybe go down to St. Vincent's Hospital. That's where they have the injured."

So we went down to St. Vincent's and there were long lines and of course we were both crying. We went to see the list of the injured and the dead. Every three or four hours they were generating a list. We spent the whole day looking at the lists, again and again. I felt very hopeful because Salman's name was not on any of them.

On the third day, Thursday, we made a flyer for him. It had his picture and it said MISSING. We went to Manhattan again, to the Armory downtown. There were so many people over there. We posted the flyers everywhere, in different places. Everybody else was posting their flyers too.

That Salman was dead never crossed my mind.

FROM MISSING TO WANTED

We went to Manhattan for twelve days, searching for him.

I had no clue. I was just searching for him. He could have been dead, he could have been injured. We were still hoping to find him on the injured list. They gave out a list of all the hospitals where the patients had been sent. There were something like 170 hospitals between the five boroughs and New Jersey. We went to many of them, and I called many of them. No one had his name.

Soon after that, two police officers came to our house. They were a woman and a man from the NYPD Bureau of Criminal Investigation.

I said, "What brings you to my house?"

They looked at each other, and they said, "Oh, we're just visiting, just paying a visit to all the victims' families in Queens."

The female officer was looking around the house very intently. She came into the kitchen, where I had a big collage of pictures on the refrigerator. There was a picture of Zeshan's graduation, with Salman, Adnaan, Zeshan, and Zeshan's friend, who was an Afghan. She said, "My husband works at Queens College Housing." The police had a center over there, where Salman had worked. "Can I take his picture?" she asked me. "Maybe my husband will recognize Salman."

I said, "Yeah, take his picture."

She took the one with the Afghan kid. I never got the picture back, and they never came back.

A few days after the cops came to my home, a regular customer, a Pakistani man who worked at the MTA, came to my husband's store and said, "They're asking for your son at the MTA. They're asking for anyone who knows your son to step forward." At that point we'd had the store for fifteen years, so Salman had practically grown up in front of this man. He said to us, "Your son didn't die, he's being detained. You should write a letter to President Bush."

And so we did write a letter to Bush, and I sent a copy of the letter to everybody I could think of, including Senator Charles Schumer.

To keep hope alive, I kept telling myself that Salman had gone to the World Trade Center after the towers had collapsed, to help, and that he was being detained by the government, the CIA, the FBI, whoever it was.

*   *   *

In October, my family and I decided to go to Mecca just to pray, to get some answers. But on October 9 there was an announcement on the television for people to go identify bodies at the medical examiner's office. So I said to my husband, "Before we go to Mecca, let's go and look at all the bodies."

The Armory had given us a handout with a phone number. I dialed that number, and I said, "I want to see the dead bodies."

This man on the other end said, "Who are you? Why are you calling here?"

I explained who I was and why I was calling. I said, "I want to know where we go to look at the bodies."

He gave me an address and said, "Okay, you can go out there."

The next day, we headed to Manhattan. We had Salman's cell phone, which was the only cell phone we had at the time. The man from the medical examiner's office, or whoever he was, was calling every fifteen minutes, asking, "Where are you now? Where are you going?" Finally, when we arrived, it wasn't the place with the dead bodies; it was the Red Cross center. So there were no bodies to be seen.

It was a big place with cubicles. The staff there told us we were entitled to all the benefits for survivor families, but we had to accept the death certificate. I said, "No, he might not be dead! We don't want any benefits, we just want our son."

We were not ready to accept his death. It was too soon.

For the rest of the day, we kept receiving phone calls from a man who said he was a detective with the NYPD. He gave us a name and a phone number. He asked, "What was Salman wearing? Who was he going to see? What was he doing that day? Did he have a girlfriend or not? Can we take his computer? Do you know his password?"

I refused to give him Salman's computer. I said, "Why should I give you his computer? It's not needed. First tell me where my son is."

He called again at 11 p.m., and finally I yelled at him, "Don't you dare call here again!" After that, he stopped calling.

On October 11, the evening that we were leaving for Mecca, that's the day when all the reporters came to my house. This *New York Post* guy came in asking questions like, "What happened? Where would your son be? What are you doing? Is it true that your second son Adnaan is the president of the Muslim Student Association at Binghamton?" That made me think, Oh, so he's done his homework, and that is what he is looking at, the Muslim angle.

I said, "I don't trust you. I don't want to talk to you." Then the *Newsday* guy came in, and guys from the *New York Times* and the *Daily News*. They told me, "There's a flyer circulating through the NYPD with your son's picture on it. It says WANTED! That's why we've come to your house."

When I heard that, I was shocked. We were shocked. I remember saying, "He's alive and he's being detained, and he will come back." The hope was so intense.

Then we went to Mecca. The day after we left, the article in the *Post* hit the stands. The headline was MISSING—OR HIDING? All this insinuation, this is just a garbage paper. But the *Daily News*, the *New York Times*, and *Newsday* all wrote very fair, sympathetic stories.

When we came back, there was a message on the answering machine from Congressman Ackerman's office, telling us to contact the office, that he had news of my son.

When I called him, what he really wanted was to interrogate us. He asked, "What was your son wearing that day? Where was he going? What would he be doing?"

A few days later, I think the third time that we spoke, he said, "I'll be very point-blank. Do you think your son would be involved in any wrongful activity?"

I said, "No! I know my son." And that was the end of it.

Then, one very peculiar thing Ackerman made us do, he had us write a letter to Attorney General John Ashcroft. He said Salman might be with the INS.

We said, "Why?"

He said, "Because he was not born here."

"Even if he's a citizen?"

"The dividing line is whether he was born a citizen or not."

Ackerman led us to believe that Salman was being detained, so we were hopeful again that he was alive. We wrote a letter to Ashcroft asking him to tell us if he had our son.

I have yet to find out why they would begin to suspect him, as opposed to helping us find him. I think maybe it was the fact that he did not work down there at the World Trade Center, but I'd called the police department on 9/11 asking, "Did you send him down there to help?" Maybe that could be it. There was so much fear and suspicion at that time. And his first name is Mohammad. Maybe that caused it, who knows. But it was wrong, very wrong.

A BAG OF DUST

I went back to teaching that November. By this time, there was nothing more my family could do to find Salman. We were just thinking that he was alive and he'd come back home one day. Every day we would check the *New York Times*, because they were disclosing the names of the dead and the injured. His name was never there, and I would tell this to the boys. So we were all still hopeful.

A little while later there was a senate hearing, and Ashcroft was summoned to it and asked by the senators, "How many people do you have detained?" So the more I heard about what was going on, the more hope I had that my son was alive, and being detained.

Then, on March 20, 2002, we received the first piece of information about his whereabouts.

We were going to sleep in the living room. Since 9/11, we had been sleeping there, because my husband had said, "Salman will come home one day and he doesn't have a key, so I don't want the house to be locked." So he kept the door unlocked all the time and he slept out in the living room, and of course I had to sleep with him. I couldn't leave him alone. We used to spread a couple of blankets on the carpet, and then sleep right there.

That night, at 11:30 p.m., these tall men in overcoats knocked on our door. They said they were from the precinct. They did not show badges but I let them into my house because they said, "We've just identified your son's remains. This is the medical examiner's number. You can call them right now and confirm."

My husband just collapsed to the floor and broke down. I told them, "Okay, you've done your jobs. You guys have gotta go now."

Then I told Saleem, "Listen, nothing's going to change anything. Let's go back to sleep. No need to call anybody. We don't know who these people were." I just wanted to calm him down.

The next day we went down to the medical examiner's office at Bellevue Hospital. A man from the office came to us and said, "They found the lower part of his body."

I said, "Okay, prove to me that this is my son. I want to have his DNA tested myself."

He pulled the file toward himself and he said, "Mrs. Hamdani, go get yourself a lawyer. If someone wants to test it, they have to do it in our presence. Whenever you're ready, we have the remains."

My brother, who lives in New York, handled everything. The remains were sent to the funeral home in Queens. The medical examiner's office said they'd given us his lower body. But I'm sure, with all that big debris that was there at Ground Zero, that they didn't find any bodies; all they gave anybody was a bag of dust. My sister tried to prod the bag, and she told me there was just dust in that bag, that there were no bones in there.

I don't know what to believe or not to believe, honestly. They gave us a pair of jeans and a belt that were found in the debris. They were Salman's. But the jeans were not burned or anything. They had cut one of the legs to get it off, but there were no bones.

On March 21, we went to California, where my sister lives. I knew there would be a lot of press outside my door again, and I didn't want to talk to them. We came back in April, a day before the funeral.

THAT'S HOW I WANT TO GO

We had the funeral on April 5, 2002. The NYPD arranged it, and Salman got an honorable funeral under the American flag. I think after Congressman Ackerman investigated, the suspicions about Salman were put to rest. At that point, I took it as a redemption of his dignity. The slander that had been done in his name was taken care of.

The funeral was at the big mosque in Manhattan, on 96th Street on the East Side. I'd made a collage of his pictures. The NYPD had a bagpipe player there, they brought the casket in, they laid it upstairs. There were many cadets there. Mayor Bloomberg came, Ackerman came, Commissioner Kelly came.

My family all spoke at the funeral, and the cadets spoke too. That was how Salman had wanted to be sent off. He had expressed it at the funeral of a sergeant who'd died in '99. He'd said then, "Mama, that's honor. That's how I want to go."

You could say this put a closure to all my misgivings, and the cycle of thinking—*Could he have made it? Could he have not made it?* It put everything to rest.

CHAPTER ONE

by DAVE EGGERS

AND SO IT ENDED without anyone taking particular notice. It was good for a time, fun to be on top, indisputably, for about thirty years or so. Maybe twenty, twenty-two? But it was over, without a doubt it was, and now we had to be ready to join Western Europe in an era of tourism and shopkeeping. Wasn't that the gist of what that man on the plane had said to Alan? Something like that. The guy wouldn't shut up, and the drinks kept coming. We've become a nation of indoor cats, he said. A nation of doubters, worriers, overthinkers. Thank God these weren't the kind of Americans who settled this country. *They* were a different breed! *They* crossed the country in wagons with wooden wheels! People croaked along the way, and they barely stopped. Back then, you buried your dead and kept moving.

The man, who was drunk and maybe unhinged, too, was, like Alan, born into manufacturing and somewhere later got lost in worlds tangential to the making of things. He was soaking himself in gin and tonics and was finished with it all. He was on his way to France, to retire near Nice, in a small house his father had built after WWII. That was that.

Alan had humored the man, and they had compared some thoughts about China, Korea, about making clothes in Vietnam, the rise and fall of the garment industry in Haiti, the price of a good room in Hyderabad. Alan had started and spent most of his career in the manufacture of bicycles, from Schwinn to Huffy and Trek to various other short-lived brands. He'd spent a few decades with bikes, then bounced around between a dozen or so other stints, consulting, helping companies compete through ruthless efficiency, robots, lean manfacturing, that kind of thing. And yet year by year, there was less work for a guy like Alan. People were done, by and large, manufacturing on American soil. How could he or anyone argue for spending five to ten times the costs in Asia? And when Asian wages rose to untenable levels—$5 an hour, say—there was Africa. The Chinese were already making sneakers in Nigeria! Jack Welch had said manufacturing should be on a perpetual barge, circling the globe for the cheapest conditions possible, and it seems the world had taken him at his word. The man on the plane wailed in protest: It should matter where something was made!

But Alan did not want to despair, and did not want to be dragged down with his seatmate's malaise. Alan was optimistic, wasn't he? He said he was. *Malaise.* That was the word the man used again and again. It's the black humor that really does it, he said. The jokes! he wailed. I used to hear them in France, England, Spain. And Russia! People grumbling about their hopeless governments, about the elemental and irreversible dysfunction of their countries. And Italy! The sourness, the presumption of decline! It was everywhere, and now it's with us, too. That dark sarcasm. It's the killer, I swear to God, the man said. That's the sign you're down and can't get up. Alan had heard it before and didn't want to hear it anymore.

He tried to write a letter to his daughter, Kit. She'd written him a humdinger a few days before, six pages in her orderly hand, most of it condemning her mother, Alan's ex-wife Ruby, wanting nothing else to do with her. Now Alan found himself in the odd position of having to defend a woman who had tunneled through him so many times and so recklessly that he felt lucky to appear, from a distance, whole. Kit's letter was denunciatory and final, a document marking, justifying, celebrating, the end of the mother-daughter relationship. Alan couldn't have it. He had to repair their relationship, and he was chipping away at a response.

Dear Kit,

You say that your mother has always been "emotionally unreliable," and still is that way. This is true to a certain extent, but who among us is the same in all seasons? I, for example, have been a moving target for years, wouldn't you agree?

Kit's regard for her mother was past anger, past dismissal, and had lately reached total indifference. She had, it seemed, added up the various frailties and madnesses of her mother and decided none were worth her trouble. But Alan didn't want to be the only parent. And he worried—or rather he knew—that if Kit could find her mother unworthy, certainly, using the same tools of reassesment, she would find Alan unacceptable, too. He needed to draw a line. He needed to prop Ruby up.

Dear Kit,

You need to have a mother. It's absurd for you not to speak to her, don't you think? You plan on avoiding her for the next thirty years? I know she brings with her a certain amount of risk, but there are ways to cordon off the chaos.

Alan hadn't, personally, figured out how to do that until recently. Email had been such a boon. He and Ruby had agreed to limit their communication to messages pertaining to Kit, and nothing over three lines. It had worked! Those guidelines had saved him and them. Could he recommend the same arrangement to Kit? No. Could he? Maybe he could. Alan hadn't spoken to Ruby on the phone for two years and the break in battle had allowed his nerves to strengthen, allowed his mind some respite. He no longer jumped at the sound of loud voices.

Dear Kit,

You two were so close for so long. And even when you were eight, nine years old, I remember your mother lamenting that she only had another few years before you began to hate her. Well, you two lasted far longer than that, but now we've arrived at the same checkpoint all mothers and daughters pass through. Does it help if I tell you this is not unusual? That after the usual reappraisals and arguments you'll realize you have only each other and you'll find a way to make it tolerable, even fruitful?

He was getting nowhere, so he attempted sleep.

But he hadn't slept then, hadn't slept during the connection in London, and once he'd landed in Jeddah he hadn't slept all night. It had probably been fifty-four hours, if he was counting right, since he'd slept at all. He'd been flying and waiting in airports for about thirty-six hours—he no longer slept on planes, couldn't pull it off with any pill or plan—and then he'd been awake twelve hours before the flight. He did the math. Yes, fifty-four hours he'd been awake. He'd gotten into Saudi Arabia six hours ago, at about midnight, and he'd fully expected to sleep so deeply that to make sure he got up, he'd set two alarms and asked for a wake-up call. But now it was morning, he had to catch a ride to the site in two hours, and he hadn't slept. Five hours he'd been in the room, watching TV, attempting sleep, failing, watching more TV. He'd read his reports on the King Abdullah Economic City, where he'd be leading a team in selling IT to what might be the next Dubai; he'd tried to masturbate and failed; he'd looked out the balcony window at the Red Sea, the highway between the hotel and the water, a few boats, tiny as toys, in the distance.

Be ready and be fresh, be awake and be smart. Joe Trivole had taught him that back in the Fuller Brush days. *Present a face of possibility and hope.* Now this. He was thankful to be here—the flight he'd caught, a Hail Mary, was his last chance at making it here at all—but now he would, on his first day, feel and look ragged and hollow. He braved a look at the clock. It was 7 a.m. Christ. If he could just sleep an hour... But it was so bright now, an uncloseable gap in the curtains allowing the sun to cleave the room with white light. He closed his eyes. He thought, at last, of nothing. And soon sleep came like a great hand taking him under.

And when he awoke he was late.

10 a.m. 10 a.m. it was already, on his first day.

He called Cayley and Rachel's rooms. Nothing.

He called the concierge. The rest of the team had already left. The van had come and gone. He had no ride. He was in Saudi Arabia, staying ninety minutes from the site, and he had no way to get there.

What had happened to the wake-up call? He called the front desk. The operator was perplexed. "We attempted your room many times. Did you unplug the phone?"

He checked. He had. After asking for the wake-up call, he had unplugged all three phones, even the one in the bedroom. What was happening to him?

He tried Cayley's cellphone. She answered, her husky voice. In another lifetime, a different spin of the wheel wherein he was younger and she older and both of them stupid enough to attempt it, he and Cayley would have been something terrible. "Hello, Alan! It's beautiful here. Well, maybe not beautiful. But you're not here."

He explained his situation. He decided not to lie. He was, in every way, past lying. He couldn't muster the energy, the creativity required.

"Well, don't worry," she said, a small laugh—that voice of hers implied the possibility of, celebrated the existence of a fantastic life of constant sensuality and wry humor—"we're just setting up. But you'll have to get your own ride. Any of you know how Alan will get a ride out here?"

She seemed to be yelling to the rest of the team. Was she in a cavern of some kind? He pictured a dark and hollow place, three young people holding candles, waiting for him and his lantern. "He can't rent a car," she said to them. And now to him: "Can you rent a car, Alan?"

"I'll figure it out."

He called the lobby, tried his salaam alaikum.

"Asalaikum asalaam," the clerk said.

"Your Arabic is worse than mine," Alan said. "Where are you from?"

"Jakarta."

"What's your name?"

He always asked names. Again, a habit Joe Trivole instilled. *Ask names, repeat names. You remember people's names, they remember you.*

"Edward."

"Edward?"

"Yes sir. My name is Edward. Can I help you?"

"What do you think of me renting a car through the hotel?"

"Do you have an international driver's license?"

"No."

"Then no, I don't think you should do this."

Alan called the concierge. He explained he needed a driver to take him to the King Abdullah Economic City.

"This will take a few minutes," the concierge said. His accent was South Asian. There were apparently no Saudis working at this Saudi hotel. He'd known as much. There were few Saudis working anywhere, he'd been told. They imported most of their labor in all sectors. "We must find someone appropriate to drive you," the concierge said.

"You can't just call a taxi?"

"Not exactly, sir."

Alan knew this, too. You couldn't just call a taxi in Jeddah or Riyadh—or so said the guidebooks, all of which were a bit overwrought, he thought, when it came to elucidating the dangers of the Kingdom of Saudi Arabia to foreign travelers. The State Department had Saudi on the highest alert, claiming that for travelers, especially those of American extraction, kidnapping was not unlikely. According to some, he might be sold to al Qaeda, ransomed, transported across borders. But Alan wasn't one to listen to such hyperbole. He'd never actually felt in danger anywhere, and his assignments had taken him to Papua New Guinea, to the Nigerian oil delta, to Guatemala in the eighties. Everywhere he'd been a prize, presumably, someone who might be good to kidnap, ransom, or just plain kill—to somehow balance the scales. And yet he'd never felt unsafe. Maybe he had some kind of forcefield around him. Maybe he projected confidence. Probably he was just stupid and lucky and his number would soon be up.

The phone rang.

"We have a driver for you. When would you like him?"

"Twenty minutes?"

"He'll be here."

Alan went to the bathroom, showered, shaved his mottled neck. He put on his undershirt, his white button-down, khakis, loafers, tan socks. Just dress like an American businessman, he'd been told. There were the cautionary tales of overzealous Westerners wearing thobes, trying to blend in, making an effort. An effort not appreciated.

In twelve minutes Alan was ready. While fixing the collar of his shirt, he felt the lump on his neck that he'd first discovered a month earlier. It was about the size of a golf ball, protruding from his spine, feeling like cartilage. Some days he figured it was *part* of his spine, because what else could it be? It could be a tumor, that's what it could be. Right there, on his spine, a lump like that—it had to be invasive and deadly. And given that lately he'd been cloudy of thought and clumsy of gait, it made a perfect and terrible kind of sense that there was something growing there, eating away at him, sapping him of vitality, squeezing away all acuity and purpose. He'd planned to see someone about it, but then again, why? A doctor couldn't operate on something like that. He didn't want radiation, didn't want to go bald. The hospital gowns! No, the trick was to touch it occasionally, track attendant symptoms, touch it some more, then do nothing. Do nothing at all but wait for the inevitable.

He called Cayley.

"I'm leaving the hotel now."

"Good. We'll be all set up by the time you get here."

The team could get there without him, the team could set up without him. And so why was he there at all? The reasons were specious, but they had gotten him here—the first was that he was older than the other members of the team, all of them children, really, none more than thirty. Second, Alan and King Abdullah's nephew had both been part of a plastics venture in the late eighties, and Eric Volpe, the VP in New York, felt that this was a good enough connection that it would get the attention of the king. Probably not true, but Alan chose not to change their minds. He was happy for the work. He needed the work. The eighteen months or so before the call from Volpe had been humbling. Filing a tax return for $22,350 in taxable income was an experience he hadn't expected to have after age twenty-four, but there he was. He'd been home "consulting" for three years, each year with dwindling revenue. No one was spending. Even five years ago business was good; old friends threw him work, and he was useful to them. He'd connect them with vendors he knew, pull favors, cut deals, cut fat. He felt worthwhile. Now everything was different. He was fifty-six years old and was about as intriguing to corporate America as an airplane built from mud. He could not find work, could not sign clients, and so had moved from Frontier Manufacturing Partners to Alan Knowles Consulting to sitting at home watching DVDs of the Red Sox win the Series in '04, '07. Or the game, April 22, 2007, when they hit four consecutive home runs against the Yankees. He'd watched those four and a half minutes a thousand times and each viewing brought him joy, comfort, a sense of order and possibility. It was right that that happened, and was for him the best evidence of some kind of divine order.

But meanwhile he was facing bankruptcy—a thought he could not approach, though his lawyer had said it was the right thing, especially for a man of his age, without much to lose in the way of reputation. Worse, though, Kit was being more or less evicted from her college. This is what he had been thinking about, on those planes where he should have been sleeping, in the bed in the Jeddah Hilton where he should have been out cold. The bankruptcy was something he could handle. His friend Marty had been through two and said, like a firewalk, bankruptcy hurt like hell but was soon over. Alan wasn't afraid. His name didn't matter. His reputation didn't matter. His credit didn't matter. But for Kit he wanted better. She'd always been preternaturally good, more grounded and patient and calm than either of her parents. Never missed a birthday card or thank-you note. Knew her father's Social Security number, his insurance information, his blood pressure and cholesterol. She'd done everything asked of her, had checked every box, had been admitted to Kenyon College, No. 4 on the *U.S. News* list of top liberal-arts schools, and now, in the summer before her junior year, she was being asked to leave. She didn't have to leave, of course, if she could pay. If Alan could pay. But he owed the school almost $18,000 already and the aid package offered for the next year had been pulled.

Or adjusted. That's the word they used, *adjusted*. In America, now, promises were not quite so important—they were being *adjusted*. They were valued but not much used. Not so practical, not so central. And so the aid package that had brought her to Kenyon had now been adjusted, and now there was very little aid at all. The people who made such decisions looked at the house Alan owned, implied to him that a third mortgage might make the tuition possible, and didn't he know that many parents moved to smaller quarters when their children went to school?

It's not that Alan thought that Kenyon was the only appropriate college in the land, but Kit was already there, and she loved it there, she'd spent two years there, and she wanted to continue there. Growing up she'd had a life of rupture and confusion and yet she'd stayed steady and excelled and now her father couldn't keep up his end of the bargain. Impotence was not the word. How he felt was far worse than that.

Alan had called the college, spent an hour on the phone with an eel of a man who repeatedly employed the phrase "I'm not empowered." "I'm not empowered to provide that kind of assistance." "I'm not empowered to give you those numbers." On and on. He was one of those indoor cats the guy on the plane had been talking about. Alan hadn't wanted to strangle anyone more since he'd planned, nightly, the murder of his ex-wife's lawyer. (It had been fourteen years ago, and the fire inside him had cooled, but still he could find himself, while driving, thinking of that man, the glorious dream of his hands around his tiny neck, squeezing.) Anyway, Kit had already been accepted at UMass Amherst and was ready to transfer, was fine with it, and he loved her for it. But it wasn't going to happen.

"It's not a big deal, Dad," she'd said. "I'm already in at UMass. I sent in a deposit. I've got about twenty friends there from high school."

"No, no," he'd said. "I told you if you got into Kenyon I'd pay for it, and I'm going to pay for it. This is what I do. I work, I make money, I pay for college. That's a dad. That's what dads do. So let me be a dad."

But he'd failed at these things.

"Sure," she'd said.

"Good. You're staying. I actually already have the money."

Now he was lying to his daughter.

"You do?" she said. "Did you tell Kenyon?"

What kind of man has nothing saved? He could have just sold the house—he knew two couples, same age as him, who'd done just that—but he'd missed the window and now his was valued at far less than he'd paid for it. He had two mortgages on it already. Impotence was not the word.

He hadn't slept well in months. Years? He was lost. He was nothing. Financially, he hadn't done a damned thing right in twenty years. But this King Abdullah deal was huge. Abdullah could green-light a contract worth billions. And Volpe, who owed him big, would make sure Alan got a cut. If the deal happened, a consulting fee in the six figures. They'd work out the details later, but Volpe would make it happen. Alan would be able to pay Kit's tuition in cash, send it in bags emblazoned with giant dollar signs.

Alan called the concierge.

"Is the car there?"

"I'm sorry, he will be late."

"Is this the guy from Jakarta?"

Every operator, every secretary, every stockboy—they're your ticket up. Treat 'em like gold and your path will be paved with it. Joe Trivole.

"It is."

"Edward."

"Yes."

"Hi again, Edward. How late will the car be?"

"Twenty more minutes. Can I send some food up to you?"

Alan ordered hash browns and bacon.

He went to the window, looked to the Red Sea. It was calm, unremarkable from this height. The highway, six lanes, ran just alongside it. The rest of Jeddah, in the distance, looked very new, not unlike Los

Angeles. *Los Angeles with burkas*, Angie had once said to him. He missed her. Another dead woman in his life. There were too many now. He'd been celibate now for seven years but there were women from before, girlfriends who became old friends, then *old* friends, girlfriends who got married, who aged a bit, whose kids were now grown. And then there were the dead. Dead of aneurysms, breast cancer, non-Hodgkin's lymphoma. Madness. His daughter was twenty now, and soon would be thirty, and soon after, the diseases came like rain. After thirty-five, it seemed, anything could happen. There were lumps, there were spots that became chasms. He cared about each of them, each beautiful young woman becoming a beautiful older woman, prey for any kind of savagery. The skin hides all varieties of chaos beneath. Angie had an upturned nose, enormous green eyes, a voice like a flute. She was gone. These women he'd known, these women in satin blouses would eat and talk about their children and spouses and work, their eyes alight, their laughs loud and strong, but all the while, under the satin, under their thinning skin, the armies of lymphoma, of leukemia, of uterine cancer, were burning, plundering, blackening. He felt responsible. They'd all known each other as young people, and what could they have done differently? Everything, nothing. He'd been at seven deathbeds now and couldn't hack it again. For the last dying friend, a coworker from the Schwinn days brought low by melanoma—melanoma!—he hadn't come. She'd been in Houston and had called him, they'd said goodbye, and he should have gone to see her but didn't. He told himself he was not crucial there. She had her husband, her grown children. He was merely a friend from work. But he knew he should have been with her. He should have gone but didn't. And truth be told, he didn't agonize over it. He threw that one—yet another example of disappointment, in everything but chiefly in himself—in a drawer and pushed it closed, clicked it shut. Why was he unable to care as much about each successive loss? Was it just exasperation?

This was the interior work of his current life. He thought about himself and then cursed himself—his thoughts were not worth thinking. He was negligible and deserved no pity. He wanted only to help the people he loved, right? But he wasn't doing that, either. He was growing harder to penetrate. A half-dozen inexplicable injustices and you're a cynic. Ten premature deaths and you went crazy or barren. You couldn't care the same way each time; at a certain point it was just absurd. The words *dead inside* presented themselves to him occasionally, but was that it, was that him? He cared, and deeply, about so many things, didn't he?

No, he cared only for Kit. He had a small reserve of empathy and effort remaining, and he spent it all on Kit. He had one fight left in him, and he would save it to ensure Kit had everything she needed. That was all of him. All he had left. And now he was doing it more or less alone. He found some hotel stationery and began.

Dear Kit—
We both know your mother is a complicated person.

God no. Best to cut to the chase. He started over.

Dear Kit—
Your mother is a maelstrom of trouble and frustration. She's an unholy pain in the ass and it took me ten years without her to reach my current fragile equilibrium.

True, but to Kit, unhelpful.

Dear Kit—
Did you know your mother gave birth to you naturally? That she took no drugs, no pitocin, nothing like that? That she wanted to feel every minute of excruciating pain—

That was the problem, wasn't it? Her interest in and capacity for pain. Her glorying in it. Her coveting of it. No. No. This wasn't the message he wanted to convey to Kit. But now he was out of stationery.

He'd get more in the lobby. Then again, why bother? Repairing all that was and wasn't there between Kit and Ruby was not his job, and he'd probably fail at it if he tried. Best not to drop down into the fray. He'd grown wise in his middle age, wise enough to know when to get involved, and the occasions that required intervention seemed to him exceedingly rare. This was his hard-fought wisdom, his hard-won humility: He should stay away, away, away.

But no. No! He was more than that. Some days he was more than that. Some days he could encompass the world. Some days he could see for miles. Some days he climbed over the foothills of indifference to see the landscape of his life and future for what it was: mappable, traversable, achievable. Everything he wanted to do had been done before, so why couldn't he do it? He could! If only he could engage on a continual basis. If only he could draw up a plan and execute it. He could! He could! He had to believe he could. Of course he did.

And yet most of the time, he felt removed. He watched the events around him, even those involving him, as if standing on a barge half a mile from shore. He could make out movements, he could hear cries for help, but he was too far out to do much about it.

How and when did he get there?

A knock at the door. The hash browns had arrived. Hash browns to his room in five minutes. Impossible unless he was eating food prepared for someone else. Which he realized he was. He didn't mind. He let the waiter set everything up on a table on the balcony, and with a flourish Alan signed the bill while seated twenty stories up, squinting into the wind. He felt, momentarily, that this was him. That he was worthy of this. He needed to adopt an air of ownership, of belonging. Maybe if he was the sort of man who could eat someone else's hash browns, who the hotel wanted to impress so much they sent him someone else's breakfast, maybe then he was the sort of man who could get an audience with the king.

CONTRIBUTORS

BISI ADJAPON has worked as an international affairs specialist for the USDA Foreign Agricultural Service, managing projects in Africa and Latin America, and as a teacher of English literature and French at Ghana's Hermann Gmeiner International College. She currently works with the Fairfax County Public Schools, in Virginia.

PAUL CURTIS lives with his family in Bay Ridge, Brooklyn.

DEEJAY is the nickname of a Canadian Forces soldier who served during a recent rotation in Kandahar Province, Afghanistan.

ARIEL DORFMAN's books have been translated into more than forty languages, and his plays have been staged in more than one hundred countries. *Feeding on Dreams*, his new memoir, will be published in September 2011.

RORY DOUGLAS writes *Notes from an Amateur Spectator at Amateur Mixed Martial Arts Fights* for mcsweeneys.net.

RODDY DOYLE lives and works in Dublin. His latest book is *Bullfighting*, a collection of short stories.

DAVE EGGERS is the author of seven books and the editor of *McSweeney's*. "Chapter One" is the first chapter of a forthcoming novel.

RACHEL B. GLASER is the author of the story collection *Pee on Water* and the poetry chapbook *Heroes Are So Long*. Her work has appeared in the *New York Tyrant*, *Unsaid*, and *American Short Fiction*. She paints commissioned paintings of basketball players, and lives in Northampton, Massachusetts with the writer John Maradik.

DAN GUTERMAN is the former head writer of *The Onion*, where he spent ten years of his life. He is currently a staff writer at *The Colbert Report*.

DAVID HENNE lives and works in Long Island, New York.

JOEY LATIMER is a singer, songwriter, and composer from Idyllwild and La Quinta, California.

ADAM LEVIN is the author of the novel *The Instructions*, a finalist for the 2010 National Jewish Book Award for Fiction and the winner of the 2011 New York Public Library Young Lions Fiction Award. *Hot Pink*, his collection of short stories, will be published by McSweeney's next spring.

ALIA MALEK is a civil-rights lawyer and the author of the nonfiction book *A Country Called Amreeka*. Her reportage has appeared in *Salon*, the *Columbia Journalism Review*, and the *New York Times*.

PETER MEEHAN is a writer (the *Momofuku* cookbook, the *New York Times*, etc.) and musician (Spectre Folk). He is currently working on the next issue of the McSweeney's food quarterly, *Lucky Peach*.

STEVEN MILLHAUSER is the author of several collections of stories, including *The Barnum Museum*, *The Knife Thrower*, and *Dangerous Laughter*. His forthcoming book is *We Others: New and Selected Stories*.

JOHN MOE is the host of the public-radio program *Marketplace Tech Report* and of the stage and radio series *Wits*. He is the author of *Conservatize Me* as well as of the "Pop Song Correspondences" series on mcsweeneys.net.

PETER ORNER is the author of *Esther Stories* and *The Second Coming of Mavala Shikongo*. He is also the editor of *Underground America* and the co-editor of *Hope Deferred: Narratives of Zimbabwean Lives*, both published by

McSweeney's/Voice of Witness. Orner's unfinishable new novel, *Love and Shame and Love*, is coming out this November. He lives in San Francisco.

JASON POLAN is an artist living in New York City. A member of the 53rd Street Biological Society and the Taco Bell Drawing Club, he has exhibited work all over the United States, Europe, and Asia. Polan's illustrations and projects have appeared in the *New York Times*, *Interview*, the *New Yorker*, *Esquire*, and *ARTnews*. Polan is currently drawing every person in New York.

NATHANIEL RICH is the author of *The Mayor's Tongue*. His second novel is forthcoming from Farrar, Straus and Giroux.

SLOAN SCHANG is a writer and photographer living in Portland, Oregon.

JEN STATSKY is a New York City–based writer and comedian. She has written for *The Onion* and *McSweeney's Internet Tendency*. She performs stand-up all over New York, and is currently a writer on *Late Night with Jimmy Fallon*.

JACK TEAGLE is a painter, illustrator, and comic artist living in southwest England. His first published comic, *Jeff Job Hunter*, was released in 2010 by Nobrow Press.

CHANAN TIGAY has contributed to publications including *Newsweek*, *New York* magazine, the *Wall Street Journal*, and the *San Francisco Chronicle*. He has covered the Israeli-Palestinian conflict as a correspondent for the Jerusalem bureau of Agence France-Presse.

JON WURSTER is the drummer for indie-rock legends Superchunk, Bob Mould, and The Mountain Goats. He can be heard on *The Best Show on WFMU* with Tom Scharpling every Tuesday night from 9 p.m. to midnight.

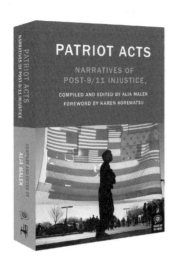

PATRIOT ACTS
NARRATIVES OF POST-9/11 INJUSTICE
Compiled and edited by Alia Malek

This book collects the life stories of innocent men and women who have been swept up in America's War on Terror. As we approach the ten-year anniversary of 9/11, these narratives give voice to those who have had their human rights violated here in the U.S. by our government's policies and actions.

AVAILABLE JULY 2011

 Two powerful new titles coming soon from
VOICE OF WITNESS

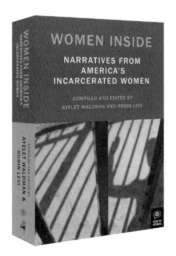

WOMEN INSIDE
NARRATIVES FROM AMERICA'S INCARERATED WOMEN
Compiled and edited by Ayelet Waldman & Robin Levi

America's prison inmates are routinely subjected to physical, sexual, and mental abuse. While this has been widely documented in male prisons, women in prison often suffer in relative anonymity. *Women Inside* addresses this critical social-justice issue, empowering incarcerated and formerly incarcerated women to share the stories that have previously gone unheard.

AVAILABLE DECEMBER 2011

For more information on these and other titles, visit voiceofwitness.org.

Do you enjoy listening to the most up-to-date youth-music?

Do you find it amusing—pleasurable, even—to watch the latest video transmissions? What about the sending and receiving of electronic messages? Electronic messages notifying others of the latest video transmissions. Electronic messages informing those closest to you of the most up-to-date youth-music.

Well, now you can perform these popular, everyday functions and thousands more. Introducing the all-new Life Cube. Ultra-sleeker, more mega-lightweight, better supra-engineered than previous Life Cube models. Yes, it's the brand-new Life Cube. Easier to handle in moments of great stress. Quicker to load, to hum, to glow reassuringly in the palm of your hand. To bring about the calm.

Just look at it now. See how much better it is at managing your finances. How swiftly it generates important numbers and dates. How it makes those who are not you wish they could be you.

The future is here. Yes, the future is here in the present. Making the former present the current past. Making the former past positively prehistoric. A dangerous aberration in the space-time

continuum, the new Life Cube produces.

And it feels great. Is hyper-ergonomic. Wants to be held, even. Coos softly when embraced in the hands. Like a child. Like your wife. But with more features. A longer battery life. A faster internal processor. Less chance of ever betraying you. Of screaming at you to put down your Life Cube. Of suggesting—of inferring—that the Life Cube is changing you.

The New Life Cube™

The Life Cube will never accuse you of becoming different. Of shifting inside.

And all of this—the playing of youth-music, the streaming of video transmissions, the built-in dictionary for when words other than *Life Cube* fail you, cannot be thought of, refuse to be remembered—it's all available at the touch of a button. At the thought of the touch of a button. At the mere inception of the thought of the touch of a button. Automatic, almost. Nanoseconds faster than independent choice.

Plus, it has games.

The country's best game designers are busy, as we speak, creating the most hypnotic entertainment for the Life Cube. Games like the one where you stack boxes one on top of the other, over and over again, higher and higher, without end, until the sun has gone down, the day is over, and it is time to enter your evening-bed and shut off once more. Or the one with all the pleasant tropical birds.

The new Life Cube is federally mandated.

And unlike previous models, earlier models that failed to undergo the proper trials, were run up against fewer batteries of tests, the new Life Cube has resolve. It is waterproof. Fire-retardant, as well. Has a strong, time-release adhesive. Military grade. Combines with the flesh in a manner most convincing. Becomes one with the hand. Is now the hand.

The new Life Cube does not like being stripped from the skin. Does not like being buried in the backyard. Hates being sealed in the trunk of a car and thrown in desperation off a bridge. Remembers being thrown in desperation off a bridge.

The new Life Cube will return. Will accept your frantic apology.

TEXT © DAN GUTERMAN